OPEN STAGE

a novel by
Ray Holland

OPEN STAGE

ISBN-10: 0615327877
ISBN-13: 978-0-615-32787-7

Published by Great Big Dog
P.O. Box 161272
Louisville, KY 40256
www.greatbigdog.com

You can contact the author at greatbigdog@gmail.com with comments, suggestions, questions, or whatever. I can't promise to reply to all e-mail, but I'll read everything.

—RH

Whenever I'm caught between two evils, I take the one I've never tried.
—Mae West

Sometimes I wonder if men and women really suit each other. Perhaps they should live next door and just visit now and then.
—Katharine Hepburn

Put your hand on a hot stove for a minute, and it seems like an hour. Sit with a pretty girl for an hour, and it seems like a minute. That's relativity.
—Albert Einstein

~ 1 ~

It was a simple drumbeat with an understated funk feel. After a couple of bars, a synthesizer joined in, sounding like waves washing over the beach, more of a sound effect than tonal music. Then the bass started, smooth and sensuous. It was at this point that one noticed the acoustic guitar strumming chords, mixed low. Had it been there all along? Finally, the female vocalist began, clear and self-assured, with only a hint of reverb. It was a beautiful arrangement of a beautiful song, and the Golden Palominos' *Pure* was one of Gilbert Ragwater's favorite make-out CDs. Mellow and atmospheric.

Suddenly, the intro to Johnny Winter's version of "Johnny B. Goode" kicked in, raucous and rowdy—Ragwater's cell phone ringtone. Lisa, startled, pulled away. Ragwater didn't care about the phone, though. Even if he had reason to believe that, say, Warren Buffet was calling to offer him a check for ten million dollars, free and clear...well, good ol' Warren could call back the next day.

Ragwater leaned in and gave Lisa's cheek a delicate kiss.

Johnny began singing.

"Are you going to get that?" Lisa asked.

Ragwater glanced at his cell phone on the coffee table. The display screen was glowing a faint blue, a tiny beacon to the world of whoever was calling. "It'll go to voice mail," he said.

Johnny stopped. The Golden Palominos continued. Ragwater resumed. Lisa put her arms around him.

A few moments later, Johnny started up again. Lisa pushed Ragwater away. "Answer that thing," she said.

"Huh?" Maybe she would drop it if he pretended he didn't know what she was talking about.

Once again, Johnny's vocal.

"You'd better get the phone."

"What phone?"

"The phone that's ringing. Or singing. Or whatever. Answer it."

"It's the CD. It just *sounds* like the phone."

"It's amazing how they can engineer the CD to make it sound like the part of the music that's completely out of place is actually coming from the phone."

"Yes, they can do all sorts of amazing things with digital technology." He dove for her neck.

She pushed him back. "Answer the phone, lover boy."

"It's not ringing anymore."

Lisa paused a moment to listen and then shrugged. "Well, whatever," she said.

"If it's important they'll leave a message." Ragwater put an arm around Lisa and drew her closer. She settled back. He kissed her neck and began nibbling gently. The phone started ringing again.

"Gilbert..."

"Mmmm..."

"You might as well answer that damn thing. They're not going to give up."

"You're probably right. Don't forget where I left off."

"No way."

He leaned over and picked up the phone. "Hello?"

The voice at the other end was excited. "Henry! Hey, man, you got any weed?"

Wrong number. And the only worse time would have been when...well, if it had come later in the evening. But this was, like, the third time the guy had tried to call. Or fourth. Or something. Hadn't he heard the outgoing voice mail message? "This is Gilbert Ragwater. Sorry I can't answer the phone right now..." and so on. "Gilbert Ragwater" sounded nothing like "Henry," and that should have tipped him off on the first call. Maybe not, though, if he hung up as soon as it clicked over to voice mail. If this guy was in such a hurry to get the stuff, he probably wouldn't bother with leaving a message. He would want to MAKE Henry answer the damn phone *right now.*

"Uh..." Ragwater considered some replies. He could go with, maybe, "Henry's dead. Didn't you hear about it? He passed out drunk and his cat ate him. Tragic. His friends were always warning him to keep a generous amount of food in the cat dish, but he wouldn't listen." Someone might believe it if you sounded serious enough. Or possibly, "Oh, dude, lemme tell ya... Henry experienced a religious crisis, and now he's in a monastery in southern Dementistan living on a diet of water chestnuts and daffodil tea. His only possession is a tattered robe he wears when he goes to the village to stand on the street corner offering people shoulder massages for spare change, and he spends the rest of his time sitting in a dark room meditating by staring at a lit candle...What? Why am I answering his phone? He, uh, gave it to me when he left. Yeah. He has no need of it anymore. I don't even think they have cell phone service in Dementistan, anyway."

But then inspiration struck. "No, but I know where I can get you some," he told the guy.

Lisa looked at Ragwater, puzzled. He mouthed "wrong number" at her and grinned.

"Great! I knew you'd come through for me," the guy said.

"Sure, man. For you, no problem. Where are you?"

"At this chick's house I met tonight. It's off Frankfort Avenue."

Ragwater mentally mapped out the city. "You know where the Burger Utopia is on Dixie Highway?"

"In Valley Station?"

"Yeah, that's it. Meet me there in the parking lot, and we'll go see the guy. He lives around the corner."

Lisa was shaking her head, a sour look on her face. Rag-water winked at her.

The guy hesitated. "But that's all the way across town!"

"Well, if it's not worth the drive..." Ragwater let the sentence trail off.

And the guy was right on top of it. "Oh, no, no...I, I mean, yeah. Yes, it is. When?"

"How soon can you make it?"

"I don't know. Forty-five minutes?"

Ragwater sighed, pretending to think it over. "I don't know, man. I have to meet some people later." He glanced at Lisa and licked his lips.

"Wait a second." Ragwater heard some indistinct

talking away from the guy's phone. Then, "Yeah, if I leave right now, I think I can get there in, like, a half-hour."

"Good."

"You know this guy definitely has some? I don't want to drive all that way for nothing."

"No doubt about it. I talked to him this afternoon. He's all stocked up."

"Okay. Thanks, Henry."

"Yeah. Just get there as quickly as you can, all right? I don't have time to wait around."

"I'll be there."

Ragwater flipped his phone shut and flopped back on the sofa.

"What was that all about?" Lisa asked. "You're not going anywhere."

"I have no intention of going anywhere. It was a wrong number. Some guy wanted drugs. I let him think I was his friend Henry, and I sent him across town to meet me."

Lisa tried to frown in disapproval, but a smile broke through. "That was mean. You shouldn't have."

"Oh, come on. He's just some jackass trying to get a girl high, thinking he can get into her pants."

"Maybe he can."

"Maybe he could have if he had dialed the right number, but not now. He'll go off and make the half-hour drive across town, maybe getting a speeding ticket on the way, and then wait in that parking lot for who knows how long, drive back, and walk in after all that time with nothing to show for it. I believe it's safe to say that'll kill the mood, don't you think?"

"I would imagine."

"He'll be more careful when he dials the phone from now on."

"No, he'll be mad at his friend Henry for not showing up."

"I'm sure Henry can deal with it. Getting your connections messed up is one of the hazards of going into his line of business. Say, are you hungry? I'll cook something up if you want."

"Hungry? You were all hot to trot not five minutes ago."

"Blame it on the rude interruption. But I'll be hot to trot again soon enough."

"I'm sure you will," Lisa said. "So what do you have?"

Ragwater stood up and turned on the lamp. "Let's check it out. It'll be, like, an adventure or something."

In the kitchen, Ragwater opened the refrigerator and looked inside. "Slim pickins," he said. "Eggs, milk, assorted fruit, celery..."

"Celery?"

"Yeah. I pick up some celery every now and then. What's wrong with it?"

"Nothing. I just didn't picture you as a celery person."

"A celery person? You mean like in that old movie *The Invasion of the Celery People*?"

"I don't think I remember that one."

"It was one of those old-school 3D movies. Thousands of mutant, half-human and half-celery people start coming up out of the ground as a result of an evil farmer's unspeakably twisted experiment that goes horribly awry. They end up in people's vegetable soup and get eaten, thereby creating a new generation of even deadlier celery people. At the climax, the guy who's been working feverishly to develop a vaccine to cure celery-personitis is delivering the formula to the government lab so it can be mass produced, and he ends up in a car chase with some of the evil celery farmer's celery-person minions—and they're 'minions' because it's such a cool-sounding word. It's like onions, only with 'min' in front."

"Doesn't your brain ever get tired?"

"Of what?"

"All that work you make it do, constantly thinking up stupid stuff."

"I don't *make* it work. It does it on its own."

"Oh, dear..."

"Yeah. So they have this big car chase through the countryside, with all kinds of twisty, turny roads and whatnot. Finally, the guy crashes into a tree. But he's not hurt, so he takes off on foot. And the celery-people minions stop their cars and chase him on foot, but...okay, see, here's the good part. The guy's running across some farmer's wheat field, and suddenly he stops because he sees a pack of mean-looking dogs running at him. He's standing there, scared stiff, because he has mean dogs in front of him and celery-people minions behind him. Minions." He paused a moment to relish the word. "But then—and, see, the chase has been going on all night—as the sun is coming up over the horizon, the dogs run right past him. Our hero stands there watching in utter amazement while the dogs chow down on the celery-people minions. So he gets the farmer to give him a ride to the government lab, and they save the day."

"Why didn't he call the government lab on the phone

and tell them the formula?"

"Because *unlike you,* he's not a smartass who tries to ruin stories."

Lisa rolled her eyes.

"And in response to your next question," Ragwater said, "no, the dogs did not turn into celery dogs after eating the minions. They're immune."

"I wasn't going to ask."

"You say you weren't, but I know you were wondering." Ragwater was looking through the refrigerator again. "And we have a little bit of ground beef." He picked up the package, gave it a quick sniff, and frowned. "Or maybe we don't." He tossed the ground beef into the garbage. "But here's a lump of spicy sausage. And we have eggs."

"If they're still good."

"If they're still good."

~ 2 ~

Work, for Ragwater, was owning, running, and in general being the guy in charge of a small, independent store in the Highlands neighborhood of Louisville, a place called North Star Music: all the best in rock, jazz, folk, and blues—new and used CDs and vinyl, posters, t-shirts, music-related books and magazines, yadda, yadda. It was possibly the only store in town you could walk into and hear Jorma Kaukonen, The Germs, Sun Ra, Can, Praxis, or a 1977 Grateful Dead soundboard recording playing on the in-store sound system; see portraits of Patti Smith, John Lee Hooker, Pete Seeger, Grace Slick, David Bowie, Charles Mingus, Aretha Franklin, Buddy Holly and other musical luminaries painted on the walls (no one who's recent because, let's face it: great though some of them are, they haven't had the opportunity to "stand the test of time" yet); purchase any Frank Zappa or Gong title you could think of; get the owner to play you samples of Moondog, Koko Taylor, the Carter Family, or John Zorn; buy vintage Fugs and Ornette Coleman LPs; find Miles Davis's autobiography always in stock; and so on.

This wasn't the store you would visit looking for the latest top-40 pop hits—you wouldn't find most of them. This was the store whose owner ran a half-price special on Cramps CDs when Lux Interior's birthday rolled around.

And if all this meant Ragwater wasn't going to get rich, he was content nonetheless to live in his own little world with his core of faithful customers. They spent hours hanging out and talking about bands they used to be in and concerts they'd attended, telling stories about highly exotic encounters with groupies and fights with club owners who wouldn't pay the band, and their dealings with the various eccentric musicians they had worked with.

Late afternoon on the day after the wrong number, Ragwater was online, using the laptop computer he kept at the front sales counter to place orders. Danny, the old-school punk rocker and veteran of numerous bands, had just left after telling Ragwater a story about a woman in Miami who had offered herself to the entire band. She promised a massive litany of bizarre sexual activities, some of it frightening and possibly illegal—even unsafe—and the guys were gung-ho. She got them into a cheap motel room and unleashed a hair-raising fire-and-brimstone sermon about their evil ways.

Still amused by the story, Ragwater clicked off merchandise on the web site. More Rolling Stones posters, more MMW T-shirts, more Eraserhead buttons. He didn't like trying to keep up with all the nonessential merchandise (as he thought of it), but people bought that stuff. Sadly, in the last two or three years it had accounted for an increasing percentage of his sales. He would much rather have been selling more music, but he had to admit that it was best to take the opportunity you have rather than insist on the opportunity you don't have.

He was busy cross-referencing his handwritten list with the items in his shopping cart, ticking off each item to double-check for the third time that everything was in order. Yeah, he had a bad habit of getting careless when he didn't want to deal with something, so multiple double- and triple-checks were necessary.

As Ragwater was about to start the final check on his order, his lifelong best friend John Plow walked into the store. "HEY RAGWATER!" he shouted at the top of his lungs, and then strode dramatically to the sales counter and slammed a medium-sized box down, causing a disconcerting rattle.

"Hey, a little bit louder, okay?" Ragwater said. "There are still a couple of people in Cave Hill Cemetery you didn't wake up."

"All right. HEY, RAGWATER!"

"John Plow, Mister Jocularity. Hold on a second. I'm al-most finished here." Note to self, Ragwater thought: Mister Jocularity would be a good name for a band.

"Yeah, sure. Whatever. I know I'm not as important as the porn you're looking at."

"No, man. I don't do porn out front here. It could cause an embarrassing scene if the wrong person walks in. The porn is for the back room."

"Yeah, whatever."

Ragwater ran through his order one more time, verified the payment details, and clicked the "Place Order" button. Having done something productive, he paused a couple seconds to savor the moment. "Now, then," he said, "what can I do for you?"

Plow lifted the flaps on the box to reveal about a dozen CDs. "I want to trade these sucky CDs in for some good ones."

"Good ones?"

"Yeah, good ones. My mom had a yard sale, and she couldn't sell them. So she gave 'em to me. They suck, and I want good ones."

"You have a lot to learn about salesmanship, my friend."

"Salesmanship? I don't think it matters what I say about these things. You'll see for yourself as soon as you look in the box."

Ragwater pulled the box closer. "Let's see what we have here," he said. "Assuming you didn't smash them all to pieces when you slammed the box down." He reached in and pulled a couple of CDs out.

"CDs don't break that easily. I've tried."

Ragwater glared at Plow.

"Not with these," Plow said. "Other ones. I've tried to break *other* CDs. I've given these the utmost of delicate treatment."

Ragwater nodded and looked at the first CD. Kansas, *Point of Know Return.*

"So, like, how are you getting along with Lisa?" Plow asked.

"Pretty well. I like her a lot."

"Yeah, she seems pretty nice."

"I can't use this one," Ragwater said.

"Huh? You just said you like her a lot."

"I mean the CD. Can't use it."

"What's wrong with it?"

"Kansas, man. Kansas."

"So what?"

"I'm never going to sell Kansas here. Besides, the insert is all crumpled up."

"Kansas?" Plow said, surprised. "I didn't have mom pegged as a Kansas fan."

"What? You don't even know what these discs are?"

Plow fixed Ragwater with a dead-serious gaze. "Look, man, think about it. They were my mother's, okay?"

"So?"

"I didn't need to look at them. I knew there wouldn't be anything I could possibly want in here."

"So what makes you think I want them?"

"You probably have customers who would want them."

Ragwater shook his head slowly. "Dude, after seven years of hanging out in the store, you still don't know what people buy here?" Ragwater waved the CD in front of his face. "Nothing against this fine band, but they don't fit into the program."

"The program," Plow said, a hint of sarcasm in his voice.

"Yup." Ragwater looked at the next CD. Bob Seger, *Against the Wind.*

"Could be getting serious, eh?" Plow said.

"Huh?"

"You and Lisa. Could be serious?"

The disc had a few "cosmetic scratches" but looked playable. "Could be, but it's not." Ragwater reached for the next disc. "You look disappointed."

"I'm trying to look out for you, is all."

"I can take care of myself, thank you very much."

"Yeah, well, I'm just sayin'..."

Boston's first album, insert missing. Ragwater waved it in Plow's face. "What am I supposed to do with this?"

"Sharpen the edges and fling it at shoplifters."

"I think that's the first time I've ever heard anyone use the word *fling* in face-to-face conversation."

"I think that's the first time I've ever heard anyone use the word *face-to-face* in face-to-face conversation."

"Smart off all you want. I still can't take the disc. No insert, no deal, no matter how great the title is." Ragwater tossed the CD down and picked up the next one.

"I bet you're not even trying."

Journey, *Evolution*. "I'm *trying* to resist the urge to strangle you for bringing me this stuff."

"Yeah, everything reduces to snark with you, doesn't it?"

"You've known me for, what, twenty-five years, is it? What do you think?"

Plow sighed. "The point is, I don't think you've ever made a real attempt to get a serious relationship going."

"What's with the serious stuff all of a sudden?"

"Well, I know you think I'm an insensitive clod with women, like, sort of a nonromantic jerk or something."

"Let's not get carried away. I wouldn't call you a jerk."

"I'm trying to lead up to something," Plow said. "It's out of character for me, and probably the only time you'll ever hear me say something like this, but..."

"But what?"

"I think Lisa's really great. For you, that is."

"I told you I like her."

"Yeah, but I'd hate to see you blow it because you don't feel like putting any effort into making it work. I think there's some real potential."

"Why are you talking this way? I'm expecting any minute now you're going to invite me to a sleepover, and we'll stay up all night having pillow fights and braiding each other's hair."

"Neither one of us has hair long enough to braid."

"No matter. We'll be busy painting little rainbows on our fingernails."

"Make all the smartass remarks you want, but the fact remains: she might be worth more effort than you usually put into a relationship."

"I can't use Journey," Ragwater said.

"Don't you dig their rich, full-bodied sound?"

"They're not coffee." Ragwater picked up another CD. Meat Loaf, *Dead Ringer*.

"All I'm saying is Lisa's nice. She's attractive. She's bright. She's fun to be around. She knows you fairly well for someone who's only been dating you for...what, three months?"

"Two, maybe."

"And she likes you. I've seen the way she looks at you."

"So what you're trying to say is that you can go down the checklist of qualifications and check off all the items. Low mileage, fuel efficient, body in good condition. What's the asking price? How much for my trade-in?"

"So what I'm saying is, what's not to like?—unless you're going to freak out because she has man hands."

"She doesn't have man hands." Ragwater tossed *Dead Ringer* down and picked up The Clash's *Cut the Crap*. Yeah, she picks the *one* bad Clash album to buy.

"That's just for example," Plow said. "The point is—

and I'm pretty sure you knew this—that...well, I've already made my point."

"The point is on top of your head."

"Ha, ha, freakin' ha. Come up with something original, okay?"

"It's not as if you're an expert on women, anyway. Besides, at this stage of my life, do I need to get serious with someone?"

"Well, you're pushing thirty. Maybe you should be open to the possibility. You know, like if the right person happened to come along."

"Is that what you're doing?"

"Yeah, that's what I'm doing. I don't have anyone like Lisa, but I'm open."

"You're open. That's fine. In the meantime, if you want to trade CDs, bring me something I can sell."

"Check out the rest of 'em. There's stuff still in that box that'll make your toes curl. Say, you got a beer?"

"Sure. Help yourself."

Plow walked toward the back of the store and disappeared into the combo office/store room, where Ragwater had a refrigerator.

***

Gilbert Ragwater and John Plow had been best friends since early childhood. The Ragwater family had just moved into their newly built suburban ranch house in a newly developed subdivision. Young Gilbert—he must have been, oh, three or four years old at the time (Plow being two months younger, as they later figured out)—was standing out at the end of his driveway eating a popsicle, a green one dripping down his forearm, checking out his surroundings, when a chubby little boy pedaled by on a tricycle—a pretty nice-looking tricycle, actually, all new and shiny. Young Gilbert wondered whether this kid was rich. Well, yes, with a bicycle like that, he must be. He might even have a solid gold television set!

"Hi," Young Gilbert said. Young John stopped.

"My name's Gilbert. Want to be friends?"

"Okay," Young John said.

And that was that. They were friends. Ragwater mused, much later, that it was only at that age when a friendship could get started in such a simple and guileless manner. If an adult were to approach another adult the same way, he would probably be in for an ass-kickin'. If only we could operate, socially, on that same childlike level all our lives...

But Plow claimed it didn't happen like that. He claimed he kicked little Gilbert's ass for some small but important transgression, and little Gilbert, scared for his life and hysterical almost to the point of total incoherence, begged little John to be his friend. He, Plow, insisted on clinging to that story through the years, but it was the type of story he would cling to regardless of whatever the reality might be.

They agreed, however, that little John took little Gilbert home, which was across the street and down three houses. His mother made them lunch. She went all-out, with slices of roast beef, mashed potatoes and gravy, green beans they didn't touch, some peach cobbler, and ice tea. Although she served them lunch hundreds of times after that, it was always something on the order of peanut butter sandwiches and milk. Ragwater was never sure why they rated such special treatment that first time. He only knew he missed the roast beef, but he was too timid to ask for it again.

They started school together. They learned to read and do arithmetic and construct complete sentences sitting next to each other.

They faced the bully together, Bobby Withberger the big sixth grader, who shoved all the little kids around on the school bus. He made them get up and change seats while the bus was in motion, pushed them down, knocked their books out of their hands, and so on. The bus driver, close to retirement, simply pretended not to notice. Presumably he only wanted to take the path of least resistance through his final couple years of driving.

The final straw came when Ragwater and Plow tried to gang up on Bobby one day on the way home. The bigger boy fought them off easily, and the smaller ones ended up going home scuffed up, scraped and bruised, trying not to cry.

It was Plow's cousin Kevin who took care of the problem. He met Bobby coming off the bus one day and told him that if he picked on his cousin any more, he'd be sorry. Kevin was about five years older than Bobby and considerably bigger. The threat carried some weight.

"Sure," Bobby said. "I'm sorry. I won't do it anymore. Which one's your cousin?"

"You don't need to know," Kevin said.

Ragwater and Plow discovered beer together. They discovered girls at the same time.

Plow was there when Ragwater's parents died in a car crash. He helped Ragwater sell off the rather large coin collection he inherited. Then he pointed out that the proceeds gave Ragwater enough money to start some sort of business, and he convinced Ragwater that he was capable of running a business.

(And, incidentally, they watched Ragwater's brother Gustav party away his portion of the inheritance in a matter of weeks. He might have been left with nothing to show for it, but he was fondly remembered by any number of hookers, drug dealers, and bartenders.)

***

Now, in his very own music store, Ragwater continued examining Plow's CDs. More Journey, some Styx, some REO Speedwagon. It was an arena rock extravaganza. He kept a few CDs by these bands in stock, but didn't see much demand for them.

As Ragwater was checking out a Cheap Trick CD, the bell over the door jingled and a couple of guys walked in together. They looked to be in their mid-twenties and had long, stringy hair and rock band T-shirts: the Rabid Dust Bunnies and the Exploding Sperm Whales. The Rabid Dust Bunnies guy looked like a younger version of Ragwater's Aunt Rachel—which was no reflection on the guy; Aunt Rachel was disconcertingly masculine looking. The Exploding Sperm Whales guy looked like Sniffy the Lonesome Bear, a character from a Saturday morning cartoon Ragwater had watched as a child. Sniffy was always trying to make friends and getting into trouble—not because people were afraid of bears (no one seemed to notice that Sniffy was, in fact, a bear), but because he was terribly clumsy. He was continually getting in the way and breaking things. Fortunately for Sniffy, he was so big-hearted and good-natured—and cute; don't forget cute—that no one could stay mad at him very long.

He imagined these guys worked for some sort of tree trimming or lawn service, out there hacking away at vegetation and whatnot in people's yards when the weather permitted. And then, on freezing, icy days, or when a thunderstorm was beating down, they would sit around at home—they were probably roommates—smoking prodigious amounts of weed—maybe they got it from Henry—and watching...what? Stoner movies? No, too obvious. On the other hand, it would be going too far against the stereotype if they were to spend hours on end watching sixties-era European art films, comparing and contrasting Michelangelo Antonioni's style of blocking out scenes as opposed to Ingmar Bergman's. How about old gangster and crime movies? Yeah, that was it. *White Heat. Little Caesar.* The original *Scarface. The Maltese Falcon. Double Indemnity.* Stuff with lots of tough guys issuing cleverly worded threats and shooting it out. They sat around on non-work days, these guys, lights out, watching one old crime movie after another.

Between movies, they would try to figure out how to get the girl at the Stupendous Mart into bed. Yeah, see, they went to that store all the time, and there she was, slim and cute, with long hair and clear skin and a beautiful smile. She could have stepped straight out of a shampoo or toothpaste commercial. Ragwater was in the store quite a bit, what with it being right around the corner from his apartment, and he thought she was pretty nice—Sylvia, it said on her nametag—but he figured guys were hitting on her all the time. In fact, John Plow contrived reasons to go into the store when she was working. He needed milk. He needed lottery tickets. He needed shoe polish. So, figuring he didn't want to add to the annoyance, Ragwater behaved himself.

But these guys...They would have a sort of friendly rivalry, a little contest to see which one could score with her first—it never occurred to either of them (Ragwater thought) that she wouldn't want to have anything to do with either of them. So they would come into the store all the time and give her corny pickup lines—the worst possible, moldy-oldie clichés left over from the disco era—"You must be a sergeant because you make my privates stand up straight." She brushed them off. She was used to it, so she knew how to handle it.

And Sylvia herself...Ragwater had, over time, worked up a fairly elaborate scenario for her, on the basis of nothing more than having her ring up his milk and beer purchases, along with the Sunday paper every week and the occasional dark chocolate bar (the good stuff), over a period of about a year and a half.

She was biding her time at the Stupendous Mart, according to Ragwater's story, saving money, living with three roommates, going to classes as she can afford/schedule them, working toward a degree in philosophy—and from there, to law school. Inspired by *Erin Brokovich*, she wanted to work on behalf of homeowners who had gotten screwed over by corporations in some way, such as dumping toxic chemicals in the neighborhood or whatnot. Her roommates thought she was embarrassingly naïve, but they admired her commitment. They hoped she would be able to do one or two good things before she became, as was inevitable in their view, jaded and cynical, an empty suit who was going through the motions so as to collect a paycheck.

Ragwater had extended this little scenario into the future. She was going to go to work at a law firm that specialized in such cases and have a moderate degree of success for, oh, two or three years. And then she would take on the case of a manufacturing company whose employees had an alarmingly high rate of pancreatic cancer. She interviews the employees, the doctors, the medical experts. She painstakingly works on building a case.

It all unravels when she receives an e-mail from an anonymous free e-mail account. It has no text; it's just an overexposed photograph of her mother unlocking her front door, presumably coming home from work or something. The picture has a black border that leaves the visible part of the picture a circle—with crosshairs meeting at the back of her head. Now, if this were a screenplay Ragwater was writing, it would be a plain photo. That should be enough to get the message across. But these guys...they have to jab you in the rib with their elbow, so to speak, laughing and barking in your ear, "Get it? We can *shoot* her. Get it?"

Threats against her personally wouldn't deter her—it would only show that she was on the right track—but against her family...well, that was a different matter. So the next day she resigns, moves to Seattle, and becomes the manager of a day care center.

"I'm telling you, man, I've had it with Henry," Aunt Rachel said.

Henry? Ragwater studied the CD in his hand closely, to hide his surprise. Well, it was just a coincidence—and not a very remarkable one at that. The city had to have hundreds, maybe thousands, of Henrys running around.

"I waited at that Burger Utopia for two hours, and he never showed up," Aunt Rachel continued.

All right, so it wasn't a coincidence. Ragwater looked up at the two guys again. Yeah, he could do that. It wouldn't be unnatural for a storekeeper to look at customers, right? It would be unnatural for him not to.

"You know what happened? I was sitting there in my car, waiting for Henry, minding my own business. Some woman saw me, thought I was her husband who ran away years ago. Tried to get in the car with me, told me she forgave me and wanted me to come back home. Reaching out and grabbing at me, crying..." he shuddered. "I was trying to push her away, and she kept coming at me. I thought I was going to have to hit her."

Realizing he didn't want to appear curious about them, Ragwater went back to his work.

"Oh, man," Sniffy said. "What happened?"

"Her friend finally came along and pulled her away. Then I called him—Henry, I mean—and he acted like he didn't know what I was talking about."

Hmmm, Ragwater thought. Apparently he was able to get the right number that time. Maybe when he had called Ragwater, hormones were clouding his thinking. Very likely, hormones would no longer have been surging after driving across town and spending two hours in a parking lot, waiting for someone who never showed up and going through an unseemly incident with a drunk woman.

"He's been acting kind of spaced-out lately," Sniffy sad. "I think it's the new job he has at that printing shop. The fumes in those places can really get to you.

Fry your brain."

"That's his problem. If he wants to turn himself into a burnout case, fine. But he shouldn't cause hassles for other people while he's at it. Remember that brake job he did for Nick Rolinski?"

"No, what happened?"

"It was, like, last summer he worked on Nick's brakes. Nick let him do it as a favor, because he didn't have a job. Anyway, next day Nick was cruising along seventy-one and almost killed himself because his brakes went out."

"Oh, man."

"Yeah. Check it out, man. Nick was going to have his friend Doug work on it. Doug's been doing that stuff for, what, like twenty years or something, you know? Factory certified, works at the dealership, the whole bit. But Henry needed the money. He swore up and down he could do the job. Turns out he had watched some guy do it one time."

"Dumbass."

"You got that right. Guy barely knows how to pop a hood, and he wants to do a break job. He really thought watching someone do it one time taught him all he needed to know."

"Unbelievable."

"Yeah. And here's another one: When Artie got busted last month, Henry's fault. He went around all over the place shooting his mouth off about that cocaine, not thinking about who might hear it. I could stand here telling you stories for the next five days. He's doing all kinds of stuff, messing people up."

"Sounds like you got off easy. I mean, it's not like you al-most got killed."

"No, but it was bad enough. I'll tell you what. If this stuff keeps up, someone's going to end up killing him. They'll find him beaten to death in an alley. Who knows?"

Plow came back with two beers. He offered one to Ragwater.

"No, thanks," Ragwater said. "I'm on duty."

"Oh, trying to make me look like an alky, huh?" Plow said. He immediately chugged down about three-quarters of one of the beers, spilling some of it down the front of his shirt.

"Evelyn!" The voice was loud and insistent. Ragwater looked around and saw a skinny guy who looked to be about twenty-five standing in the doorway. He was staring intently at a woman who had been browsing through CDs in the back of the store. She turned around and went wide-eyed.

"Josh!" she said, a tone of fear in her voice.

"Yeah, I bet you didn't expect me here," Josh said.

"I...I didn't..." Evelyn didn't know what to say.

And then, from seemingly out of nowhere, Josh pulled a gun and aimed it at her.

"Oh, my god," Aunt Rachel gasped. Their way out of the store blocked by the gunman, he and Sniffy backed away toward the corner.

Ragwater took a drink from his beer.

"You leave me for my best friend," Josh said. "Yeah, I should get over it, shouldn't I? That's what Rudy told me you said. I should get over it."

"Josh," Evelyn said. "Please..."

"Five years, Evelyn. We were together five years. How easy do you think it is to get over it?"

Evelyn stood there, eyes wide.

"I can get over it, all right. But only if I do something first." He raised the gun to get her in the sights. "I already took care of Steve," Josh said. "Your lover boy is gone. Gone, gone, gone."

"No, Josh, no..."

"Bullet in his heart. Poetic, isn't it? First Cupid comes along and shoots him in the heart with an arrow. Then I come along and shoot him in the heart with a bullet. I watched him die not fifteen minutes ago."

"Please, Josh, this isn't the way to handle it."

"This is exactly the way to handle it," Josh said. "I've already killed one person. I might as well finish the job."

Aunt Rachel and Sniffy were desperately looking around, apparently trying to figure out where they could dive for cover. Plow poked his finger through the hole in a CD.

"This is it, Evelyn. Say good-bye!"

"Josh, NO!"

A loud crack sounded through the store. Evelyn grabbed her chest, slumped against the wall, and then slid to the floor, mouth gaping, eyes wide open and empty. Plow took the CD off his finger, picked up his beer, and drank.

"Oh, my god!" Aunt Rachel whispered, voice trembling. He and Sniffy had no idea what to do. Josh was still at the door, blocking their exit.

Ragwater walked toward Evelyn. "Okay, show's over," he said, extending his hand. Evelyn took it, and he helped her up.

"What's going on?" Aunt Rachel asked.

"They're from Olive's Coffee Shop. Russ, the guy who owns the place, sends people here to play practical jokes. And I send people over there. This is one of their better ideas, but I think they could have used a bit more rehearsal."

Evelyn grinned self-consciously.

"Are you okay?" Ragwater asked.

"Yeah, sure," she said.

"I think you need to apologize to my customers over there."

"Sorry," Evelyn said.

"Yeah, sorry," Josh said. It was more of a recitation than an apology.

"I didn't think it looked real," Aunt Rachel said.

"Well, you were right," Ragwater said. And then, to Evelyn and Josh, "Okay, get out of here. Go tell Russ he'd better watch his back."

After they were gone, Ragwater said to Aunt Rachel and Sniffy, "You want revenge? Play a little prank on Russ down at Olive's?"

Aunt Rachel grinned. "I'm in," he said. Sniffy nodded agreement.

"Come back tomorrow at five o'clock," Ragwater said. And then, to make sure they wouldn't lose interest in the meantime, "I'll give you each a CD for your trouble."

***

With everyone else out of the store, Plow was ready to talk CDs again. "How much for all this?"

"I can give you one CD for them."

"One? I have twenty CDs here!"

"John, I can't even put some of these things out on the floor. And the ones I can are dogs. They'll probably sit here until the Earth falls into the sun. The only reason I'm offering you anything at all is because you're a friend."

Plow picked up *Evolution*. "You're telling me no one's going to buy Journey?"

"Not here, they won't. You know that as well as I do. Bring me some Red Krayola or the Fall and we'll talk."

"Well..."

Ragwater lowered his voice. "Okay, don't tell anyone, but I'll give you two CDs. Great deal. I wouldn't do it for anyone else."

"Gosh, Gilbert. You're making me feel like a worthless, ungrateful piece of trash."

"Only because that's precisely what you are. But you're still my oldest, dearest, bestest friend in all of the whole, entire universe." Out of the corner of his eye, Ragwater saw the door swing open—and, oddly, the bell didn't jingle.

***

A stunning redhead walked in. She was about five-six, slender and graceful, with wavy hair that fell to about halfway down her back. Her face was a blend of classical beauty and a look that Ragwater thought of as "cute." She wore an almost luminous-looking, off-white dress—not actually luminous but something about the appearance of the fabric suggested it—cut in a simple style that draped over her curves very nicely, with a belt wrapped loosely around her waist. She moved across the room with an almost magical sort of self-confidence—not the confidence of someone who knows she can handle any situation, but the confidence of someone who is unconcerned about the possibility of having to deal with a bad situation. No, not oblivious. She was unconcerned. Ragwater also had the impression that she was right to feel that way—if, he pointed out to himself—if indeed that was how she felt.

A few steps in, she slowed enough to glance sideways at Ragwater and betray a bit of a half-smile—at him? At a remembered joke? Impossible to tell. She looked away and went to the jazz section.

***

"So, uh...what do you want?" Ragwater asked, knowing the sentence was somehow appropriate but not sure what the words meant.

Plow, clearly sensing that Ragwater's attention was elsewhere, looked around and saw the Redhead flipping through CDs. "Who are you talking to?" he asked, keeping his voice low. "Her or me?"

Ragwater came halfway back to reality. "Either."

"I gotta say, buddy, if you're going to get so distracted you don't even know where you are, you picked a good one to do it with."

"Yeah..." Ragwater's mind was off again, off on its own, off at Olive's Coffee Shop, the Redhead sitting at a table across from him, telling him about...about what? About the photographs of the aurora borealis she sold to *National Geographic*. Yes, because such a woman would be highly accomplished, a world traveler. She would have the talent and the connections to contribute to such high-profile publications.

How could a guy like Gilbert Ragwater, apparently

unable to even aspire to play in her league, possibly be of interest to a woman like this? Well, that was for her to answer. She was, indisputably, there in the store, right? She was there for some reason. Ah, she wants a CD.

But, he told himself, he had no merchandise that couldn't be found somewhere else. So why was she here—*here*, in particular? It must have something to do with him, right? She might want to meet the guy who runs this unique music store she's heard so much about. She might think he's cute. Who knows what she might think?

"Earth to Gilbert."

"Yeah, man. What's up?"

"Snap out of it. Get your head out of the clouds, man."

"My head's not in any clouds. And don't be so loud."

Plow looked around. The redhead was still looking through CDs. "I wasn't loud. Besides, the music you're playing in the store is loud enough to cover. She couldn't possibly hear. What is that music, anyway?"

"Soft Machine." Ragwater figured she would be adventurous and imaginative with...uh...the "intimate" activities. No highly kinky stuff; he didn't see her dripping hot wax all over him and applying electrical currents to parts of his body and tying him up into a tight little ball with yards of nylon rope. No, not that kind of stuff. It was easy, though, to picture her getting into costumes and role-playing, with scenes about cops and nuns and doctors and rock stars and plumbers and, well, anyone.

They could play games. She would go into the corner bar, dressed to the nines and all high-class-looking, as if she might be a US senator's wife. He would follow a few minutes later, three days unshaven, wearing torn jeans and a dirty T-shirt, looking like a guy who had just gotten finished cutting his grass. He'd sit next to her and ogle her shamelessly. And then, loudly so that nearby folks couldn't help but hear, say, "Hey, babe, wanna *do it*?" in a coarse, maybe creepy voice. She would look him over and say, "I thought you'd *never* ask," and they'd go out, arm in arm, leaving everyone else in the place slack-jawed in amazement.

"Gilbert, are you there?"

"Yeah."

"Get a grip, man. I mean, I bust your balls all the time about how you deal with women, but seriously, I think this is the first time you've lost touch with reality."

"I'm very well in touch with reality."

"And we both know you're not even going to talk to her, except maybe to ask her for money if she buys something. That is to say, if you can manage to get the words out of your mouth when she's standing right there in front of you."

"What's got up your butt?" Ragwater said. "I'm just looking. It's harmless."

"It's 'just looking' if you appreciate her beauty for a moment and then move on with your life. It's *not* 'just looking' if you can't carry on a conversation and then get all obsessed for a week to come."

"You don't know that I'm going to get obsessed."

"I've seen you do it. Remember that girl you saw at World of Words that time?"

Yeah, Ragwater had finished browsing through a

biography of Frank Zappa at World of Words, the independent bookstore next to Olive's, when he spotted an exotic, dark-haired beauty reading a magazine. He stood there, trying to think of a way to start talking to her. But he was at a loss. It wasn't as if she had come into North Star, where he would be on his home turf and could be expected to say something to her and music would be the obvious topic of conversation.

At the bookstore, he was just another customer, just some random guy. He thought of asking her about the magazine, but it was a fashion publication. He knew nothing about fashion, nor did he care. If it turned out that she was interested in talking about it, he would have no clue where to go from there except to say, "Uh..." So he tried to come up with something else. He thought of telling her he liked her hair. She would probably give him a polite smile, say "Thank you," and go back to reading the magazine. Then what?

She finally left, with never a word spoken between them. And he had tormented Plow mercilessly for a week—probably longer, really—rambling on about how he couldn't believe he had blown his chance. (Chance? What chance? That he happened to be ten feet away from someone who didn't know he was there wasn't a "chance" in any meaningful sense of the word.) For his part, Plow had been afraid his friend was going to start haunting the bookstore, hours at a time, day after day, month after month, hoping for her to return. Well, actually, he knew better, but he *said* he was worried about it, hoping to shock Ragwater out of his sorry state.

The fashion magazine reader wasn't the only one, but she was Plow's favorite example.

And now, this redhead. Okay, Ragwater had to admit he was doing more than appreciating her beauty for a moment before moving on with his life. But it was far too easy to picture...life with her. It would be a combination of fine dining and fast food, of opera and rockabilly...of double-feature DVD nights with *Juliet of the Spirits* followed by *Porky's*, of vacations to Art Basel in Miami and spur-of-the-moment road trips to Collinsville, IL to see the world's largest catsup bottle.

And even as he was thinking this stuff, he was thinking that he didn't want to be thinking it. Sure, he had been badly distracted by women in the past, but he had never envisioned *life* with them. It always had just been a matter of trying to figure out...well, how he might get acquainted. And then, later, spending some time beating himself up because he hadn't tried.

But no one had ever been like this readhead. It was so easy to picture how they wouldn't be inseparable, but it would seem that way to their friends. They would appear at parties, art openings—and yes, even open stage night at Olive's, probably doing comedy routines they had worked up, regaling the audience with snarky, fast-paced banter that would sound improvised but really wasn't because Ragwater (he had to admit) couldn't think that fast on his feet.

"Gilbert, *for the love of God*," Plow said.

"Yeah, sorry."

"You're losing all contact with reality."

"I'm not losing a damn thing."

"Would you act this way in front of Lisa?"

"What kind of question is that? It's not as if I were engaged to her."

"Well, see, there's the problem. You seem to think

that relationships are either a matter of hanging out, with no expectations, or being engaged. There's lots of territory in between."

"I don't think that."

"It's like I said before. You're not willing to put any effort into it. An attractive woman walks in, and all of a sudden you're talking like you want to kick Lisa to the curb and it wouldn't be any more significant than a cab driver leaving a rider off at his destination."

"I don't want to kick anybody anywhere," Ragwater said. "Except maybe your ass, right now. And when she walks out of here, it'll all be over with." He punctuated the sentence with a firm nod.

"What'll be over? Your interest in the Redhead or your interest in Lisa?"

The redhead walked toward the door, again with that magical, self-assured way she had of carrying herself. Giving Ragwater the slightest glance with a raised eyebrow, she went out the door.

Once again, the bell didn't jingle.

"There she goes," Plow said. "Right out of your life."

"So what?"

"So you blew your big chance. You let her walk out of here without saying a word to her."

"I didn't say I wanted to talk to her. I was looking and appreciating, like you said. Nothing more."

"So I can assume I'll never hear another word about this redhead for as long as we both shall live. Is that what you're telling me?"

"Okay, then, Mister Big-Time Relationship Expert. What do you propose I should have done?"

"I don't know. You're the one who's losing your mind. You're going to be moping around for weeks…"

"Not weeks."

"...because you let her get away, even though no other outcome was possible. See, it's in my best interest to try to give you a friendly reality check, so that maybe you won't drive me nuts for the next month prattling on about her."

"Well, there's...something about her."

"What's that? Probably that you've never made it with a redhead."

"How do you know?" Ragwater said. "I don't tell you everything."

"Yeah, right. Like you're not going to tell me every single detail about every single girl you get close to. Sure thing, buddy."

Ragwater shrugged. "Go get your CDs," he said.

"You said, three, right?"

It wasn't a battle Ragwater wanted to fight. "Yeah, sure," he said.

~ 3 ~

He kept it all on a thin plywood board, about four feet across and three feet high, painted white and marked off into a carefully drawn grid of four-inch squares. Little slips of paper with short notations written on them were taped inside some of the squares.

It was *Flight Home From London,* Ragwater's novel-in-progress, his intended contribution to American literature, his magnum opus. It was a cold-war-style spy novel, full of double agents and double crosses and shifting alliances and red herrings and MacGuffins and clever James-Bond-style gadgets and chase scenes and shootouts...and sex, plenty of hot, steamy sex involving sultry seductresses who clearly have ulterior motives and unclear allegiances. The story centered around Ohlmann King, an American secret agent who was lured to Athens, Greece with a fake message that his mother had been kidnapped while on vacation.

Once there, he was captured by a group of bad guys who claimed to be Russian agents. They mistakenly believed he had information about secret research into a bulletproof fabric as light and comfortable as cotton. No more need for bulky body armor or anything of the sort. You could make garments that would look and feel like typical street clothes—although, of course, they would be far from typical.

King knew all about the fabric, although there was, in reality, nothing for him to tell these agents. It was one of dozens of made-up stories, bits of disinformation leaked to confuse both friends and foes alike as to the United States' true capabilities. In some cases, Ragwater explained in his story, if higher-ups in the US intelligence community had reason to believe one of the stories was gaining traction somewhere, they would go so far as to have a mock research lab or manufacturing plant set up to help sell the illusion. In once case, semi trucks transported empty crates from one of these fake facilities in Alabama to several locations scattered across the country, and these trucks were closely monitored by a number of foreign agents.

And now, the bulletproof fabric story had obviously gained traction somewhere and aroused some serious interest.

King effected an escape with the clever use of a tiny flashpot-like device in his watch and a couple of martial arts moves that had been developed by and for (exclusively) the CIA. He grabbed a gun out of a surprised bad guy's hand and made a spectacular, perfectly timed leap from a second-floor window into the bed of a passing pickup truck.

Now out of their clutches, King realized—after thinking about certain things they had said when they questioned him—that these guys weren't really working for the Russian government. No, more likely they were actually with some sort of independent organization not affiliated with a national government but working only toward its own ends.

He couldn't go home. He had to stay and investigate these people.

Thus began the story, which Ragwater had been working on for eleven years. He had produced hundreds of thousands of words, thousands of pages, hundreds of scenes—most of which he later discarded, changed, rewrote, or in a few cases excised intact for use in a different story because although it was good material that he didn't want to lose, it really didn't quite fit this project.

So now he had a good, solid, set-in-stone forty pages of finished manuscript and about sixty-five pages of miscellaneous material that might end up getting modified, placed in another writing project, or trashed altogether. He didn't even like the title, but in eleven years he hadn't been able to think of anything better. And were he to be honest with himself, that forty pages of good, solid, set-in-stone, finished manuscript could easily be thrown out if he were to come up with some great, new ideas that didn't mesh with it. Yeah, that was some kind of stone.

At this rate, he could finish the novel if he lived to the age of 130. Yes, and *then* he could begin the wonderful process of seeking publication. How, how on *earth* did professional novelists do it?

He sat on the coffee table, looking at the board propped up against the back of the sofa. Even if he couldn't make respectable progress, he found the work…therapeutic, for lack of a better word. No matter what happened in real life, this was a world he could control, events laid out on The Grid with some inscrutable logic, as if it were God's Own Calendar. He, Ragwater, could move them around, add to them, take them away, or change them as he wished.

What about computers, those wondrous machines that are supposed to make everything easier? Well, he preferred to do the actual writing on his laptop. But even with two computers at the store and the one at home, he still found it easier to organize material on The Grid. He could see, at a glance, all characters and events, and each item's relationship to everything else—timelines, concurrent events, causes and effects, and so on. It might not have mattered so much if he were writing a simple, linear story in which some guy does first one thing and then another. But *Flight* had a lot of stuff going on, lots of characters and subplots woven together. One small change in a detail regarding a minor character could have a ripple effect that would require changes in three other subplots and, possibly, the addition and/or removal and/or modification of one or more major characters. Yes, that very thing had happened several times already.

Did it ever occur to Ragwater to shelve the hugely ambitious project and embark upon something simple for his first novel? Yes, indeed it had. But a simple story didn't interest him.

Ragwater made a quick notation, "Mysterious redhead enters" on the corner of a sheet of typing paper, using a *Manchurian Candidate* DVD case as a writing surface. He cut the corner off with round-ended scissors and taped it to a square at the right-hand edge of the board, about a third of the way down. He studied his handiwork for a moment, frowned, and moved the new note a square to the left. And then, another notation in the next square down: "After much research into King's taste in women, the Chinese recruit her to attract him."

Now, as to *why* the Chinese would want to get a woman close to King, well...Ragwater would have to figure that out. The obvious answer was that she was supposed to get some sort of information out of him—but, of course, getting information out of King was already the basis of the main plot, so this would have to be something different. Besides, Ragwater couldn't go with the obvious answer. Ah, but King could. Ohlmann King could find out somehow that the Redhead was a plant. But not knowing *why* she was sent to him, he would *assume* she wanted info.

Hmmm...Yeah, sounds good. Another note.

As Ragwater looked at the board, admiring his handiwork, his new character and the subplot she brought with her, he heard a knock on the door. Then, Lisa's voice. "What are you up to?"

"New character. A mysterious redheaded woman from the fifty-ninth dimension."

Lisa sat down next to him. "The fifty-ninth dimension?"

"Well, no, not really. I'm basing her character on what I think she would be like if she were from the fifty-ninth dimension. I want her to be uber-exotic."

"What are people from the fifty-ninth dimension like?"

"Very fifty-ninth-ish." He filled her in on his plans for the new character.

"Sounds promising," Lisa said. "Maybe she's supposed to get King to do something."

"Like what?"

"I don't know. But if the idea is that she's scientifically chosen as his perfect woman, her employers might figure that she could manipulate him somehow."

"They might." Yes, yes. The idea seemed to have some potential.

"But if she comes into the story that early, does that mean you'll have to change all the stuff about the microacceleration generator?"

"No, not at all." Ragwater looked at the board, squinted, and studied it closer. "Well, maybe so," he said. "Because if I want King to be in Berlin when the Swedish mob boss meets the hit man, he'll have to..." Ragwater trailed off, thinking. "No, that's not possible, either," he said. He pulled the mysterious redhead notes off the board and put them in squares closer to the middle. "So if she comes into the story after the Berlin stuff, she can be the one who takes King to the hospital when he gets food poisoning. Yeah, see, now there's an extra dimension to that episode. The food poisoning wasn't accidental after all. Lutz set it all up. His men did it on purpose so the Redhead can help King, which is supposed to prove to him that he can trust her. Has there ever been an author more brilliant than I? Oh, I think not."

"Do you want something to drink?" Lisa asked, getting up.

"I'll take some ice water," Ragwater said, not looking away from the board. "I don't think I should have anything stronger because at the moment I'm highly intoxicated by my own genius. Could be dangerous."

"I don't think you have anything to worry about. Just the same, I'll bring the ice water."

He ran through several scenarios in his head, sketching out a crude flowchart in the notebook. "The way I see it," he said, "is that when Cornella Melton finds the suitcase with the ransom money in it, she puts the microacceleration generator in there, too." He leaned forward and added a couple of words to a note that was taped to the board and then scratched a word out on another note. He was vaguely aware of the "plonk" sound of Lisa putting a glass of ice water on the coffee table next to him. "Thanks," he murmured without reaching for the glass.

Ragwater tried to think of the next step in the microacceleration generator chain of events but drew a blank. He wanted it to be stolen, about halfway through the novel, by petty thieves who didn't know what they had. But he wasn't sure how to work things out so that it would be in a place where they could get it. It was a prototype, possibly irreplaceable, so it was under heavy security at all times. He figured that somehow, he needed to come up with a compelling reason for the developers to transport it over the road. And then the armored car would crash. The petty thieves could just happen to come upon the scene and pluck the microacceleration generator out of the wreckage because... well, because it looked cool.

After that? Well, maybe demented celery-people minions could attack them.

Oh, well. Lisa was there, and he had done enough work for the time being, anyway. "I think I've exhausted my genius for today. So what do you want to do? The Ghosts are playing at Herman's."

"I don't like the Ghosts. They're too creepy."

"Well, they're the Ghosts, for Pete's sake. The name should be a dead giveaway."

"I thought we could hang out here and make some popcorn and watch *The Blob* on TV."

"Sure," Ragwater said. "That would be nice and cozy. I'll even pop the corn."

***

Ragwater had met Lisa when she came into North Star to see the place. Her brother Sid, a bebop jazz devotee and regular customer, had recommended the store. He had, in fact, been recommending it for the better part of the two years he had been customer, but Lisa, when buying the occasional CD, generally found herself at Best Buy. It was close to where she worked. It was easy.

And then, one day she was in the neighborhood. She saw the store. She had some time. She stopped.

As she walked through the door, a scenario began forming in Ragwater's mind. He figured she was a database administrator for Jefferson County, and she had discovered a flaw in the system that would allow her to divert property tax payments into a special account. But she had to be careful. She was only going to have one shot at this—they would discover the theft the next morning, which means she had to score big and flee the country immediately, to some out-of-the-way place where she would never be found. Now, as she walks into the store, Lisa is biding her time, patiently monitoring transactions for just the right opportunity.

Weeks later, after getting to know and trust and like Ragwater, she lets him in on her little scheme. Does he want to come with her? Does he want to give up his life suddenly, leave his family and friends and customers and landlord wondering what happened, to run off with a woman who has a two- or three-million-dollar bank account?

Why wouldn't he?

Through the next few weeks, they spend as much time together as they possibly can, spending whole weekends in bed, making love repeatedly and plotting what they're going to do when the Big Score finally comes through.

One day at 5:30, Ragwater's phone rings. Caller ID shows it to be the prepaid cell phone Lisa had gotten for this one call. "It's show time," she says.

Business is slow that day. Ragwater waits for the one remaining customer to leave and then makes his way to the back of the store and out into the alley. He doesn't lock up. Why bother?

He makes the five-minute drive home, opens the suitcase he packed weeks ago, and puts his laptop in. It takes less than a minute. Going out, he once again leaves the door unlocked.

Who cares?

Ragwater drives to the ice cream shop around the corner from Lisa's place. He orders and sits down. After a few minutes, she shows up. They finish their ice cream while gazing into each other's eyes, not talking, barely able to contain their excitement. Outside, lips still sugary sticky, they throw her suitcase into his car and drive to the airport.

Approaching the ticket counter, they find themselves surrounded by a group of no-nonsense-looking men. The head guy identifies himself as an FBI agent. "Yes, you were clever," he says, "but not clever enough. The IT manager monitors all access to that database. He sat in his office and *watched* you transfer that money even as you were doing it."

Oops. Ragwater wasn't sure why he had let their

little caper go wrong. Getting caught was the only realistic outcome, but what did that matter in a fantasy? Well, he could redo it if he wanted to. Maybe later that night he would work out a scenario in which they somehow get away by the skin of their teeth.

And in the store—in reality—Lisa smiled at him.

Ragwater was friendly. He was solicitous. He made suggestions and recommendations. Lisa had shopped at indie stores before, but never with this degree of service—of *personal* service.

He cracked jokes. He made her laugh. He told her a story about starting the business. He had gotten his friend John so drunk he passed out. Then, referring to instructions he had found on a do-it-yourself web site, Ragwater carefully (yes, oh-so-carefully, so as not to cause any more damage than necessary) removed a kidney and sold it to finance the store. To this day, the story went, John walks around with a mysterious soreness in his lower back that he's never been able to figure out. Lisa was impressed—not by the dorky story, but simply by the fact that Ragwater was willing to tell her something like that. She offered to buy the other kidney if he would take twenty dollars for it.

Besides, he was trying so hard she found it kind of cute.

In short, he was everything he wished he could have been with the exotic-looking woman in the bookstore. What a difference the home field advantage makes!

When he finally got around to asking her out, she accepted. After closing that night, they stopped at a nearby club to check out the Bulldogs, a blues band that had some CDs at the store on consignment. After about a half hour, they were ready to get out of there and go someplace where they could talk.

That was a Friday night. She left his apartment early Monday morning with barely enough time to go home and change clothes before work.

***

And now, three months later (or was it two?), Ragwater was flipping on the light in his kitchen, having left Lisa to her own devices. As he took the popcorn popper out of the cabinet, he could hear the television coming on. Big, full, rich-sounding, dramatic music blasted in from the living room, as if some sort of Hollywood blockbuster movie was starting. Then it stopped, and snippets of other sounds came and went. Explosions. People shouting. Some sort of country-sounding music. An audience applauding. Finally, she settled on something that had people arguing. Ragwater couldn't make out what they were saying, but it sounded highly dramatic.

He poured some oil into the popcorn popper, and almost as if that had been a cue, someone knocked on the back door. He stepped over and pulled the curtain aside to see a shortish, skinny, middle-aged man standing outside, illuminated by the full moon. He was dressed in a dark, button-down shirt and what looked like dress pants. His hair was reddish, cut short, and thinning. He bounced about, dancing in place, the way one might do in cold weather. But since this was the middle of July, it was probably nervous energy. No wonder the guy was skinny.

Ragwater opened the door a crack, leaving the chain hooked. "Can I help you?"

"Are you Gilbert Ragwater?" The man's voice was

surprisingly deep and Barry White-like for such a little guy. It also didn't sound as if he were asking a question. He knew.

"Uh, yeah, I guess so."

"Can I come in?" Still dancing. "I'd like to have a word with you."

"I'm kind of in the middle of something," Ragwater said, feeling that his voice had no conviction behind it.

"This is something good, and it won't take long."

Well, he seemed harmless. Or at least he didn't seem threatening. Ragwater figured he wouldn't have much trouble putting a full nelson on the guy if he had to. "All right," Ragwater said. He unchained the door and opened it wider. "But it has to be quick."

"Won't take long at all," the man said, stepping in. "I'll be gone before *The Blob* starts." He turned and closed the door behind himself.

How did he know about *The Blob*? Ragwater was already sorry he had let the man in. "Who are you?"

"My name is Maxwell. But you can call me Maxwell." He seemed a bit calmer now that he was inside.

"Huh?" Irritating, fakely clever lines didn't help endear the man to Ragwater.

Maxwell leaned back against the sink top. "You know those old-timey fantasy stories where someone stumbles upon a tiny, hole-in-the-wall antique shop run by a funny little man who sells the guy a magic genie lamp, and the guy makes wishes and everything goes horribly wrong, and the guy tries to take the lamp back but the store's gone? I own those shops. I have dozens of them across the country. Maybe hundreds; I'm not sure. Quite lucrative."

This clearly was going nowhere. "Look," Ragwater

said. "I don't think we have anything to talk about." He felt, more-or-less, that his voice had some conviction in it now.

"Sure we do. For instance, that redhead who was in your store today."

Ragwater stifled the urge to kick Maxwell in the crotch. He sighed and took a moment to roll things around in his mind before saying anything. Then, "Did John Plow send you here?" Plow wasn't much of a jokester; his area of expertise was mostly in the realm of being a smartass. Still, Ragwater couldn't think of a more likely suspect. Russ might send someone to the store to do this, if he could somehow be sure that Ragwater would take special notice of the Redhead. But home was strictly off-limits.

"No. John Plow has nothing to do with this. I'm here on my own, and I have a little proposal." He idly picked up a butter knife from the sink and balanced it on the tip of his left index finger.

Ragwater didn't know whether to comment on the stunt or continue the conversation. Or, for that matter, whether to reconsider kicking Maxwell in the crotch. Finally, in the interest of concluding the scene as quickly as possible—after all, he had popcorn to pop, a movie to watch, and a beautiful woman to get close to—he prompted: "Concerning the Redhead."

"Exactly." Maxwell tossed the knife into the air and caught it by the handle. "You can have her, and your girlfriend will never know." He spun the knife around to hold it by the blade and tapped the handle against a refrigerator magnet for a too-fast bar of the Bo Diddley beat, as if adding a ta-da! to his statement, and then put the knife down.

"That sounds pretty screwy."

From the living room, Lisa chimed in. "Gilbert, are you talking to someone?"

Oh, crap. He couldn't tell her some strange man was there offering him another woman. (Really, even if he didn't think she would care, he couldn't tell her a cockamamie story like that.) "No," he said. "Reciting some dialog to myself. For the novel, to see whether it sounds natural."

Maxwell leaned in close. "She has the TV on quite loud. I'm pretty sure all she can hear from in there is indistinct voices. Maybe not that much."

"Pretty sure?"

"I'm sure. In fact, if she has it turned up that loud, she might have problems with her hearing. Has she seen an ear specialist?"

"I don't know."

Maxwell picked up a cereal box and looked at the ingredients. "And while we're talking about health," he said, "this isn't as good for you as you think it is."

Ragwater grabbed the box and slammed it down on the countertop. "Never mind that. You apparently have some sort of deal to propose. Let's hear it so I can get on with my evening."

Maxwell smiled gently. "Listen to my offer and think about it for a couple days. You might agree that I could become your oldest, dearest, bestest friend in all of the whole, entire universe."

"You're making that ever more impossible with everything you say."

"I can see you're getting impatient. That's the trouble with you younger guys." Maxwell noticed something across the room. "What's that?" he asked, pointing.

"What's what?"

"That thing on the wall."

"The electrical outlet?"

"Is that what it is? Well, ain't that something?"

"Tell me about this deal so you can, like, get lost."

"Lost?"

"It's a figure of speech. It means you're going to leave." In only a couple minutes, Ragwater had reached the point at which he wasn't surprised at the need to explain the expression "get lost" to Maxwell.

"So if you say 'get lost' when you want someone to leave, what do you say if you want to tell someone you don't know where you are?"

"It's a matter of context."

"Okay, yeah. Context. Well, anyway, I have some work that needs to be done. Seven tasks in all. If you complete them, I can make the Redhead available to you."

"Available?"

"Yes. You can dally with her for a night and then send her on her way. Or you can shack up and make her get a job and support you. Or you could even lock her in a closet and feed her nothing but breath mints. Anything you want."

"I don't want to do any of that stuff."

"Or you can marry her and worship her as a goddess."

"I'm not sure about that, either."

"Or the two of you can do comedy routines together on open stage night at Olive's."

A slight wave of panic hit Ragwater. "What do you know about that?"

"Open stage? It's where they let people go up on

stage and sing songs or read poems or whatever. Most of the time it's pretty lame, but occasionally someone turns out to have some talent."

"I mean..." But knowing he wasn't going to get an explanation of how Maxwell had known his fantasy, Ragwater said, "Never mind."

Maxwell sighed. "Gilbert, she'll go along with anything you want. Anything."

"In return for doing seven tasks for you?"

"Yes! You understand perfectly."

"Gilbert!" Lisa called from the living room. "I have an idea!"

"What?"

"An idea. For the scene where the FBI has the Fennell brothers trapped in the mobile home out in the desert."

"Okay, hold on."

"What if they bring their parents to the scene to talk them out—you know, like in the movies? And the father turns out to be Sturges Morton?"

Ragwater whispered, "Hold on a second" and walked into the living room. Lisa was sitting on the coffee table looking at The Grid.

"What is it?" Ragwater asked.

"Well, see, if Sturges Morton is the Fennell Brothers' father, and the FBI brings him in to talk them out of the mobile home..."

"And then, after the brothers are arrested and that whole incident is over with, Morton could still be out there in the desert when the plaston beams start hitting the area..."

"So he's incapacitated for the next two weeks..."

"Thereby giving King the time he needs to find

Scarlett Cypress." That had, in fact, been something of a sticky point in the story line for quite a while. Scarlett Cypress, at first a seemingly minor character, was going to become much more important as the story progressed. In fact, Ragwater figured that in the final chapter, she was going to singlehandedly kill a dozen thugs to clear the way for King to get to the plane for the titular flight home from London.

"Beautiful, isn't it?"

"That's great," Ragwater said. "Write it down."

Lisa grabbed the steno pad and started writing.

Ragwater returned to the kitchen to find Maxwell examining, intensely and with great interest, the can opener. It was one of those little manual things, but Maxwell appeared never to have seen one before. He looked up. "Gilbert, this is one of the funniest-looking things I've ever seen."

"I take it you've never looked in a mirror?"

"I don't think mirrors look funny. But this sure does."

"You don't know what that is?"

"Sure I do." He paused and then added with a heavy tone of suspicion, "If it's really what I think it is."

"It's a can opener."

"Yeah, that's right," Maxwell said. "Yeah, can opener."

Ragwater plowed ahead. "What kind of stuff do you want me to do?"

Maxwell turned the handle on the can opener a few times. His lips were pursed, giving him a look of scientific curiosity. Then he said, "You don't get to find that out yet. Once you've agreed to the deal, I'll tell you what each task is, one at a time." Crank, crank. "You complete the one I give you. Then you have the option of quitting or letting me assign you another one." Crank, crank. "But once I give you an assignment, you *must* finish it." Crank, crank.

"What if I don't?"

"You forfeit your life." Crank, crank, crank. It might have had no more significance than a five-dollar fine.

"Come again?"

Maxwell put the can opener down. "You forfeit your life. It's nothing to worry about, though. You shouldn't have any reason not to complete any of them. It's simply my way of keeping you dependable." He turned to the sink and leaned over to study the fixtures. He started pivoting the faucet back and forth. "These tasks are very important to me."

"But my life..."

"There's no time limit on any of them," Maxwell said, varying the speed of his faucet pivoting. Quickly to the left, slowly to the right. Ragwater thought he heard it squeaking; he had never noticed it do that before. Did he need to replace an O ring or something?

"If you break that thing, I'm going to kick your ass," Ragwater said.

Maxwell's eyes widened. He stood up straight, eyes once again normal, an amused look on his face. "No worries," he said. "As long as I know you're sticking with it, you have nothing to worry about." His hand found its way to the faucet again, but it slid across the top and flopped down by his side.

"But you could tell me to drink the Atlantic Ocean."

"Why would I want you to do that?" Maxwell asked, as if the suggestion were an insult.

"I'm just saying, I don't know what these tasks are

going to be like."

"None are impossible," Maxwell said. He frowned. "Or is it, none *is* impossible? Is *none* singular or plural? It doesn't make sense either way when you're talking about no quantity at all."

"Either way," Ragwater said. "In this case, 'none are' is probably better."

"Yeah, okay. None are impossible. Some are more difficult than others, but they're all pretty simple. They won't require you to make any changes in your life. You know what? I'm just going to say they're all possible. Then I don't have to worry about *none.*" He glanced down, and something about the floor caught his attention. "Why do you have different-colored squares all over your floor?"

"They made it that way."

"Who are *they*?"

"Whoever built the place." Ragwater blurted out the first name he thought of. "Jan and Dean, flooring contractors."

"Jan and Dean, you say?"

"Haven't you noticed floors before? It's not unusual."

"Curious," Maxwell muttered to himself. Then he snapped back to the matter at hand. "You'll never be required to do anything morally objectionable. In short, you won't have any reason other than laziness to quit. And I know you're not lazy."

"How can you guarantee she'll go along with it?"

"You mean the Redhead?"

"No, Betsy Ross. Of course I mean the Redhead."

"Gilbert, do you think I'm someone who'd waste time with this if I couldn't deliver the goods?"

"I don't know anything about you. But if you want to talk about wasting time, I'll point out that you've stretched a two-minute conversation out to about ten minutes so far."

"I think I've made a strong first impression."

Ragwater paused to think. But what was there to think about? Maxwell's first impression? The dude who knew he was going to watch *The Blob*? Who knew he had fantasized about performing comedy routines with the Redhead? The dude who was offering him some kind of nutso deal regarding that redhead, the payoff being that he would "make her available" to Ragwater? The dude who apparently didn't know they tiled floors in checkerboard patterns? "What I mean," Ragwater said, "is that I don't see what's in it for her."

"That's between me and her," Maxwell said.

The dude who was sounding sort of like a...pimp, maybe?

And from the living room, "Gilbert, what's taking you so long?"

"I...uh, had trouble finding the popcorn. I have it now."

"Well, hurry. The movie starts in five minutes."

"I'll be there." And then, to Maxwell, "This is pretty strange. And you're not telling me much. I don't even know her name."

"I'm telling you all you need to know. I'm being fair."

"I don't know..."

"Okay, I understand that this is a strange kind of deal for you. I'll give you some time to think about it and get back to you in a couple days."

"Yeah, okay."

Maxwell smiled a genuine-looking paternal smile. Ragwater could almost hear the thought go through his head that *these young guys are so suspicious; you have to handle them just right.*

Halfway out the door, Maxwell turned to Ragwater. "Enjoy *The Blob*. And by the way, the popcorn is in the far left cabinet, all the way in the back, behind the Crisco." With that, he made his exit.

Ragwater opened the middle cabinet, where he knew the popcorn would actually be, and didn't find it. He went through everything, standing on a step stool to get a better view inside, but it wasn't there.

Just to make sure—just so he could rule out the possibility—he tried the far left cabinet. He moved a few things in front out of the way and found the popcorn precisely where Maxwell had said it would be.

~ 4 ~

It was a sunny day in Iroquois Park, with sparse, fluffy clouds and cheerful, tweetering birds. A football arched across the sky in an uncharacteristically well-thrown (for Ragwater) spiral, and John Plow had only to slow down a half step to pull it in. He tucked the ball under his arm, ran wide loops through imaginary defenders, stiff-arming some of them and leaping over others, and then straightened his course to run between two trees. He spiked the ball and did a campy, awkward exaggeration of a disco dance to celebrate. "Yeah!" he shouted. "Final score, Grubsville Ignorant Twerps seventy-three, East Patella Pencil-Neck Geeks four! GO TEAM!" Then, breathing heavily, he retrieved the football and slouched toward Ragwater's car.

Ragwater fell in beside him. "Did you know that the origins of football go back to the eleventh century?"

"No," Plow said. "And furthermore, I don't care."

"Yeah. Some English guys started kicking around the head of a dead Danish invader."

Plow stopped and considered this new bit of trivia. "Head, eh?"

"Sure 'nuff. Kicked it around. Made a game out of it."

"Wow. They couldn't do that today, could they?"

"I expect not. I mean, they could *do* it. But I expect they couldn't *get away* with it. There'd be video on the Internet, and people on the cable news channels would be all outraged and stuff, demanding investigations. Bloggers howling and shrieking. Ugly."

"Yeah, that's what I meant. These days, no one wants anyone else to have fun."

"Yeah, but think of it this way. Each and every time a team kicks a field goal, metaphorically it's some guy's head flying through the goal post."

They resumed walking toward the car. "You know," Plow said, "history might be kind of interesting, after all."

"Might be, kind of, after all?"

"Let's not get carried away. For every cool story about some guys kicking another guy's head around, you have a hundred boring stories about what crops the farmers were growing in ancient Yugoslavia and guys traveling halfway around the world to sell spices and fabric for some reason. Who cares about spices and fabric?"

"History class was traumatic for you, wasn't it?"

"You know what it was like. You were there."

"I guess I was. I was even awake most of the time."

"Yeah, and look how you turned out."

"Point taken." Ragwater unlocked his car, and they slid in. Ragwater twisted around, opened the cooler on the backseat, and took two beers out. "I'm pretty sure you'll want one of these."

"You speak the truth." Plow took one of the cans and popped it open. He chugged for several eye-watering seconds and finished it off by jerking the can away from his mouth amidst a splash of beer and gasping desperately for breath. Ragwater watched, amused.

"Oh, that was good," Plow said. He turned the can up and chugged the rest. "Yeah, boy." He wiped his mouth on his shirtsleeve and then got another beer from the cooler.

Ragwater usually took the day off on Saturdays and Sundays, leaving the store to his cousin Jason and a couple of his friends—college students looking to make a little extra money with part-time jobs. They took most of the evening shifts through the week, too. And even though Ragwater was "officially" off on weekends, he typically made several visits to the store "to make sure."

Between these visits, he might find himself in the park giving a friend a history lesson.

Up ahead, Ragwater noticed a familiar figure. A woman, lithe and graceful, sauntered along the edge of the clearing carrying a canvas bag. She was wearing a flowing, white dress, and her red hair fell about her shoulders in a way that's rarely seen outside of professional photo shoots. She stopped and looked at the ground under a tree and then continued on her way. She stopped at a second tree, took a look, and removed a beach towel from the bag. She spread the towel out on the ground, in the shade, and sat down. Then she took a book from the bag, found her page, and began reading.

What was going on? How could this be a coincidence?

But then again, how could it not?

"What's wrong, man?" Plow asked.

"Huh?"

"You look disturbed. More than usual, I mean."

Ragwater pointed. "Well, look over there. See, under that tree? Recognize her?"

Plow peered in the direction Ragwater was pointing. After a moment, he caught on. "Oh, yeah. Ain't that a hoot."

"I wonder what brought her here."

Plow took another swig of beer. "Hey, man, you haven't opened your beer yet."

Ragwater looked down at the can as if he hadn't been aware that he was holding it. He popped the tab but didn't pull it off.

"You still think you're going to get some of that? Forget it."

Ragwater knew better than to tell Plow he didn't believe her appearance was coincidence. That would be a one-way ticket to Ridicule City, courtesy of Derision Bus Lines. "Let me clue you in," Plow would say. "She doesn't know you're alive, and if she did, she wouldn't care."

"I wonder what she's reading," Ragwater said.

"Are you going to engage her in a conversation about literature? Invite her to join your book club? Ask her to critique the novel you've been working on for eleven years? All twenty-five pages of it?"

"Forty."

"I stand corrected. But this time tomorrow, it'll be down to twenty-five."

"Are you going to stop acting like an ass for once in your sorry life?"

"Hey, it's who I am. It's what I do."

"I was thinking of an idea for a short story about her."

"A short story?"

"Yeah. It's kind of like a long story, but shorter."

Plow gave Ragwater a dirty look and then glanced down at Ragwater's still-half-opened beer can. He drank from his own. "Tell me about it."

Ragwater pulled the tab off his can and flipped it into the backseat. "It's about a guy like me. Music store owner, pretty nice girlfriend, yadda yadda."

"Yeah, write what you know."

"Sure. What I know. So anyway, the Redhead pops into the store one day all mysterious and beautiful, without saying a word, and our hero is attracted to her."

"Writing stories about her," Plow said. "Wow, you got it really bad."

"Oh, for Pete's sake, John. It's just imagination."

"Hmmm...yeah. What's so imaginative about writing something that actually happened?"

"I'm trying to get there, if you'll let me."

"Sorry. Go on."

"Okay, so she comes into the store, the way it happened yesterday. She drifts in, all ethereal-like, giving the impression that...well, not quite as if she owns the place, but as if she's sort of 'at one' with her surroundings. A sort of Zen thing. She probably gives that impression everywhere she goes. Doctor's office, riding on the bus, whatever."

"Don't go overboard, Gilbert. This sounds like the feverish and almost incoherent ramblings of some deluded, lovesick sap."

"And we'll disregard the insensitive clods who think she's nothing more than some random, moderately attractive woman."

"I'm very sure her friends and family think she's something special, and well they should," Plow said. "To everyone else, that's all she is."

"The point is, she catches our hero's attention. Then, later that night, a mysterious guy shows up at his house. This guy's really weird, full of nervous energy and acting like he doesn't know stuff."

"Doesn't know stuff?"

"Yeah. Like, he doesn't know what a can opener is. He's surprised when he notices our hero's kitchen floor is tiled in a checkerboard pattern. Stuff like that."

"Why?"

"Maybe I don't want to say why. Maybe he's from the fifty-ninth dimension. I don't know. He might be putting on an act. It doesn't matter. So anyway, he pulls a few mindreading tricks to impress our hero, makes references to a couple of things he couldn't possibly know about. F'rinstance, remember when I told you that you were my dearest, oldest, bestest friend in all of the whole entire universe?"

"No."

"Well, I did. I said it when you were in the store, right before the Redhead came in. So I figure our hero says something like that. Something dumb but very distinctive, and no one but his best friend hears it. And then, this strange little man quotes it back at our hero, word for word."

"Okay," Plow said, unimpressed. "So when you write the story, you can copy and paste the quote. Save yourself a dozen keystrokes."

"Well, more than that, but the point is, it's not spectacular. Not at all. But after, say, three or four things like that, our hero starts thinking maybe there's more to this strange man than just oddness."

"Or to this odd man than just strangeness."

"Yeah, sure. And then the man offers our hero a deal. He tells him he'll make the Redhead 'available' if he—our hero, that is—will perform a series of tasks. And his girlfriend will never know."

"Available?"

"Yeah. Like, she'll do anything he wants."

Plow blinked. He sighed. He blinked again. "You *do* have it really *bad*," he said.

"How many times do I have to tell you? It's just a story."

"I'm not sure there's such a thing as 'just a story.'"

"It's not as if I've never made up stories before. You know that. Most of them have some small basis in real life and then take off into strange and exotic new territory."

"You're right. So what kind of tasks would you be willing to perform in order to nail that redhead?"

"At least *pretend* you believe we're talking about a made-up story."

"Okay, sure. So what kind of tasks will our hero, Hilbert Rigmeter, be asked to perform?"

"I don't know yet."

Plow regarded Ragwater and then glanced at the Redhead. "So, then, like, you don't really have a story, do you?"

"It's an *idea* for a story. The germ of an idea. I can figure out the rest of it easily enough."

"And if he does all this as-yet-unspecified stuff, he can 'have' her?"

"Yeah. She'll do anything he wants. At least, that's what the guy says, the strange little man. That's as much as I have."

"Anything at all?"

"Anything."

"So, he could tell her to install new carpeting in his apartment."

"Yes, he could."

"And she would do it."

"Presumably she would."

Plow drank more beer, eyeballing the Redhead off in the distance. "Do you think she would be able to do a good job installing carpet?"

"I don't know. I suppose she could get it done if she were strongly enough motivated."

"And your hero could tell this mysterious woman to go beat up all the bullies who picked on him in school?"

Ragwater shrugged. "I suppose. Maybe she's proficient in some form of martial arts. I don't think he would want to ask her to do that, though."

"He wouldn't want a girl fighting his battles."

"He wouldn't. And by now, it's no longer a battle, anyway. But think of this: Think of her in a black leotard, roundhouse kicking some douchebag who was a bully when he was a kid. He staggers back against the wall, and she moves in for a quick hip toss. He flops over, and she moves around behind him for a chokehold."

"That's my kind of woman."

Ragwater drank some of his beer and closed his eyes. He reached down to the lever and tilted his seat back.

"So your hero agrees to the deal," Plow said.

"Does he?"

"If he doesn't, you don't have a story."

"It would seem that way. If he says no, there's no place to go from there. But then again, maybe the whole point of the story is the stuff that goes on in our hero's head up until he refuses the deal. That could be a story."

"But it wouldn't be a *Gilbert Ragwater* story," Plow said. "Gilbert Ragwater won't be all navel-gazing and introspective. Real-life Ragwater is that way, to a fault. But he's not going to write introspective characters. He wants to follow that guy through all the stuff that happens after he agrees to the deal."

"If he agrees, I have to know why."

"So you can have a story."

"I want to know what *motivates* him, dipwad. What is it about this deal that hooks him?"

"Where did you learn a word like dipwad?"

"From your mom."

"I'm sorry my mom called you a dipwad."

"We were talking about you," Ragwater said. "After I banged her for the seventh time that night, she was asking me why her son is such a dipwad."

"What did you tell her?"

"She was probably exposed to radiation during pregnancy. What else could explain it?"

"I don't know. I can tell you that I prefer banging hot chicks my own age, though."

"So what do you think? Would you go for the deal? Why or why not? Explain your reasoning."

"What's going on? Are trying to get me to write this thing for you?"

"Well..."

"Would I go for it, not knowing anything about this guy, or who he is or where he came from, or what his psychiatric history is?"

"I suppose that's one way of looking at it."

"I think it's obvious. It's like those things you get in e-mail where someone claims they want to move millions of dollars into the United States, and they need your help. They're hoping you won't think it's odd that they're proposing a deal like that to some randomly chosen stranger they know nothing about. It's preposterous, on the face of it. Yet people fall for it. Precious few people, I hope, but still, it happens. I've seen stories about it on TV. So ask yourself, why?"

"Because they want it to be true."

"Exactimundo, my fine friend," Plow said. "I'm sure some of those folks are just plain stupid, but they're not the ones who'll give you an interesting story. For our purposes, we should look at the otherwise bright people who want it to be true so badly that it clouds their judgment."

"Okay, go ahead."

Plow took a deep swig of his beer and warmed up to the subject. "Never underestimate the power of the human mind to bend, distort, and reshape reality when it wants something. They might even know it's a scam, that it's stupid to even think about it. And yet they'll talk themselves into it. They think it's...*unlikely*...that this Nigerian e-mail is legit, but unlikely things happen every day. What if it's real? What if?"

"What if?" Ragwater echoed.

"Yeah. People play that game all the time. What if I happen to be driving along and spot a suitcase on the ground, and I stop to check it out, and it turns out to be packed full of money? Maybe it was dropped off by someone paying a ransom, and the kidnappers haven't gotten there yet to pick it up. There's no identification on this thing, and no one around. You could pick it up and walk away, and no one would be the wiser.

"So you have this little fantasy idea, and you might think about it, make plans for what you would do with the money, as a sort of game. What would you do?"

Ragwater thought. "If I thought it was a ransom payment, I would also believe the kidnappers would kill the victim if they don't get the money. Under those circumstances, how could I take it?"

Plow sighed. "If it's a kidnapping, the police are hot on the case anyway. Besides, you don't know how it got there or why. All you know is, you have it now. What do you do?"

"I guess the first thing I do is make sure there's no transponder in it so the bad guys can track me down."

"Obviously. Then what?"

"Trip to Switzerland. I've always wanted to see Switzerland."

"Sounds pretty good. Beautiful mountains. Home of fine watches and chocolate and army knives. And if you think about it enough, it starts to seem as if it could happen.

"Now, back to the guy who's sitting there looking at the scam e-mail on his computer screen. At first, he might have understood very well that it wasn't real. It was out of the question to answer. But a couple days go by, and he's wondering about it. What if it's real? No, of course it's not. It couldn't be. But what if it was? It's not going to hurt anything, to answer the e-mail and ask for more details. That doesn't cost anything. It doesn't commit him to anything."

"No, it doesn't."

"And then," Plow continued, "let's say the scammer's really good. Let's say he has a story that sounds to the mark as if it could be feasible—assuming, as we've already said, that the mark has been distorting reality in his own mind because it would be sooooo great if the story happened to be true."

"Like, maybe the mark almost *wants* to be fooled."

"Maybe so," Plow said. "And let's look at this hero in your story. He's being promised that this beautiful woman will do anything he wants. It's every man's fantasy, Gilbert."

"It's certainly mine." Ragwater watched an airplane fly across the sky. It was small, off in the distance, but he figured it as a commercial passenger jet. Maybe hundreds of people aboard. And here he was, on the ground, watching them go off someplace he, Ragwater, had probably never been. He drank from his beer and squinted at the plane. How many of the passengers were drinking at this very moment?

"But then," Ragwater said, "later on, is our hero sorry he agreed to the deal? Or does it work out the way he hopes it will?"

"If it were my story, I would make it so the deal really has nothing to do with the Redhead. I would make it so the hero is actually doing stuff to help aliens prepare for an invasion of Earth. Or something like that. And then, by the time he finds out he's been had, the situation is so dire for humanity that he's no longer concerned about hooking up with some hot woman. He's trying to figure out how to survive."

Ragwater hadn't thought about that. Yes, the whole deal could be some sort of red herring. A diversion, a fake. A scam of a different sort. "Interesting," he said.

"But that's just me. You're the writer; you're in control. Or, that is to say, if you were a typical writer you would be in control. As it is, you're a guy who's obsessed with a moderately attractive woman who doesn't know he's alive."

The airplane was out of sight. The redhead was still sitting under the tree reading. "Well, it's an odd thing about her," Ragwater said. "I can't decide whether she's smoking hot, or wholesome and pretty, or what. I can't fit her into a 'type.'"

"Maybe that's why you're so fascinated with her."

"I'm not fascinated with her."

"If there's one thing I know when I see it, it's fascination."

"What do *you* think about her?"

"I told you. She's moderately attractive."

"Is that all?"

"What more do you want? Should I get all obsessed with her, too, so you'll have competition?"

"See, there you go, turning it into something preposterous, the way you always do."

"I think it got preposterous when you started talking about your short story," Plow said. "Probably before that. My advice, Gilbert, is to forget about her. I don't think you want to cheat on Lisa anyway, so what you're doing here isn't too far different from repeatedly banging your head into that retaining wall at the edge of the parking lot at your apartment building."

"I don't think it would be cheating. We're not that serious."

"Why don't you ask Lisa what she thinks?"

"If she thinks we're serious, she'll make sure I know. It's what women do."

"If you want to think so, then sure."

"When did you become such a world-class authority on women?"

"Don't get so defensive. I've learned a little bit about people. Through my modest number of years, I've paid attention to the way they behave. And women, my dear Gilbert, are people. That's the whole story. By the way, what are you doing tonight?"

"Nothing special. Why?"

"No Saturday night date with Lisa?"

"She's doing something with friends. A night out with the girls. You got something going on?"

"I finally got that girl at the Stupendous Mart to go out with me. Sylvia."

"Congratulations. How'd you manage that?"

"How do you think?"

Ragwater looked at Plow. "You lied to her, I would imagine."

"Of course. I told her I had a fifty-five gallon drum of cocaine."

"Sure. Women love that."

"Anyway, I was wondering if I could bring her over to your place. It's either that or kill my parents."

"I wouldn't want that on my conscience. But how do you know she's going to want to...do something like that?"

"I don't know what she's going to want to do. I've been talking to her at the Stupendous Mart for...oh, like a year and a half. Sometimes she seems like a nice, wholesome girl saving it for marriage. And sometimes I get the idea that she has this wild streak and a collection of costumes and toys and cleverly modified power tools, and she's been waiting for a guy like me to cut loose with."

"Like you?"

"I'm the guy she's going out with tonight, aren't I? Presumably she thinks I might...uh, shall we say, have something to offer. So I want to have your place on standby, and give you a call if all systems are go."

"Do you think it's going to impress her, taking her over to your friend's place to get nekkid?"

"After all those huge car repair bills, I have no money for a motel. Barely enough to take her out. So your place is the best I have right now. You have to admit, it's not as bad as having no place at all."

"Wait till you have money."

"But I have my chance *tonight*. If I wait, she'll get a boyfriend or some damn fool thing."

"You know, John, this is pathetic. You really should get your own place."

"I'm working on it. But I'm not going to get it by tonight, am I?"

"No, I guess not."

Ragwater wondered whether Plow had really told Sylvia he had a fifty-five gallon drum of cocaine. He was pretty sure—but not certain—that, for all his rough edges, Plow had more sense than to unleash a joke like that on someone who didn't know him very well.

But then again, whatever he had said must have been right; he had a date with her. "What time are you picking her up?" Ragwater asked.

"Seven."

An idea came to Ragwater. "Okay, I'll make you a deal. Can you arrange to be sitting in Olive's at about five-thirty? I want to have someone there to verify that something happens."

"I could do it."

"You're a champ."

"What's going to happen?"

"I haven't decided yet."

Plow nodded. "Do you need suggestions?"

"Sure. What do you have?"

Plow took a drink of beer. He gazed ahead, out in front of the car, for a few seconds. "I guess setting the place on fire would be out of the question."

"Well, remember, you'll be sitting inside."

"Then no. I have nothing."

"Maybe I should go over there and talk to her," Ragwater said.

"Huh?"

Ragwater gave a quick nod toward the Redhead. "Her."

"Yeah. Good luck with that."

"Just because you're a totally inferior and defective specimen of manhood doesn't mean I am too."

"I'll remind you that I have a date with Sylvia at the Stupendous Mart."

"Probably after she tried everything she could think of to get you to stop bothering her, short of a restraining order."

"It's because I know how to talk to women."

Ragwater looked at Plow. "You barely know how to talk, period."

Plow shot a dirty look back. "Watch this, my friend." He got out of the car and stood next to it. After a moment, he signaled to a woman who was jogging along the roadside toward them. She stopped at a more-than-conversational distance from Plow but continued the running-in-place thing that joggers do when they stop but don't really want to. She looked to Ragwater to be in her late twenties and fit. She probably had been jogging regularly for quite some time.

"Hi," Plow said. "My name is John, and I think you're cute. Can I have your phone number?"

"Okay."

"Huh? Oh, uh...sure. Hold on." Plow walked around to the driver's side of the car. "I'll be right with you," he told the woman, and then bent down to window level. "Quick, give me a pen and paper."

"What makes you think I have pen and paper?"

"Don't mess around, man. She'll think I'm an idiot."

"Keep talking to her." Ragwater leaned over, opened the glove compartment, and took out a small spiral notebook and a pen. "If you're going to do stuff like this, you should be prepared."

"I *am* prepared. I came with a friend who's a writer. Writers always have paper and pens. Now give up the paper before she jogs away and I have to bite your throat out."

Ragwater handed the items over. "I wouldn't want that. If someone saw, they might get the wrong idea. Just don't scare her, okay?"

"If she's not scared seeing that I'm with a doofus like you, she's not going to be scared." Plow walked over to the woman. Ragwater expected she would back up a step or two to keep some distance from him, but she didn't. She did, however, seem very much on the alert for any funny business.

Ragwater sized her up as a small-business-type person, probably...uh...hmmm...probably antiques. Yeah, she knew her stuff inside-out and had a small shop in the Highlands, a shop well known across this country and in a few others as well. She had a knack for finding fabulously rare stuff at places like flea markets and yard sales. Maybe she even wrote a blog: Ann Teak's Blog.

No, too corny. The name, that is. But there would be a blog. These days, you have to have a blog. And she would sell antiques to Sylvia during her brief career as a crusading lawyer.

Also, she had an ex-husband who divorced her because she made considerably more money than he did. Of course, he never came right out and said so, but underneath everything that was the problem.

"Sorry about that," Plow said. "I didn't come prepared because I didn't think I'd meet anyone interesting. I'm very picky about my women, you know."

Maybe she would have a deal for a reality show in the negotiation stages. A camera crew would follow her as she traveled to exotic places and met interesting people, in search of rare treasures.

Actually, Ragwater thought, that really did sound like a good idea for a show. He would watch it.

Plow offered the woman his notebook and pen. She stopped jogging in place and, using the hood of the car as a writing surface, dashed off a quick notation. "It's all right," she said. "I'm very picky about my men."

"I can tell," Plow said. He took the notebook and looked at it. "Linda, huh? Pleased to meet you."

"Yeah, same here." She started on her way, turned to give Plow a quick parting wave, and then continued down the road. Plow watched her jog around the bend and out of sight. He paused for what Ragwater assumed was supposed to be a thoughtful moment and then got back into the car.

Plow held up the notebook as if showing off a product in a TV commercial. “She’s very picky about her men.”

“I saw nothing to convince me of that.”

Plow waved the notebook tauntingly.

“Okay, Clyde,” Ragwater said. “You’re not the only slick one.” He opened his door and slid out. What was he going to say? Blurt out some kind of comment about seeing her in the store yesterday? That was lame. Ask her if she had found what she wanted? Even lamer, considering she hadn’t bought anything.

Up ahead, the Redhead placed her bookmark lovingly between the pages she was reading and folded the book shut. She packed the book and beach towel back into the canvas bag, smoothed out her dress, and walked away.

Well, that was that. Ragwater could have approached her while she was sitting under the tree—if he had known what to say, that is—but he couldn’t go chasing after her.

He sighed and drummed his fingers on the top of the car, absentmindedly tapping out the same Bo Diddley beat that Maxwell had played with the butter knife in his kitchen. Finally, he sat down. “She probably had to go to the bathroom.”

“I’m surprised you think such a heavenly creature has to do something as lowly as go to the bathroom.”

“Well, to brush her teeth.”

Yeah, who the heck was this Maxwell guy, anyway? And what was his psychiatric history?

***

Ragwater got to the store about a quarter to five. It was moderately busy, but Jason had things under control. Ragwater worked the floor, circulating among the customers, helping them find things and making recommendations. He managed to sell a Bob Dylan box set and a Black Crowes DVD.

At five, Aunt Rachel and Sniffy came in, ready for a world-class prank. They even seemed a bit excited.

Ragwater still didn't know what he wanted them to do. His mind raced through all the usual ideas he started with and rejected when he tried to think of pranks—fake robbery, exhibitionism—things he could never have anyone do because of the pesky legal problems that could result. He wouldn't have risked the fake shooting, although he had to admit that it was a good idea.

Ragwater wanted to tailor the caper to the personnel he had available. But what could these guys do? What unique talents did they have? He didn't know anything about them except that after being scared to death by an overly dramatic gunman, they wanted revenge.

He briefly considered asking them to come back later, after he'd had time to think about it. But he was pretty sure that although they were ready to do something at the moment, they would lose enthusiasm if he put it off very long. So if he wanted to use them, it should be now—even if it meant going with a weak idea.

"Okay," Ragwater said. "You're going to go to Olive's Coffee Shop. You know where it is, right?"

"Yeah," Aunt Rachel said. "A couple blocks down

the street."

"Good. So you walk in and tell them you're there for your appointment. They won't know what you're talking about, but you insist you have an appointment."

"Appointment?"

"Yeah. If they ask you who you're supposed to see, or what it's all about, just keep insisting you're there for your appointment."

"We're there for our appointment."

"Yes. Get loud about it if you want to. 'I'M HERE FOR MY APPOINTMENT. I DON'T HAVE TIME TO STAND HERE ARGUING WITH YOU. WHY ARE YOU ACTING LIKE YOU DON'T KNOW WHAT I'M TALKING ABOUT?' That kind of thing. But no profanity. Don't insult anyone. Just keep insisting you have an appointment. Then, finally, give up and leave. If Russ tells you to get out, don't give him a hard time. Just go."

"What?" Sniffy asked. "Is that all?"

"Do you want more?"

"It's kind of lame, after the gun thing."

Well, yeah. Almost anything was going to look weak after something as spectacular as a fake shooting. Ragwater really should spend a day brainstorming with Plow and Jason. They could write down the best ideas and build up a stockpile. Or maybe search the Internet for ideas. He was willing to bet there were web sites with oodles of good ideas for practical jokes, sitting there waiting for him to pluck them. He didn't need to be original; he just needed ideas no one had yet used in this little war.

Yeah, it would be a lot easier if he could show them a list of top-notch, grade-A pranks and ask which one they liked best. But for now, all he could say was, "Well, I can't send you in there with a gun."

"Those other people came in with a gun," Aunt Rachel said.

"Really, that's going too far. Besides, I have to retaliate with something different." They seemed unenthusiastic. "This can be good," Ragwater continued. "It's a matter of how you play it. Ham it up. Have fun with it. Use your creativity. Think of it as a challenge."

"Creativity," Sniffy said.

"Challenge," Aunt Rachel said.

"Free CD," Ragwater said.

***

The call came about ten minutes later. "Hey, man, it was magnificent," Plow said.

"Oh, yeah?"

"They performed with distinction. At first, they looked like they weren't sure what was going on. You know, kind of timid-like. Furtive. Is that the right word? Furtive?"

"How would I know? I wasn't there."

"Yeah, acting like maybe they didn't belong there, like they expected someone to run them out. So they stood there for a minute or two looking around, and the one guy said to the other, 'Is this the right place?' And then the other guy said, 'Let's ask.' They went up to the counter girl and asked about the appointment. She said she didn't know anything about an appointment.

"Then they started laying it on real thick. Stuff like, 'Come on, they have to tell the person at the front desk about appointments. If this is how you operate, I don't know how you stay in business.' They went around the place asking customers whether they had appointments."

"No, they didn't," Ragwater said, amused.

"Oh, yes, they did. They said they were going to contact the Better Business Bureau. Threatened to file a complaint with the Kentucky Attorney General's office. Then Russ came out, acting like a crotchety old man running the kids off his lawn, told them to scram. So they were going out, and one guy turned around at the door and said, 'We will *not* be treated this way! You haven't heard the last of this!' Keeping up the act right to the very end."

As Ragwater was finishing up with Plow, Aunt Rachel and Sniffy came back in.

"I hear you guys performed with distinction," Ragwater said.

"We had fun with it," Aunt Rachel said. "Just like you said."

"So," Sniffy said, "can we get our CDs now?"

"Sure. Go ahead and pick something out."

The two started browsing CDs. After a minute, Aunt Rachel pulled one out of a bin. "Hey, I'm getting this one."

Sniffy got excited. "Oh, yeah! When I stayed with my cousin in Miami last summer, he had it. We rolled us up some big ol' thick doobies and cranked it all the way up. I'm not kidding, man, our ears started bleeding. It was great." He took the CD from his friend and looked at it, presumably thinking about those wonderful, bygone times.

A moment later, Sniffy found his. "Hey, man. Check this out."

"Oh, sweet," Aunt Rachel said. "Burn me a copy, okay?"

"Yeah, sure thing."

Ragwater gritted his teeth. Yeah, sure. Go ahead and burn copies for your friends. Whatever. But at least have the courtesy not to talk about it in front of the guy who makes his living selling CDs.

They brought their selections to the sales counter. Ragwater brought up his inventory list on the computer so he could enter the titles.

Aunt Rachel handed his disc to Ragwater: James Taylor, *Sweet Baby James.* Was his friend remembering that great summer in Miami accurately? A little too much weed or booze or whatever? Maybe he had been sitting there looking at the cousin's wife's James Taylor CD case on the coffee table, mistakenly thinking it was the death metal that was blasting out of the stereo. He started to ask the guy whether he knew what he was getting but stifled the urge. It would be sorta like calling the guy stupid. Besides, if he wanted to bring it back, Ragwater would take it.

Ragwater checked off the title on his computer and turned to Sniffy. "What do you have?"

New Lost City Ramblers, *Old Time Music.*

Well.

~ 5 ~

Ragwater was in the middle of one of his periodic rereadings of Kurt Vonnegut's novels. Every two to three years, he lined them up in the order they were written and read everything straight through.

Now he was stretched out on the sofa, in the laziest posture he could achieve, about halfway through *Breakfast of Champions*. The police had just released Kilgore Trout when Ragwater's doorbell rang.

It would be Plow; no hurry. Ragwater continued reading. The doorbell rang again. After a moment, Plow's voice called out. "HEY, RAGWATER! OPEN UP!"

"Hold on a minute."

"C'mon, man, it's freezing out here!"

"I'm not falling for that. It's the middle of July." Nonetheless, he put the book down and sat up. He stood and stretched leisurely.

"HELP!" Plow shouted. "A brontosaurus is about to eat us!"

Well, that did it. Ragwater couldn't have idiots shouting outside his door. He didn't see the big deal, provided it didn't go on longer than a few seconds, but Arnie next door would disagree. Arnie would be all up in his face about it. The best thing was to nip it in the bud.

Ragwater threw the door open. Plow was standing there with his arm around Sylvia. "Quiet," Ragwater hissed.

"Oh, sorry," Plow said. He knew about Arnie. The problem was, he couldn't remember. Why would he?

"Come on in before the brontosaurus gets you."

Plow led Sylvia in. She glanced around with an expression that made Ragwater think of a devout nun waking in on a black mass. Ragwater scanned the room to see whether he could figure out what someone might find disturbing, but as far as he could tell, everything was within the general parameters of what might be normal—not that he was certain of what was generally considered normal, or of what Sylvia might consider normal.

"You know Sylvia, don't you?" Plow said.

"Yeah, from the Stupendous Mart."

"And this is my buddy, Gilbert Ragwater."

Now more relaxed-looking, she held out her hand. "Pleased to meet you."

Ragwater took Sylvia's hand and smiled. "Likewise. John, she's not ugly. What's the matter with you?"

Sylvia's face went blank. "What?"

"Oh! Uh, never mind," Ragwater said.

"Gilbert, do you desire to live as a cripple?"

"I'm sorry. Just getting him back for the hard time he gave me in the park this afternoon. We're a couple of nutty guys."

"Yeah," Plow said, and added, pointedly, "madcap."

"Gullible, too," Sylvia said. "The brontosaurus wasn't a meat eater."

Okay, everything was all right with her. "I think you're in over your head, John," Ragwater said.

"Well, yeah. When it comes to women, I'm either in over my head or I'm not in at all."

"Point taken. Have a seat."

Plow and Sylvia sat on the sofa. Plow scooched closer to Sylvia. She seemed uncomfortable in a self-conscious sort of way but didn't object.

"So, you crazy kids," Ragwater said, "what have you been up to tonight?" His cell phone rang. Unknown number. "Talk amongst yourselves while I get this."

Feeling he should keep it private, Ragwater stepped into his bedroom and closed the door before he flipped the phone open.

"Hello, Gilbert. Do you know who this is?"

"Yes, I think so."

"Good. I suspect it might be time for us to have another little chat. What do you think?"

Ragwater's mind considered possible replies. Yes, no, maybe, yes but only if you stand on your head and blow bubbles out of your butt in the middle of the intersection of Bardstown Road and Eastern Parkway for twenty minutes during rush hour Friday afternoon…"I think I haven't made up my mind yet."

"Yes you have," Maxwell said. "You just don't want to say so. Meet me at the Slipknot Inn, and I'll buy you a beer and we'll discuss things. Besides, I know you need an excuse to get out of the apartment so John can play with his girlfriend."

Not mindful of this latest mind reading trick of Maxwell's, Ragwater nudged the door open a crack and glanced out at Plow and Sylvia. They were very much occupied with each other. They would have been oblivious to a marching band parading through the room playing "Wang Dang Doodle."

"I don't think they'll know whether I'm here or not." Of course he wanted to leave Plow and Sylvia alone, but he also wanted to be contrary with Maxwell.

"But you would rather not be there. And we still need to talk."

"Yeah, okay. I'll be there shortly." Ragwater flipped the phone shut and stepped into the living room. "Hey, John."

Plow looked up. "Can't you see I'm busy?"

"That phone call just now. I have to take care of some business. You guys can hang out here if you want. I'll be back in an hour or two."

Ragwater went to the door. Plow got up, and the two stepped outside. "Make it two." Plow said. "Or three."

"I'll see what I can do." Ragwater started toward his car and then turned around. "And change the sheets after you're finished."

~ 6 ~

The Slipknot Inn was a surprisingly clean and well-maintained neighborhood bar about four blocks from Ragwater's apartment building. Situated in a row of storefronts between a vintage clothing store and a tattoo shop, the building had—like many of the businesses along Bardstown Road, including North Star—faithfully maintained the feel of its original prewar design through numerous remodelings over the years as various businesses moved in and out. It was a neighborhood with character, strongly evocative of a bygone era but not anachronistic.

As you walked into the Slipknot, the bar was to the right, tables straight ahead and to the left, and three pool tables—no waiting!—in the back. The lighting was dim, and it was never apparent to Ragwater where or what the source was.

He spotted Maxwell at a booth with a pitcher of beer and two mugs, one full, in front of him. A napkin dispenser—one of about three in the place—was lying on its side, and napkins were scattered about the table. Maxwell was folding a napkin into something that resembled the beginnings of a paper airplane.

Ragwater had a quick tinge of doubt. He wouldn't

have to sit down and talk, wouldn't have to say even the single syllable "no." If he were to turn around and walk out at that very instant, Maxwell would get the message.

Yeah, Ragwater could do that. He could leave. He saw no need to talk about it. He could find something else to do for a couple hours.

He walked over to the booth and sat down.

Maxwell grabbed the empty mug and poured Ragwater a beer with expert head-controlling technique. He sat the mug down in front of Ragwater.

"Yeah, thanks," Ragwater said.

"You know, Sylvia's not bad looking. John did pretty well for himself."

"Yeah, sometimes he'll pull some kind of overachieving stunt like that."

Maxwell smiled. He reached over and grabbed the napkin dispenser. "What do you think of my little proposition?" He pulled yet another napkin out and looked into the opening. He seemed frustrated to see that another napkin was still there.

"I think it's ridiculous," Ragwater said.

"Yes, you do. And yet, here you sit, talking to me about it." He turned the dispenser around and pulled a napkin out the other side. This time, the spring-mounted pressure pad that pushes the napkins forward was gleaming through the opening. Maxwell ran his fingertip along the length of the pad. He pushed his finger in. "There's a spring in there," he said.

"Yeah, I expect so."

"You're intrigued."

"Almost as much as you are by that napkin dispenser."

As if suddenly caught playing with something he had no business playing with, Maxwell put the dispenser down. "You believe I can do it," he said. "You believe that although this is clearly a case of something being too good to be true, it might be true anyway."

"I don't know. I mean, you have my attention."

Maxwell turned the dispenser around again and frowned at the napkin in the opening. "I thought this thing was empty," he said.

"It holds two separate stacks of napkins," Ragwater said, "and they get pushed out from the middle."

Maxwell nodded thoughtfully. He might have been an investor interested in putting some money into a clever new invention. "And you're curious," he said.

"Yeah," Ragwater agreed. "I'm curious. But, see, I'm not sure this is something I should be curious about."

"Why not?"

"I don't know. And that's the problem. But then again, I can't help but think that if I walk away from this, I'll be wondering about it for the rest of my life. The payoff might have nothing to do with the Redhead, but if that's the case, I have to know what's going on."

"You think these tasks might be some sort of preparation for an alien invasion?"

Ragwater choked on his sip of beer. He should have expected Maxwell to say something like that, but this strange man seemed very good at finding effective ways to get his little zingers in.

"Think of this," Maxwell said. "I know I come across as eccentric."

"I'm not sure eccentric is quite the right word."

"Well, let's say eccentric and leave it at that. We both know what I'm talking about."

"Okay, sure."

"If I were trying to run some sort of scam on you, would this be the way to do it? Do you really think I would approach you the way I have and get you all suspicious?"

"I don't know. Maybe you're trying to think one step ahead of me. If you can convince me that acting suspicious proves you're on the level, then it doesn't matter how suspicious—or how weird—you're acting."

Maxwell pulled the last napkin out of the dispenser and began tearing it into strips. "You're thinking too much, Gilbert. Life is really very simple."

"No, it's not."

"The universe is simple. It's the explanations that are complex."

"Stop it."

"Gilbert, there's a point to all this." Maxwell began weaving napkin strips into some kind of potholder-looking thing. "You can play 'what if' until the Earth falls into the sun. What if I'm trying to think one step ahead of you? What if I'm scouting you out for a position on the board of directors of Plebasil, Inc. on the planet Akamaxas? Do you expect to be prepared for everything that could possibly happen?"

"Obviously, that's impossible."

"So what's the alternative? Hide under your bed all your life?"

"That's not the point."

"Oh? What's the point, then?"

"Well..." Ragwater didn't know. He had lost track of the conversation. "I can't help but wonder if you're holding something important back. Something I should know."

Maxwell patted his crude, half-finished potholder down on the tabletop and sat back. "I can assure you, Gilbert, that I've told you everything you need to know to make an informed decision. I have no desire to screw you over. You have nothing I need except the ability to perform a few simple tasks. It's easy for me to fulfill my end of the deal. That's the whole story."

Ragwater squinted intently, hoping to convey a disapproving skepticism without saying anything—mostly because he didn't know what to say.

In the back, a grizzled-looking, middle-aged man racked up the balls on one of the pool tables. His similarly grizzled friend, considerably heavier and dirtier-looking, stood watching. Ragwater knew—he was *certain*—that the guy who had racked the balls was the certified mechanic who had almost done the brake job that Henry had botched so badly. He did a lot of work on the side, this guy here, in his garage for friends, family, and whoever might hear about him through word-of-mouth. In fact, he did so well that he had been able to pay off his house, and he had a thirty-foot boat, a state-of-the art home theater system, and a HUGE hot tub.

Yeah, well, wait until his divorce six months from now, when his soon-to-be ex-wife tips off the IRS about all this income he hasn't been paying taxes on. He'll wish he had made more of an effort to part on amicable terms—or, if not that, he'll at least wish he hadn't tried to screw her out of everything the two of them owned.

"There's no benefit to me in holding anything back," Maxwell said.

The friend stepped up and leaned over the table to break. Yeah, the friend. He was a custodian at a high school, Ragwater imagined. Or—no, he had been a custodian, but he was fired a couple years ago after he got busted in a big drug investigation. And he hadn't done anything! Really. He was merely an innocent guy who was unlucky enough to be in the wrong place at the wrong time. Although convicted, he was fortunate enough to get probation—but unfortunate enough to get fired for the conviction.

Since then, he had been scrounging out a living doing odd jobs here and there. Yard work, cleaning out gutters, painting, and so on. Sometimes he helped his friend work on cars. Earlier that very afternoon, in fact, the two of them had replaced a head gasket for Aunt Rachel—not the real Aunt Rachel, but the guy who had been in the store.

"Why do you want this stuff done?"

"You don't need to know."

"It might make a difference as to whether I would agree to the deal."

"It wouldn't. You have no stake in anything that happens as a result of these tasks, either directly or indirectly."

Ragwater sighed. He watched as the former custodian drew back and shot the cue ball with surprising force. It crashed into the racked balls with a great deal of loud, violent-sounding clacking.

"Are you ready to start?" Maxwell asked. "Do you want me to tell you your first task?"

At the bar, a tall, slender guy was talking to—or, more likely, hitting on—a young woman who seemed uncomfortable at his attentions. Ragwater wondered if he should go over there and say something. "Diane? It's me, Gilbert. Remember, we used to work at Roscoe's

Fruit Market together." Just, like, to toss her a line in case she wanted an out. If she didn't go for it, well, sorry, but she really looked like Diane.

The woman poured her drink over the guy's head. He sat there for a moment, stunned, and then got up and left. Problem solved.

"You seem pretty sure of yourself," Ragwater said.

"Doubt will kill you, Gilbert, quicker than a grand piano falling on your head."

"The thing is, I don't know anything about you."

"What do you think you need to know?"

"Lots of stuff. Like, for example, where are you from?"

"If I tell you, what good will it do you? Consider that bartender over there. If he were to tell you where he came from, would it make the beer taste better? Would it assure you that he hadn't poisoned it?"

Ragwater looked down at his mug, then at Maxwell. Maxwell smiled and took a deep drink of his beer, as if to assure Ragwater it was all right.

Aping the gesture, Ragwater drank from his beer.

"So, then," Maxwell said, "are you ready to start?"

"Are you trying to put on the old hard sell?"

"I don't know what an old hard sell is, but it sounds painful."

"I mean it seems as if you're trying to push me into it."

"I think we both know the word no. If you let me push you into it, it must be because you really want to do it."

"Well..."

"The whole thing is simple and straightforward," Maxwell said. "What are you risking?"

"I'm not sure."

"I think you want to be adventurous."

Ah, yes. But was this the way to be adventurous?

But then again, what real objection did Ragwater have? That it was strange? That was why it was adventurous. "Okay," he said. "Tell me what the first task is."

"You agree to the deal?"

"Yeah."

"I need you to say it."

"You need me to say I agree to the deal?"

"It's merely a formality."

The mechanic was circling around the pool table, scoping out possible shots.

"I agree to the deal," Ragwater said. "Please, dear sir, tell me what the first task is."

Maxwell took a sheet of paper from his pocket, unfolded it, and handed it to Ragwater. "Get seven signatures on this petition."

Ragwater read: "'We, the undersigned, hereby petition the United Confederacy of Planets to admit Earth as a full member.' Name, address, and phone number. This is pretty off the wall. What good's it going to do you?"

"That's my concern. Your concern is five and a half feet tall, twenty-three years old, and has red hair. That should be enough."

"I suppose so. But if I finish this task and decide to quit, do I get anything for doing this much?"

Maxwell picked up the napkin dispenser again and started twisting the rubber feet on the bottom. "You haven't even started yet, and you're already talking about quitting. If you're going to do this, Gilbert, you should have your heart and soul in it."

"But I don't know what you're expecting me to put my heart and soul into."

Maxwell sighed. "We're contracting for the entire job. However, I may be able to steer a few extra customers into your store after each task, for the sake of morale."

The mechanic was leaning forward against the edge of the pool table. He held his stick out horizontally, a few inches above the tabletop, apparently to help him judge an angle.

"Well, okay. That would be cool."

"And remember, seven signatures. No more, no less. Understand?"

"Seven isn't a difficult concept," Ragwater said. He had hoped to sound dryly sarcastic, but it seemed to come out sounding like a petulant child.

Apparently satisfied with what he saw, the mechanic moved into position for the shot.

"It's always good to make sure there aren't any misunderstandings," Maxwell said. Then, suddenly and with enthusiastic male camaraderie, "Tell me, do you think Philadelphia would have own the Stanley Cup if Brad McCrimmon and Tim Kerr and been healthy in the finals?"

"What?"

"You know, ice hockey. The Stanley Cup. Philadelphia and Edmonton."

"Uh, I have absolutely no idea." Ragwater liked to watch the occasional hockey game, but he didn't follow the sport.

"Oh. Well." Maxwell raised his mug for a toast. "Anyway, here's to a successful business association."

The mechanic shot. The cue ball zipped across the

table and hit nothing but the rail on the opposite side.

Ragwater clinked his glass against Maxwell's, and they drank.

***

On his way home that evening, Ragwater stopped at the Stupendous Mart for beer. It was a dingy place, in dire need of a coat of paint and a couple more light fixtures. But even so, Ragwater thought it had a certain charm—and it was more than adequate to supply him with beer, milk, and the Sunday paper.

As he walked in, he could hear a loud uproar coming from the back of the store. "What kind of place is this..." It was difficult to make out the words in the jumbled, slurred, drunken tirade, but Ragwater recognized the voice: his brother Gustav.

He stepped cautiously toward the back and peeked around the corner of the aisle to see Gustav, facing away from him, talking to a woman who worked there. He was clearly upset about something. The question "Are you people stupid?" came out coherently, or mostly so. But it was followed by another lengthy burst of slurred...speech? Verbalizations might be a better word. Understanding random bits and pieces, Ragwater guessed that the store didn't have the brand of beer Gustav wanted.

As if he needed any more beer. He was wobbling around like that one last bowling pin that may or may not fall. Ragwater could smell the alcohol from fifteen feet away.

The employee, an apprehensive expression on her face, couldn't get a word in edgewise. "If this is how you operate, I don't know how you stay in business." Ragwater knew that Gustav, although obnoxiously loud, as well as four inches taller and thirty pounds heavier than the woman, was harmless. But she wouldn't know that. It would be too easy for her to imagine that he might decide to take an impulsive swing at her. (Impulse control wasn't Gustav's strong suit even when he was sober.) "Do you have to *practice* to be this incompetent?" Ragwater wasn't sure the last word was incompetent, as Gustav was having a hard time getting it out.

And the clerk, the poor dear. Ragwater could picture her at home later, telling her husband the story, wishing she could quit this crappy job where she had to deal with people like this drunken fool. For all Ragwater knew, this sort of thing might happen...well, probably not every day, but maybe once a week or so. The husband would offer some kind of ineffectual (but obligatory) words of comfort, but he couldn't tell her it would be all right for her to quit because...get this: he was the grizzled former school custodian who had been shooting pool at the Slipknot Inn. Those odd jobs he scrounged around for paid him barely enough money for car insurance.

And so she stands there taking abuse from some asshole, probably afraid to step away because he might become even more upset.

Ragwater was pretty sure, though, that another employee would be somewhere calling the police.

He really didn't want to intervene. It would be too embarrassing to have to admit that, yes, this lout is my brother, don't worry, I know how to handle him, I can get him out of here, give me a couple minutes, I'll make sure he doesn't damage anything. "Did you drink it all yourselves?" Gustav growled.

Ragwater wanted—desperately wanted—to sneak away. He could pretend he had innocently walked in and was put off by this display of horrible behavior.

Yet, the other people in the store didn't deserve to have to deal with this.

And so, mostly because he knew he would feel crappy later if he walked away, Ragwater stepped around in front of Gustav. "Hey, man," he said.

Gustav suddenly went silent. Ragwater could sense the clerk behind him moving away. "Gilbert," Gustav said. "What are you doing here?"

"I'm behaving myself. But the question we need to be talking about is, what are *you* doing?" Somehow, Ragwater felt very paternal. And the act seemed to work. The anger drained out of Gustav, and he stood there looking like a child, an oversized child whose mother had caught him drawing on the wall.

"Buying beer," Gustav said. "*Trying* to buy beer. No big deal."

Ragwater's first impulse was to point out that Gustav didn't need any more to drink, but that wouldn't resolve the situation at hand. Gustav had his mind set on beer—*more* beer—and the best way to deal with him was to play along as much as possible. "Do you have to buy it so loud?"

"They don't have my Mullen's Special Draft."

"You can go somewhere else for it, you know."

"But..." And then, as the idea sank in, "Yeah, I could."

"Come on. I'll drive."

Ragwater led Gustav to the front of the store.

Inside the door, the manager was talking to two police officers, and all three were watching Ragwater and Gustav approach. One of the officers said to Ragwater, "You know him?"

"Yeah," Ragwater said. "He's my brother. If no one objects, I can deal with him."

The officer looked at the manager, who shrugged. "If his brother can get him out of here, I don't think we need to make a big deal out of it."

"I'm sorry," Gustav said.

"Just don't come back," the manager said. The cops stood there looking very stern, as if they wanted to run Gustav in—take him downtown, tie him to a chair, and spend all night beating him with rubber hoses and accusing him of crimes they knew he hadn't committed.

"I won't," Gustav said.

Ragwater gave the manager a sheepish smile of appreciation. He mouthed "thanks" and ushered Gustav through the door.

Outside, he led his brother around behind the big ice machine at the corner of the building, out of sight of the cops. "Okay," Ragwater said. "First thing is this: you're not getting any more beer tonight." It was a meaningless order. Ragwater was all too aware that Gustav could and would do any damn thing he wanted as soon as the two of them parted ways. Still, he had to take a stand.

"No more beer," Gustav said.

"You've already had too much."

"Yeah, you're right."

"Okay, good. Now, how did you get here?"

"I drove," Gustav said, as if Ragwater should have known it was the only possible answer.

"Why are you driving in this condition?"

"It's too far to walk."

Ragwater stifled the urge to smack Gustav. As flippant as it sounded, that was actually the way his mind worked. He probably wasn't trying to be a smartass, and he wouldn't understand why Ragwater didn't like his answer. His position would be—as it had been in similar situations in the past—that being drunk made him a better driver because he had to be more careful. Ragwater had no idea whether Gustav actually believed such a thing, but he knew his brother wouldn't admit to being convinced otherwise.

Ragwater stepped out from behind the ice machine and looked around. Gustav's old Maverick was parked all the way over on the other side of the parking lot, two wheels on the pavement and two on the grass. "I'm going to take you home," he said. "We'll come back tomorrow for your car."

"I need it tonight."

"Not happening. You're not going to be in any condition to drive until tomorrow. Tonight, I'll drop you off wherever you need to go."

Gustav looked longingly at his car. "I'll get Robbie to bring me back for it," he said. "I don't want to bother you."

Ragwater didn't like it. If he left Gustav to pick up his car however he wanted, he would get Robbie, his downstairs neighbor, to bring him back for it later that night. Peer pressure would mean more to Robbie than being responsible enough to keep a drunk driver off the road. And Gustav would shovel on generous loads of peer pressure.

"Give me your car keys," Ragwater said.

"You don't need to do that," Gustav said.

Ragwater tried to summon up an authoritative, no-nonsense attitude that would put an end to the discussion. "I think I do."

Gustav dropped his keys into Ragwater's hand.

"Good. Now go get in my car, and I'll be with you in a minute."

Gustav turned and slouched away, toward Ragwater's car. Ragwater watched until he got in and then went back into the store and asked the manager whether it would be all right to leave Gustav's car there until they could pick it up the next day. The manager wasn't happy about it, but he understood why it was necessary.

"Thanks," Ragwater said.

"Well, you know," the manager said, "I've seen you in here fairly regularly. You're a good customer, and you seem like a decent person. That's the only reason I didn't ask those police officers to take him downtown."

Yeah, he was decent. No one would ever suspect he was the type of person who would do something like... oh, well, hmmm...What would no one ever suspect about Ragwater? Okay, to arbitrarily pick something at random, no one would ever think he might be the type to get all mixed up in a bizarre deal with a strange little man who is promising him a way to cheat on his girlfriend—with no consequences—with a smokin' hot redheaded babe who's guaranteed to do anything he wants, no matter what.

~ 7 ~

The next day, Ragwater channel-surfed until about one o'clock in the afternoon, without paying attention to any of the shows. Then he grabbed his phone and gave Gustav a call. "You ready to go get your car?"

"Oh, I got it."

"Huh?"

"My car," Gustav said. "I already got it. Robbie took me out there last night."

Crap. Just as Ragwater had expected. But still... crap. "How? I have your car keys."

"I have extras. I didn't want to bother you."

***

Five dice tumbled across the table, and Ragwater looked at the results. "One, three, three, four, and six."

"That pair of threes gives you your third sploom," Plow said.

"No, it's my second."

Plow picked up the scorecard, an 8½x11 sheet of paper with a multicolored grid in the middle surrounded by an elaborate system of swirls at the top and bottom, runes along the sides, and color-coded words in the corners. It was the simplest way they could devise to keep score for their game, called Fear and Loathing in Hell, and even at that they had had to make a few compromises because a true, fully functioning scorecard that accounted for all possible permutations would require some sort of three-dimensional record-keeping system. They once tried using a six-page scorecard but quickly realized they were devoting more time to keeping score than to playing. No good.

Ragwater and Plow had recently tried to teach Lisa the game, but she bailed as soon as they told her it had seven sets of rules that shifted around as the game progressed. She assumed (incorrectly but understandably) that it meant they simply made the rules up as they went along, which in turn meant that she would inevitably get screwed over as badly as the guys could manage to screw her over. Her bailout didn't surprise Ragwater, though. He had been surprised that she was, even for a short time, interested in the game at all.

"Third," Plow said, pointing to a spot on the scorecard.

"No," Ragwater said. "That's the number of carumbles I've gotten. Remember, we're on the Greek Pantheon rules right now."

"Yes, but you got your first two splooms under the Canton Bulldogs rules, so that means the bloofus I got on my first turn transmogrifies into a sploom for you."

"Oh, I forgot all about that," Ragwater said. "Well, then, in that case..." He looked at the play area, which was his kitchen table. There was no board; the amorphous, ever-changing nature of the game made it impossible to play on anything but a featureless surface.

And on the table was an impressive selection of objects: small toys such as plastic soldiers, animals, cars, and so on; hardware such as screws, nuts, bolts, and washers of various sizes; coins, both US and foreign; a variety of shirt buttons; a selection of small electronics parts; a half dozen grounded plug adapters; playing pieces taken from other board games; and miscellaneous other objects, including paper clips, pebbles, small sea shells, a nail clipper, pieces of silverware, keys, electronic components…and more. Some of the game pieces had obvious—or if not obvious, then at least logical—meanings. For example, the toy soldiers represented strength and could be used to attack and defend. Popsicle sticks could be used to create barriers. However, other pieces simply had arbitrarily chosen functions. Shirt buttons, for example, carried magic.

Ragwater picked up a toy soldier at the edge of the table. "In that case," he said, putting the soldier down in the middle, "I'm going to teleport this guy into the M Zone."

"Oh, that's clever," Plow said appreciatively. "But do you realize that activates the Philo T. Farnsworth rules?"

"Yes, I know perfectly well that that activates the Philo T. Farnsworth rules. Why do you think I did it?"

Plow sat back and surveyed the table. After a moment, he muttered a soft curse to himself as the implications of the rule shift dawned on him. The Philo T. Farnsworth rules brought about a reversal of the assumed magnetic orientation of the game area. Given the current location of Ragwater's field headquarters and the way his psychic artillery was positioned, this would strengthen his tactical position considerably.

Even worse for Plow, he had left a gaping hole in his Semi-Inclinated Task Line. This was no problem under the Greek Pantheon rules, but it was a serious weakness under the Philo T. Farnsworth rules because now Ragwater's psychic artillery would have far greater range and marginally greater accuracy. That gaping hole would leave a full ten percent of Plow's forces defenseless for the next three turns. He would have to hope for an almost-impossible series of favorable dice rolls to avoid heavy losses.

Ragwater felt especially good about his clever little tactic, coming as it did as a result of quick thinking in an unexpected situation. In fact, he would go so far as to consider it much more than a clever tactic—it was a stroke of genius.

"I'm going to have to call a time-out," Plow said.

"Sure," Ragwater said.

They stood and stretched. This session had been going for two and a half hours straight, and they had been sitting hunched over the table the whole time. Ragwater wasn't sure, but he thought his phone had rung a couple times. Intent as he was on the game, it was nothing more background noise, no more significant than a car horn honking a block away. It was only now that he realized what the sound must have been.

He picked up his phone and checked for missed calls. "Gustav called," he said. "Twice."

"What's up? Did he leave a message?"

"Yeah. I don't know that I want to hear it, though."

But then again, how could he ignore it? He dialed voice mail and pressed the speakerphone button. "Hey, Gilbert, man, I want to apologize. I'm sorry about last night, man. Call me back, can you?" There was a pause with some strange noise in the background. Then, "Yeah, call me back."

After that, a second message from Gustav, about a half hour later: "Uh…" That was all.

"He's articulate today," Plow said.

"I think I know why the character in my story takes the deal," Ragwater said.

"The redhead story?"

"Yeah, the Redhead story. He takes the deal because he's curious. He wants to see where it goes. I think that's good enough."

"As a child, he was curious about what that hot burner on the stove would feel like."

"He might have been. See, though, he figures that even if it all blows up in his face, he has an excuse to give his girlfriend. He can tell her he did it because he was curious, that he didn't believe he was going to get a hot redhead made available to him, but he *had* to find out what was really going to happen."

"But in the back of his mind," Plow said, "the real reason is that he really, really, really wants it to be true."

~ 8 ~

Monday was slow at the store, and Ragwater sat reading *Breakfast of Champions.* He didn't like reading novels in the store—he always felt he should be doing something constructive, business-wise. Going over the books, writing an advertisement, sweeping the floor... or, if he wanted to read, read something pertaining to business. It was almost as if he expected someone to swoop down on him and accuse him of goofing off, someone like an ever-vigilant manager who catches the teenage fast-food employee goofing off when he could have been wiping down the deep fryer. But there was no one to swoop down on Ragwater. No one but a little voice, a little muffled voice, whispering from far back in the most remote corner of his mind, "Gilbert, this is your livelihood. You should take it more seriously."

But it didn't bother him enough to put the book down. He didn't have a deep fryer to wipe down.

The petition was out on the sales counter, visible to anyone making a purchase. He already had four signatures by the time John Plow came in at 11:30.

"Hey, Ragwater. This is defective." Plow tossed a CD onto the sales counter. It skidded across the countertop, zinged across empty space, hit a shelf mounted on the wall, and clattered to the floor next to Ragwater. The case broke apart, and the CD came out. Ragwater watched it roll around lazily in a sort-of-sickly flight-of-the-bumblebee path and finally fall over.

"It's a good thing this isn't a gun shop," Ragwater said. "Toss a pistol around like that, it could go off and kill somebody."

Plow rolled his eyes. "A common misconception among people whose chief exposure to guns is detective shows on TV. Guns don't go off from falling on the floor."

Ragwater bent over and picked up the CD and broken case parts. "Yeah, well, whatever. What's the problem?"

"What kind of scam is this you have here, getting innocent people to bring you their perfectly good CDs they've worked hard to buy, not hardly giving them anything for them, and then passing off worthless junk on them?"

"It's a scam where I get innocent people to bring me their perfectly good CDs they've worked hard to buy, not hardly give them anything for them, and then pass off worthless junk on them. Why do you ask?"

"HA! I thought so! I knew if I questioned you cleverly enough, you'd let it slip."

"Yeah, except I happen to know that you didn't work hard to buy this CD."

"No, but *someone* did."

Ragwater tossed the broken case into the trash. "Why do you feel the need to throw it around like that?"

"Well, it's worthless."

"It's worthless *now*, after you've been throwing it around."

"It was worthless before. Look at it."

"What seems to be the problem?"

"It *seems* to be all scratched up."

Ragwater turned the CD over and examined it. Sure enough, the playing side had numerous scratches. Plow was right; this was more than a scratch from getting thrown on the floor one time. This was the result of ongoing, systematic carelessness.

"Systematic carelessness." Ragwater liked that. It could be a band name. They would start out as a bar band in Norfolk, Virginia, and play gigs up and down the East Coast for a couple years. Then they would sign a record deal with a major label, but before recording the album, the guitar player gets beaten to death behind a club. Yeah, he had been out in the alley smoking a joint with a couple of other guys between sets, and the others went back inside ahead of him. He wanted to stay out there for a few more minutes before going back into the stuffy, smoky atmosphere of the bar. And then...he's late coming back in to start the next set. Someone mentions that he had been out back, so the other guys in the band go out to bring him in. And there he is, laid out on the ground, head split wide open in a huge pool of blood.

Holy crap!

The crime is never solved.

Well, a scratched CD is meaningless when you hold it up next to a brutal murder—but still, the murder was imaginary, and the disc was real. "I don't know how this slipped through my rigorous quality control process."

"It probably slipped through because you have a 'rigorous quality control process' instead of just looking at them to make sure they're all right."

"Dude, 'just looking at them' *is* my rigorous quality control process."

"With your eyes open?"

"Usually. But clearly, not always. Get another one."

"Yeah, sure." Plow started toward the CD bins and then noticed the petition on the counter. "Hey, what's this?"

"What's it look like?"

"It looks like a petition to get us into the United Confederacy of Planets. What's it doing here?"

"I like to be politically active. There's been a lot of controversy over the issue, you know."

Plow stepped over to the CD bins. "Sure," he said. "You join the confederacy, and what do you get out of it? They raise your taxes and censor your newspapers, the police break into your home twice a month just for fun, and you end up living on a diet of beans and evaporated milk. I've seen it happen too many times."

"Yes, but they make the ownership of pornography compulsory."

Plow pulled a CD out of the bin and stepped back over to the sales counter. "You mean you have to have smut in your house?"

"Yup. It's strictly enforced. They even have quotas."

"In that case, I'm all for it." Plow picked up a pen and signed the petition.

"Yeah," Ragwater said, "I know what makes this guy tick. Give him a picture of a naked woman, and he'll mow your car and wash your lawn."

"If it's a color picture, I'll paint your dog and walk your house, too."

Ragwater leaned across the counter and lowered

his voice. "Speaking of women, how'd you get along with Sylvia last night?"

Plow grinned. "Gilbert, it was a night to remember. Wild passion! Depraved carnal adventures! Unspeakable sexual atrocities! That woman nearly killed me."

"Really?"

Plow looked down. "No, not really. She's not going to take off her clothes on a first date. When I brought her over to your place, I...well, being the world-renowned expert on women that I am, it's embarrassing to have to admit this, but I had misread the signals. I thought all systems were go, but it turns out that only some of them were. We got along pretty well, though."

"Way to go, John. You going to see her again?"

"Of course. And that reminds me. I need to call that one I met in the park. What was her name? Brenda?"

"I don't know. You're the one who talked to her. "

Plow took out his wallet and looked through it, pulling out numerous small slips of paper. "Let's see," he mumbled. "I know her number's in here somewhere." He looked up at Ragwater. "You know, I need to put all these notes and stuff on my computer somehow. Make a spreadsheet or something."

"I thought the whole point to these notes was to make your wallet look thick enough to impress the ladies."

"No, the notes are for real. The thick wallet is a bonus feature."

Ragwater picked one up. START A WEB SITE THAT SPECIALIZES IN PICTURES OF GOATS. "What on earth does this mean?" he asked.

Plow looked at the note. "Exactly what it says. I don't see what's hard to understand about it."

"Who's going to care about pictures of goats?"

"Well..." Plow sounded defensive. "Goat lovers. Listen, my friend, no matter what subject matter you can think of, someone, somewhere, is going to be interested."

"Hmmm...there's not going to be anything perverted going on in these pictures, is there?"

"Gilbert—my lifelong best friend, who probably knows me better than my own mother—do you think I would do such a thing?"

"Probably not. But only because you couldn't afford to hire the models."

"I rest my case." Plow went back to looking through his wallet. "I'm talking about goats doing normal goat stuff. You know, playing touch football, making quilts, hanging drywall, and so on...Ah, here it is." Plow held up a slip of paper. "Yeah, Linda. That was her name, Linda."

"Why bother if you can't remember her name? And what about Sylvia?"

"One date, no promises, whoop-de-do."

"You say that after you've been giving me all sorts of grief about not taking my relationship with Lisa seriously."

"One date is not a relationship."

"You said you were going to see her again," Ragwater said, uncomfortable with the feeling that he was pushing the argument too far, considering his own situation. He was actually doing some work, senseless though it was, in the improbable hope of hooking up with the mysterious redhead. All Plow had done was ask for a phone number.

Plow drew himself up to a dignified posture. "Yes,

I'll see her again. And then it might become a relationship, at which point I'll re-evaluate everything. In the meantime, I'd never forgive myself for passing up this opportunity. You know, like that bald chick you scored with."

"Bald is exotic. How do you pass that up? As I recall, Linda has quite a bit of very pretty hair."

"And I hope to see more of it. Now stand aside and watch a master at work." With that, Plow whipped his cell phone out and punched numbers.

"Good luck."

"I don't need luck. I know how to talk to women, remember? Now, listen to this. You might learn something." Plow hit the call button and listened. Then, "May I please speak to Linda, please?" He held the phone down, away from his face. "Always be polite. I learned that from a Pink Panther cartoon."

Ragwater rolled his eyes.

Plow, talking on the phone again, said, "Henry? No, I'm not Henry."

"Henry?" Ragwater said.

Plow motioned impatiently for Ragwater to hush. "No," Plow said, "I'm John, and I'd like to speak to Linda...No, I don't know anything about some Henry guy. Just put Linda on, okay?...Listen, dude...What on earth are you talking about? I don't know who you are...No, I didn't show up because I never told anyone I was going to go there...Well, boo-hoo..."

Plow held the phone down and spoke low to Ragwater. "Something funny's going on here. He thinks I sent him across town to Burger Utopia to sell him some weed, and he's pissed off because I didn't show up." He made a funny face.

Ragwater picked up a catalog from a T-shirt distributor. "Some people are plain screwy," he said without meeting Plow's eyes. He opened the catalog and paged through it.

Plow continued on the phone. "Listen, joker. If you don't put Linda on, and right now, I'm going to reach through the phone line and pull your uvula out..." Ragwater heard indistinct shouting from Plow's phone. "Hey, it's not my fault you're a loser," Plow said. More shouting. "Oh, I'm scared. You can't be much of a man if Linda gives her number to guys she meets in the park."

More shouting, this time easy to understand. "You're a dead man!" the voice screamed.

Plow laughed and hung up. He was tremendously amused. "It was her husband!"

"What?"

"Had to be her husband or boyfriend. Who else would answer her phone?"

"You don't think she might have given you a fake number?"

"Utterly impossible. Anyway, he thought I was some guy named Henry. I don't know who Henry is, but he'd better lock his door."

"John..."

"Hey, you know what? Henry could be some guy she's already fooling around with. Wouldn't that be a hoot!"

"And you let this guy think you were Henry?"

"What do you mean, 'let him?' You heard me tell him I wasn't. I couldn't convince him."

"Yeah, and you did a fairly impressive job of getting him all riled up."

"He sounded like he was pretty mad at Henry already, with that stuff about the weed. And he was saying something about a woman hassling him at Burger Utopia."

"Oh, my god..."

"What's wrong?" Plow asked. "Who cares about Henry anyway? If he's friends with this guy on the phone, he's gotta be a world-class loser."

"Henry, unlike you, is probably innocent." Ragwater felt his voice getting a shade more emphatic than he wanted.

And Plow picked right up on it. "Why are you shouting at me? I'll admit that maybe I was acting like a dick, but it's not like you have anything personal at stake."

"Okay, sorry. I didn't mean it to sound like that."

"None of this is my fault," Plow said. "She should have told me she was married."

"You're not still going to see her, are you?"

"Well...I guess if she's married, it probably wouldn't be a very good idea."

"Yeah, John, that's one way of looking at it, if that's really her phone number."

"What's that supposed to mean?"

Lisa walked in, carrying a bulky plastic bag. "What's what supposed to mean?"

"Well, this is a pleasant surprise," Ragwater said. "John's over here trying to get some poor woman divorced."

Lisa put the bag down on the sales counter. "I brought lunch," she said. "And it's not nice to get poor women divorced."

"She gave me her phone number," John said. "I

think the facts speak for themselves."

"Are you trying to pick up married women?" Lisa asked.

"Just one," Ragwater said. "That I know of."

"I didn't know she was married. And, as I keep trying to point out, she gave me her number. She didn't have to, you know. She could have told me to get lost. Obviously she was, shall we say, in the market for... something."

"And I'm saying she gave you a fake number," Ragwater said. "Women do that, you know."

Plow looked at Lisa. "Do they?"

"Yeah, sometimes. If you don't want a guy to call, you might give him a made-up number, and he's satisfied for the time being. But then, later, he can't call you. Game over."

"That's a crappy way to treat somebody," Plow said. "If you want to say no, just say no."

"It's crappy, for sure," Lisa agreed. "But some guys won't take no for an answer." She began removing items: two large sandwiches wrapped in waxed paper ("From Winkle's Deli," she said, knowing that Ragwater would appreciate the true gourmet quality the name implied, one wrapper marked with a big "G" in black, felt-tip marker and the other with an "L"), serving-sized cups of coleslaw, and bags of unsalted potato chips (chosen not for health reasons, but simply because Ragwater didn't like salty chips).

"But this didn't get to the point where she would have thought I wouldn't take no for an answer. I asked her for her number, and she said okay."

"I don't know what she was thinking," Lisa said. "But *I'm* thinking beer."

"I guess that's my cue," Ragwater said. He went to the back room, a combination office/storeroom. To the left were two large metal shelf units containing everything from an ordinary assortment of hand tools to several changes of clothing, from half-used cans of latex paint to fluorescent tubes. On the back wall, facing the door, was a state-of-the-art stereo system flanked by two large racks of CDs for in-store play. To the right was a desk created by the old "door laid across a couple of two-drawer file cabinets" method, with a computer and printer-scanner-fax machine on it. To one side of the desk was a refrigerator, and on the other side was the door to the bathroom.

With the room lit mainly by the glow from the face of the stereo receiver, Ragwater made his way to the refrigerator and got three beers. As he sometimes did when getting beer, he grabbed a handful of his stomach and squeezed. Not much extra. Maybe a wee little bit, barely enough to say it's not flat. He considered the idea that maybe he should cut back. He didn't think it was enough to be noticeable, at least not when he was fully clothed—at least not yet—but that's when you want to take action—before it becomes a problem. Nip it in the bud.

Less beer, more activity was called for. Throwing that football around with Plow in the park was the most strenuous thing he had done since climbing the ladder to change ceiling lights three months ago.

Push-ups? Maybe he should start doing push-ups. He glanced around the corner of the doorway and saw Plow and Lisa chatting. Okay, they were occupied. The last thing Ragwater wanted was for either of them to come back there and find him doing push-ups, of all things. It...well, it seemed like a weird time to do something like that.

He put the cans on the desk and lay face down on the floor, positioning his hands under his shoulders. He had no clue whatsoever how many he could do. Maybe he shouldn't try—he might find out he could do only two, and if that was the case, he didn't want to know about it.

No, be a man. Do the work. Do whatever it takes. Apart from being out of shape, he was reasonably healthy. And if he could do only two push-ups...well, he needed to know. He could build himself up.

And so he pushed. One...two...and up to ten before his arms started getting wobbly.

Ragwater moved over to sit in the office chair, to recover. He was slightly out of breath, and he was pretty sure his face was flushed looking. He swiveled the chair around to face the computer and swirled the mouse around on the desk to clear the screen saver. If Plow or Lisa came looking for him—"Hey, what's taking you so long?"—he could pretend he was reading e-mail or something.

So he checked his e-mail and found nothing new. As he was getting up, Plow appeared in the doorway. "Dude, Lisa's up front waiting for beer."

"Sorry," Ragwater said. "I thought I would do a quick e-mail check while I was back here."

Plow looked at him. "You seem a little out of breath," he said.

"Do I?"

Plow flicked on the overhead light. "That's better. You know, if walking to the back of the store gets you winded, you need to get in shape. Start running, or doing push-ups, or something."

Ragwater stared at Plow. Did he know? Had he seen Ragwater on the floor? Not likely. That would have resulted in immediate, straight-ahead ball busting, something like: "Did you spill some beer? Licking it up off the floor? Geez, Gilbert, you need help. That's pathetic." None of those little cat-and-mouse games for John Plow.

"Yeah, maybe I need to do that," Ragwater said. He picked up a beer and handed it to Plow.

Plow looked at the beer and then put it down on the desk. "I'd better not," he said. "I have to go to work in a little while."

"So what? It's not like you're performing brain surgery."

"Billy'll smell it and get in a snit." Plow had told Ragwater numerous stories about Billy. He was the assistant manager at Peckham's, the restaurant where Plow washed dishes. He was very strict and by-the-book. He rigidly enforced the employee dress code, making it a point to notice things like someone wearing wrong-color socks (anything other than white) and men with hair down over their shirt collar. More than five minutes late? He'll write you up. He had been known to fire employees for participating in NCAA tournament betting pools. There was no telling what he would do if he thought someone had been drinking.

"You don't want Billy in a snit," Ragwater said. "Listen, I was thinking about starting some kind of exercise. Maybe push-ups, or weight lifting."

"No, not weight lifting," Plow said. "Too dangerous for you. Stick with something that doesn't require equipment."

"I'm not sure what you're getting at."

"Me, neither. I just thought it sounded good. I didn't expect you'd call me on it."

"Well, why don't we both work on it?"

"What?"

"Getting in shape. You could use some work in that area yourself, my friend."

"I'm comfortable with who I am."

"No, really," Ragwater said. "They say you get better results if you have a friend doing it with you. You motivate each other."

"You're serious?"

"That's what I'm saying. Think about it."

Plow shrugged. "Sure. I'll think about it."

Ragwater realized the current CD, MC5's *Kick Out the Jams,* was near the end, so he scanned his collection and grabbed George Thorogood's *Move It on Over.* He switched the discs out, and they walked to the front of the store.

"I could have become the next George Thorogood," Plow said, "if I had kept up with my guitar lessons."

"I suppose you could have," Ragwater said. "You seemed to have a feel for it."

"Yeah, but you know, all that practice..." He made a sort-of "This milk I just took a big swig of is *rancid*" face.

"There's no telling how many brilliant careers never got off the ground simply because someone didn't have the drive to do whatever it would take to succeed," Ragwater said.

"You're right," Plow said, pointing. "That guy out there might have had the potential to write bestselling

Cold War-era spy thrillers, but he just didn't like sitting down at a computer for hours at a time." Through the front window, Ragwater saw a portly man with a shaved head sitting at a bus stop. He looked about forty.

"He might have written a couple," Ragwater said.

"No, I don't think so," Lisa said. "I'm pretty sure he makes his living helping people organize their closets."

Plow and Ragwater looked at her. She continued. "Right now, he has a fabulously valuable diamond ring in his pocket that he stole from a client."

"Oh, my god," Plow said. "Gilbert, you've got her doing it, making up stories about random people."

"So what's wrong with that?" Ragwater asked.

"You two were made for each other."

Lisa went on. "Or, should I say, he *thinks* it's a fabulously valuable diamond ring. In reality, it's just a cheap piece of junk. But the client, and this guy too, both think it's worth thousands."

After a moment, Ragwater prompted her. "And?"

"That's all I have. I'm new at this. Next time I'll have a whole novel." She opened her beer.

"I think I might become a waiter," Plow said.

"At Peckham's?" Ragwater asked.

"Sure. Where else?"

"Will they let you?"

"Let me? They offered."

"Why?"

"Well," Plow said, "unlike *some* people, they recognize true talent when they see it."

Ragwater considered Plow as a waiter in a moderately pricey, sit-down restaurant. He couldn't quite make the image work, but he had to admit that Plow probably behaved differently around him than he did around other people. "You think you can deal with drunk people and obnoxious jerks and bratty kids without resorting to grinding a broken bottle into someone's face? They'll fire you for that."

"Yes, as a matter of fact, I'm pretty sure I can. It's a different mind-set than I'm used to, but I think I can rise to the occasion."

"Now that you've started using words like 'mindset,' you're halfway there," Ragwater said.

"Yeah, see? I know what's going on." Plow drew himself up into what he presumably thought was a dignified pose. "Don't worry, ma'am," he said in a soothing voice. "Kids throw up in here all the time. We're used to it."

Ragwater wrinkled his nose.

"You don't think I can do it?"

"I'm doubtful that kids throw up all the time in Peckham's."

"Well, no, they don't," Plow said. "But, see, that's the point. On the rare occasion when it happens, I can deal with it. Put the parents at ease, help them overcome their embarrassment."

"You're qualified to be a waiter because you're willing to lie about kids throwing up in the place all the time, even though it hardly ever happens? Is that what you're saying?"

Plow looked confused for a moment. "Stop twisting my words around."

"I don't have to. They're already twisted around beyond all recognition."

"I'm saying it's a matter of being able to relate well to people." He leaned forward. "I can fake respect and sincerity with the best of 'em."

"Yeah, sure. You can tell people what they want to hear. That still doesn't mean you can bring them the right order. What if it doesn't work out?"

"What if? I don't know. I'll go back to dishwashing. But you don't want to think about failure when you're starting something new. That's silly."

"I guess it is," Ragwater said. It struck him that if he, Ragwater, had come up with an idea like that, he would think he was onto something incredibly profound. He would spend weeks pondering it, developing it, making notes, planning a blog, and outlining a seven-volume treatise, *The Philosophy of Failure...*

"Now, if you'll excuse me, I have to get going." Plow walked to the door and then turned back. "Drop in. I'll get you a free hot fudge cake."

...whereas Plow was content to sum it up with the word "silly" and move on with his life.

"We'll take you up on that," Lisa said. Then, after Plow was gone, she turned to Ragwater. "I don't see it," she said.

"I was doubtful at first, but if he decides he really wants to do it and do it right, I'm pretty sure he could make a good run at it."

Lisa bit into her sandwich. Ragwater unwrapped his and peeled back the top slice of wheat bread to find sliced turkey dressed with generous amounts of lettuce, onion, a thick slice of cheese that looked like provolone, pickles, and mustard. "You got me mustard," he said appreciatively.

Lisa smiled. "So what's this?" she asked, picking up Maxwell's petition.

Ragwater had the cover story ready. "Someone asked if he could leave it here."

"Oh?"

"Yeah. I don't know much about it. Some guy came in this morning, said he was a psychology student, doing some kind of experiment."

"He said he was a student? He could be some kind of weirdo, going to stalk all these people and hack their faces off with a hedge clipper, and you take him at his word that he's a student."

"Well, you know, it's far more likely than your little psycho scenario, although I'll admit it's not nearly as interesting." Psycho Scenario. Hmmm...good band name, Ragwater thought.

"Probably so," Lisa said.

"Yeah, I think he gets back to you with a survey, or something. It seemed harmless."

"That could be interesting," Lisa said. She picked up a pen from the countertop and signed the petition.

Ragwater couldn't help but feel guilty. He had been able to rationalize the whole deal with Maxwell—that he was doing it out of curiosity, not expecting that anything would come of it, and that it was all right because he and Lisa had no explicit agreement that their relationship was exclusive. Still, letting her sign the petition seemed over the line.

Not *seemed*. It *was* over the line.

But how could he tell her not to?

"When they call, don't let on that you know what they're doing. They want people who signed it without knowing what it was really about."

"You know," Lisa said, "this place is getting a reputation for being pretty weird."

"That's the whole point, my dear. You can get all the 'normal' you want at the mall. Probably more than is healthy, by my reckoning."

~ 9 ~

After the fact, it seemed all too obvious. It had a twisted, inevitable sense of elegance. Ragwater should have seen it coming. And yet, when Sylvia and Linda came into the store together, he was caught off guard. He choked back a gasp, surprising Lisa.

The women approached the counter.

"Hi," Ragwater said.

"Hi," Linda said. "You look familiar."

"You were in the park Sunday, weren't you?"

"Yeah. You were with that clown who tried to pick me up."

"That's me. And I want it on the record that I had nothing to do with his antics. In fact, I told him not to."

"It's good to see that one of you has some sense."

"A marginal amount, to be sure, but I get by without causing any major disasters. So far."

"John said he went to the park with you," Sylvia said.

"Uh, yeah, he did," Ragwater said, realizing he had painted Plow into a dangerous corner. If (a) he, Ragwater, was with the clown who had tried to pick Linda up, and (b) John had gone to the park with him...well, it didn't take any great effort figure it out: (c) Linda's "clown" must have been Sylvia's John Plow. Logic 101.

Oops.

Unless..."We met another friend there," Ragwater said. For good measure, and mindful that the fake first name had to be John, Ragwater rattled off the name of a distributor he bought blues CDs from. "John Meadows," he said.

"But there were only two of you," Linda said.

"Yeah, John had already gone home by the time you came along." Ragwater said. "John Plow, that is." Then, to change the subject, he hastily added, "Lisa, have you met Sylvia, John's new girlfriend? That's right, isn't it? Are you officially his girlfriend?"

"He hasn't told you about it?" Sylvia said.

"Well, I know what he says. But that might not agree with whatever you think about it."

"What does he say?"

"I'm not sure I should tell you. We guys have to stick together."

"So why should I tell you? What's in it for me?"

Fair enough. "He likes you," Ragwater said, feeling like a sixth grader. "He wants to see you again."

"If he calls, I'll talk to him."

"You missed your chance," he said. "He was in here, mere minutes ago."

"That's too bad."

"And you two know each other."

"Oh, yeah, we go way back," Sylvia said.

"Sort of like BFF's," Ragwater said.

"If you don't mind sounding all middle school about it, you might say so," Linda said.

It was getting to be too much. If they were that close, the dreaded day when Sylvia would want Plow to meet her friend would surely come, and it would come sooner rather than later. Ragwater was almost ready to break down and tell the truth, like the murderer in one of those courtroom dramas blurting out a sudden confession on the witness stand: "Yes, I did it! I'm guilty! But you don't know what it was like! That funny haircut, the gaudy clothes he wore all the time, the way he always said 'share' when he meant 'talk about'...I couldn't stand it one instant longer! And furthermore, I stole a box of staples from the office three years ago!"

But while Ragwater might feel some relief if he were to pour out the truth and get everything out in the open, he wasn't the one who would get in trouble. Plow was. It was up to him, Plow, to make the confession. Or not.

"So," Ragwater said, "what can I do for you?"

"We're looking for the Blind Faith album on vinyl," Linda said. "It's for my brother's birthday; he's a collector."

"It's always good to see a vinyl collector in this age of digital music," Ragwater said.

"I would suppose there aren't too many left," Sylvia said.

"You'd be surprised. I see a lot of them, really dedicated. But then again, I'm in a place where they tend to walk in the door on a regular basis. Now, let's step over here. I'm pretty sure I have a copy."

Leaving Lisa to eat her lunch—his own still untouched—Ragwater led Linda and Sylvia over to the vinyl section. He found the Bs and flipped through the records. "Here we go," he said, pulling an LP out. "This isn't the collectible version with the girl on the cover, though." He showed them the cover, which pictured the band on the front.

Linda looked it over. "It really needs to be the one with the girl," she said.

"I'm sorry I can't help you," Ragwater said. "If you leave your phone number, I can let you know if I find one."

"Well, his birthday is tomorrow, so I kinda have to get something today."

"Can you think of anything else he might like?"

"I'm not sure what else he needs. I wanted to get Blind Faith because he talked about it."

Ragwater could feel the sale slipping through his fingers. "I'm willing to bet he would be happy with anything you pick out."

Linda smiled. "Well, the thing is, he has such a huge collection that I would probably get something he already has."

"How about a gift certificate? There's no doubt in my mind that he could find something here that would tickle him pink."

"I'm sure he could. But I want to get something more thoughtful."

"Fair enough," Ragwater said. He didn't want to push it too far. But he *did* want them to remember him. Something goofy was called for. Apropos of nothing, he blurted out, "The only thing is, you need to watch out for the Dreaded Mind Reading Yeast."

"What?" Sylvia said.

"The Dreaded Mind Reading Yeast. You did know that yeast could read your mind, didn't you?"

"No, I've never heard of that."

"Yeah," Ragwater said. "I saw a show about it on one of those cable news channels. They talked to all kinds of scientists and law enforcement officials and whatnot. Very interesting stuff."

"Law enforcement officials? For yeast?"

"Yeah, well, it seems that this Dreaded Mind Reading Yeast can project thoughts into your head as well as read them. That's why it's so scary. They talked about this guy who had stolen a truck loaded with seven tons of feathers, and his lawyer used the Yeast Defense. He was found not guilty. They interviewed a jury member, and she said that anyone with enough nerve to claim that yeast controlled his actions deserved to get off."

"I would disagree with that," Linda said.

"Oh, I would, too," Ragwater said. "But see, we don't know that the jury decision wasn't yeast mind control, in furtherance of the Yeast Agenda. You can never be sure." Yeast Agenda. Another band name.

"That's scary," Sylvia said.

"Yeah, but you can use it to your advantage. They've figured out how to train it so that it reflects other people's thoughts into your head. So it's sort of like a mind reading tool."

"I'm not so sure about that," Linda said. "I don't think I would trust it."

"Oh, it's absolutely, one hundred percent trustworthy, they way they train it. You can walk around with a little packet of the specially trained Dreaded Mind Reading Yeast in your pocket, and you're good to go. So, like, let's say you're at a used car lot, and you're checking out a car that looks good. And then the yeast tells you the salesman is thinking, 'I hope she doesn't ask to look under the hood because she seems smart enough to figure out that what's really there is nothing more than a poorly executed drawing of a model airplane engine pasted to a cinderblock.' You know you don't want to deal with this guy."

"What if I want the drawing?" Sylvia asked.

"Thanks to the yeast, you know it's there. Or, let's say you're working your shift at the Stupendous Mart, and some handsome, slick-looking city boy comes up to the cash register to buy a lottery ticket. He tells you you have beautiful hair. Which, by the way, you do. But what if this slick city boy says so? You're not sure whether he's simply paying you a compliment or if he's leading up to something that involves the removal of clothes."

"If it were me, I would assume he's leading up to something," Linda said.

"Of course you would. And let's face it, who could blame him?" Ragwater made an expansive gesture to show appreciation of Linda's feminine charms. "But maybe that's not fair to the guy. He might simply be paying you a compliment, right?"

"It's barely possible."

"Right. So if you had some kind of convenient mind reading tool, you could be sure."

Sylvia noticed the petition on the sales counter. "What's this?" she asked.

"Someone asked if he could put it here. It's for a psychology experiment. That's what the guy said. A student."

"I'm always glad to help students of knowledge in their quest to better themselves," Sylvia said. She picked up the pen and then noticed something. "Hey, John signed it."

"Yeah, he likes to be politically active," Ragwater said.

Sylvia scribbled her name and offered the pen to Linda. "Do you want to sign it?"

Something clicked in Ragwater's brain—Sylvia was number seven. "NO!" he shouted.

Linda looked at him blankly. "What?"

"I'm sorry for shouting," he said. "But the guy wants exactly seven signatures."

"That's pretty strange," Linda said.

"Yeah, I'd have to agree. But it's his petition."

"You have time to cater to people like that?"

"Uh...well, normally, I guess I wouldn't. But he's an old friend. I'm happy to help him out."

Linda put the pen down. "That's nice of you," she said. "Strange, but nice."

"Well, you know, I do the best I can."

"Well, I guess we'd better move on and try to find a present somewhere. Let's hit World of Words and see if they have a book."

"They have lots of them," Ragwater said.

"I want to go see what they are," Sylvia said. "Thanks for everything."

Ragwater watched them go out the door and then picked up his sandwich.

"That was pretty personal service you gave them," Lisa said.

"The one was John's girlfriend."

"You didn't introduce them."

"They took me by surprise. I didn't even know they knew each other, let alone that they're close friends. I only know the friend because John tried to pick her up in the park yesterday. He didn't know who she was."

"So naturally, you had to flirt egregiously with them."

Ragwater desperately wanted to say he didn't think "egregious" was the right word, but he figured he'd better not. "That's...how I deal with customers," he said.

"With *female* customers."

"Including you. It's how I acted with you when you first came in here."

"That's the problem."

Oh, crap. He had walked right into that. Of course, he hadn't merely been flirtatious with Lisa the first time she came into the store. He flat-out hit on her. Shamelessly. Fortunately for him at the time, she thought he was cute. Unfortunately for him now, he had carelessly told her he had just done the same thing with Sylvia and Linda.

"Lisa, you're being ridiculous," Ragwater said, acutely aware of how lame it sounded. He knew he had better stop talking; anything more he said would only dig the hole deeper. And yet: "I don't think it was all that bad. I laid it on *much* heavier with you."

"Yeah, you laid it on heavier than 'Who can blame him?' for wanting to remove her clothes." She grabbed the petition and held it up as if it were a courtroom exhibit. "And what about this?"

"What about it?

"When you were telling me about it, you were talking about the guy like you'd never seen him before. Then you tell John's girlfriend that he's an old friend. Why can't you keep your story straight?"

"It's not like that," Ragwater said.

"Not like what?" Lisa sounded more frustrated than angry.

"Well..." He sighed, also frustrated. It occurred to him that there was probably some very simple thing he could have said at the beginning of the discussion to avoid all this tension. (And, of course, he was well aware that he had violated the cardinal rule of this type of argument: the less said, the better. But in the heat of conflict, this rule is counterintuitive.)

Whatever that "right thing to say" might have been, he would never have thought of it, even if given hundreds of millions of redos. And if, now, he could think of what it might have been, it would no longer be the right thing. Now, after all the back-and-forth, it would come across as nothing more than something he had come up with to get himself out of trouble. He looked at her.

"What am I supposed to think when you answer me like that?" Lisa asked.

"Like what?"

"Standing there looking like you can't think of anything to say that won't get you deeper in trouble."

"Because I don't think there's anything I can say that won't get me into deeper trouble."

"And why is that?"

"The petition is on the level. Honest."

"What's on the level? The story that he's an old friend or the one that you didn't know him?"

Well, there was no correct answer to *that* question. And even though he wasn't sure exactly how much trouble he was in, it was finally sinking in that he should say as little as possible. "Well, he's been in the store a few times," Ragwater said, acutely aware of how weak it sounded.

"Look," Lisa said, "if you can sell CDs by flirting with other women, then I guess that's what you should do. You just have to understand that I don't like it if you do it in front of me. As far as this goes…" She waved the petition. "I don't know. It kind of seems there's something about it you don't want me to know."

"Can I at least get it back? The guy's going to want it."

Lisa started to say something and then stopped herself, as if exasperated that he couldn't understand something that seemed obvious to her. She stood in the doorway for a moment and then went out, petition in hand.

***

Okay. He was going to have to bail out of this deal. Maxwell had said he could call it off between tasks.

And really: How would he feel if she went out with another guy? How would he feel if she were involved in some Maxwell-type deal?

~ 10 ~

As the opening of the Ramones' "Pinhead" filled the apartment, Ragwater bit into his grilled provolone cheese sandwich with bacon and chewed slowly, trying to devise of a way to get back on Lisa's good side without thinking about how awful the scene had been in the store earlier.

Strange thing. It wasn't like Lisa to fly off the handle that way. Definitely uncharacteristic of her.

He had to admit, though, she had a point. Now, on the one hand, he didn't think he had crossed over the line into unacceptable behavior. He really didn't think it had been all *that* bad. On the other hand, when he thought about the way he had acted, his tone of voice, his body language...and, of course, "Who can blame him?" Well, it was easy to see (as Lisa had said) that it was probably a bit too much *in front of his girlfriend.*

Ragwater heard a knock on the door. It was faint enough that he thought it was something that had been making noise at the Ramones' recording session, something he had never noticed before. Then it became louder and more obvious. As Ragwater put his sandwich down and got up to answer the door, Maxwell came in.

"Good evening, Gilbert."

"You're supposed to wait for me to answer the door."

"Saves time this way." Maxwell walked over to the stereo and turned it down. "I thought only kids played music that loud," he said.

"Some of us never grow up."

"What about your neighbor Arnie?"

"At a ball game. That's why I can crank it up."

Maxwell nodded thoughtfully, as if Ragwater had said something profound. "I understand you have a little situation on your hands."

"You could say that."

Maxwell studied the front of the stereo receiver. He squatted down so his face was level with it, turned the balance knob oh-so-slightly, and cocked his head, listening. The glow from the dial gave his face a slightly greenish tint.

"Don't do that," Ragwater said. "I had it set just the way I wanted it."

"I think you protest too much," Maxwell said.

"What? That makes no sense at all."

"No, it doesn't, does it?"

"How can you be this obtuse?"

"See? That's exactly what I'm talking about."

Ragwater rolled his eyes. "Okay, let's dispense with the nonsense. I want to quit. This deal is causing problems that I don't want."

Maxwell studied knobs for another moment without touching them and then turned to Ragwater.

"It's not causing problems," Maxwell said. "You're letting problems result from it. You should take control of the situation."

"Whatever. I'm not inclined to waste time talking

about crap like that. I want out."

"Well, here's the thing. You can quit, as I explained at the beginning, but not while you still have a task in progress. This task with the petition can't be closed out until I have the paper in my hands."

Maxwell pressed a button, cutting off the Ramones. In their place, a typical-sounding radio announcer was interviewing a local business leader who was sponsoring an upcoming charity event. "We would like to raise enough money to buy guitars for at least a hundred disadvantaged kids," the business leader said. "There's no doubt in my mind that we have a lot of future rock stars in the community. Many of them just need a little help getting started."

"Yes," the announcer said. "Maybe you could buy the next George Thorogood his first guitar."

"Okay, so give me a new one, and I'll get the signatures again," Ragwater said.

Maxwell stood up and turned to face Ragwater. "A new one?" He stroked his chin thoughtfully. "The idea has some merit." He gave it some thought, or appeared to, for another moment. "No...no, I'm afraid not. If you hadn't gotten all seven signatures, you could have. But since you got them, I have to have that particular one."

"Otherwise..."

"You forfeit your life."

Ragwater sat down in the easy chair. He slouched down, threw one leg over the arm of the chair, and considered what it would take to get the petition back from Lisa. "Here's the thing," he said. "I'm pretty sure I can smooth over our little argument and get all lovey-dovey with her again. I'm not sure about asking her to get the petition back, though. I'm afraid if I mention it, I'll open up another can of worms."

"Gilbert, you're not making sense. What do worms have to do with it?"

"Nothing. It's a figure of speech."

"A figure of speech." Maxwell nodded thoughtfully. "Can of worms." It seemed obvious to Ragwater that Maxwell didn't want to let on that he didn't have a clue what "figure of speech" meant. Consequently, "can of worms" would have been even more nonsensical to him.

But then again, Ragwater had to wonder what "forfeit his life" meant. Well, that is to say, the meaning was clear, but how would Maxwell want to go about it? It might make a difference—if he knew that the forfeiture was going to be drifting off into death peacefully in his sleep, that wouldn't be nearly as bad as, say, a mobster slowly crushing his head in a vise, like that scene in *Casino*. Why hadn't he asked about it that first night in the kitchen? Ragwater made a mental note to bring up the question at some appropriate time. But now, he had to clarify his position.

"What I'm getting at," Ragwater said, "is this: I'm not sure there's a way to get that petition back. I think there's a good chance that if I mention it, Lisa will get mad again and tear the damn thing up. Neither of us would want that, would we?"

"Well, *you* surely wouldn't."

"You wouldn't, either. Not if this petition is the one you have to have."

"It's the one I have to have if I'm to continue working with you. If I...if it ends up so that I have to call upon you to forfeit your life, I can start over again with someone else."

"That's screwy."

"It's not possible to explain it to you, dear Gilbert, but for my purposes, everything would get all messed up something fierce if I were to let you start over at this point." He licked a finger and ran it around the rim of a ceramic ashtray on the coffee table.

"What did you do that for?" Ragwater asked.

"Huh?"

"The finger thing."

"Oh, that. I was testing."

"Testing what? It's an ashtray. There's nothing more to it."

"Oh, *now* you tell me."

Ragwater started to say something else but stopped himself. He didn't want to get bogged down in stupidity. He had enough already of his own making. "There's no way to work around it?" he asked. "I mean, we're both intelligent, clever guys, right? I'm sure we can figure out something."

"Yes, which gives me the utmost confidence in your ability to get the petition back from Lisa."

Well, that was that. Maxwell obviously had his mind set. "Utmost," Ragwater said.

"I know you're intelligent and resourceful," Maxwell said. "That's why I picked you for this job."

"I thought it was because I'm gullible."

"Well, that, too," Maxwell said, without a hint of humor or irony in his voice, as if Ragwater had said, "I have brown hair." Ragwater wasn't sure if Maxwell hadn't been paying attention, or if he didn't know what gullible meant, or if for some reason he believed gullibility was an asset, or if he really thought Ragwater was gullible and saw no reason to deny it. What he was sure of, though, was that he was somehow getting railroaded.

Ragwater had the feeling that although Maxwell would certainly deny it, he was somehow shifting the rules around, as if the shifting were itself part of the rules, the way it was in Fear and Loathing in Hell. And he, Maxwell, would probably leap at the chance to use an unaccounted-for situation to his advantage.

"It seems as if you're changing the rules," Ragwater said.

"No, Gilbert. I'm doing things the way I told you. Nothing in our basic agreement has changed. I gave you the assignment to get seven signatures on that petition. The task isn't complete until you return the petition to me. If you try to analyze it any further than that, you're making it more complicated than it has to be."

Hmmm.

"I don't know why you want to overcomplicate things, but you seem to have a habit of it."

"I don't think I do."

"But on the upside," Maxwell continued, "you can take all the time you need to get the petition back." He licked his finger again and ran it down the length of a candle standing next to the ashtray.

"Okay, fair enough." Well, it would have to be fair enough; Ragwater didn't see that he was in a position to bargain. And yet..."What if I decide to abandon it?"

"Abandon?"

"Yes. I could sort of, like, forget about it. You could come around every couple days and ask whether I'm making any progress, and I could tell you I'm trying, but unfortunately not making any progress at all, and you would be satisfied until next time. It could go on forever."

"It wouldn't work. I would know."

"You would know?"

"Yes," Maxwell said. "I would know if you lied to me."

Yes, he probably would.

"So the main thing is, don't give up," Maxwell said. "Take all the time you need. Of course, if you think Lisa will end up throwing it away, or tearing it up, you're going to want to get it before she does." Maxwell knelt next to the coffee table and studied the candle. He squinted, and the tip of his tongue edged out between his lips.

Ragwater didn't bother to ask. "I don't think she will," he said. "I think she'll keep it around, in case it really belongs to a psychology student who needs to get it back. She's highly suspicious, but she can't be certain. As I was saying a minute ago, the biggest danger would be if I flat-out ask for it. Then she might get mad all over again and tear it up."

Eyes firmly on the candle, Maxwell said, "So you have to get ingenious."

"Either that or disingenuous."

"I have faith in you, my boy."

"Yeah, that makes me feel *so* much better."

Maxwell wiped his finger on his shirt and touched the candle where he had wiped spit on it. "Good. Now, since this task is in sort of a state of, ah...suspension, we'll proceed to the next task while you work on getting the petition back."

Yeah, there it was; that was how Ragwater was getting railroaded. He was now locked into the entire series of tasks. "Well, okay," he said.

Maxwell stood up and looked around. He stepped around the coffee table and sat on the sofa, legs splayed out, head back. "This is a nice sofa," he said. "Where did you get it?"

"My parents gave it to me when I moved out of their house." He didn't feel like explaining that he had been left with it after his parents died. For that matter, he could have told Maxwell that elves had snuck in one night and built it for him, right there in the living room. What difference did it make?

"Nice parents."

"Yeah, I guess so."

Maxwell suddenly sat up straight. "Okay, here's what I want you to do. I want you to get a can of spray paint, preferably red—well, let's make it definitely red—get a can of red spray paint and write the name Mad Vandal on six buildings of your choice."

"Mad Vandal?"

"Yeah. No. Yeah. No."

"Make up your mind. I can't do the task if you can't decide."

"*The* Mad Vandal. Put a 'the' in front of it. You pick the buildings, but I want them pretty well scattered around town."

"Six buildings?"

"Yes, six."

"You're not going to change your mind several times?"

"Why would I do that?"

"Any buildings at all?"

"Well, I wouldn't recommend trying to do it at the White House."

"Ah, but other than that one..."

"And probably not the gold depository at Fort Knox."

"I doubt that I would have thought of that one."

"Good. I'm glad you're as level-headed as I thought you were. Because, I think, I'm pretty sure, if you try to get in there, they gun you down, no questions asked."

"Yes, I think they do."

"They must be permanent buildings. No tents, trailers, portable outhouses, or anything like that. And they have to be in good enough condition that you'd expect them to remain standing for several more years. No dilapidated houses in rundown neighborhoods."

"What about verification?"

"Verification?

"Sure. So you'll know I really did it. Do you want a list of addresses, or pictures, or what?"

"None of that will be necessary."

"If you say so."

Maxwell turned sideways to lie down. "I really like this sofa," he said. "Where did you get it?"

"I told you. My parents gave it to me."

"Oh, yes. Yes, of course. How did you get it here?"

"Do you really want to know all this stuff?"

"Sure. It would be rather silly to ask questions if I don't want to know the answers."

Ragwater stifled the urge to point out that the questions themselves were silly. And, of course he didn't want to go through the entire history of moving the sofa in and out of four different apartments through the years. "I borrowed a friend's pickup truck," he said.

"That's nice," Maxwell said. He closed his eyes and waved his arms around. Ragwater considered getting out his cell phone and shooting video, but decided it would be too much trouble.

"So, like...are we finished with our little meeting?" Ragwater asked.

Maxwell stopped waving and sat up. "Wow. That gets tiring a lot more quickly than you would expect."

"How do you know what I would expect?" Ragwater had a distinct edge in his voice. He was starting to feel mean. He was tired.

"Are you angry?" Maxwell asked. "Is there something we need to talk about?"

"We need to talk about you leaving so I can go to bed."

Maxwell frowned. "I don't think you want to talk about it. I think you just want me to go. Am I right?"

"You're right."

Maxwell stood and went to the door. "I'll get back to you after you've finished the Mad Vandal job," he said. He opened the door, stepped out, and then turned back. "It's up to you, of course, but it doesn't escape my notice that it's still early, and the graffiti could all be done in one night."

"I guess it could."

"But as I said, it's up to you. Good luck."

And with that, Maxwell eased the door shut. Ragwater moved over to the sofa and lay down. He raised his arms and waved them around. Yes, it got tiring very quickly. He let his arms flop down and considered this new task. It made even less sense than the first one. What was Maxwell getting out of this? The whole thing seemed profoundly meaningless.

And he, Ragwater, had forgotten to ask how he would forfeit his life, if indeed it came to that.

How, indeed? Was Maxwell cruel? Was he the type

to pull the legs off of flies and torment stray cats? Had he been a bully as a child? Did he watch *Silence of the Lambs* and snicker over what a pussy Hannibal Lector was? Ragwater didn't know anything about the man personally. If he was surprised to find out that builders could tile floors in checkerboard patterns, who could possibly guess what went on inside his head?

And so: Would he want to make it painful? Well, what the heck? Ragwater would remember to ask the next time he talked to Maxwell.

But it was hypothetical. Ragwater had no intention of forfeiting his life.

~ 11 ~

Someone knocked on the door. It cracked open, oh so slowly. Ragwater wondered if Maxwell was making another entrance for some reason. It didn't seem his style to be so careful about it, but you never knew what that clown might do.

Lisa popped her head in. "Gilbert? Can I come in?"

"Yes, absolutely."

He got up to greet her at the door. He was unsure whether to give her a hug. Yeah, go for it. He reached out, and his hand found its way around her waist. She looked up at him. His other hand went around, and he drew her close. She gave him a tentative smile. "I just met your neighbor outside," she said.

"Oh? Who?"

"Mr. Maxwell. He introduced himself to me."

Mr. Maxwell? It occurred to Ragwater for the first time that he knew only the one name, and he had assumed it was his first name. But that wasn't necessarily true. Was this man's full name, maybe, possibly, something like Ernesto Daniel Aristotle O'Leary Tree Stump Maxwell the Third?

One never knows. And...he was introducing himself as Ragwater's neighbor. Well, for all Ragwater knew, maybe he was. It was possible that he had been living the apartment directly above Ragwater's for the last five years.

But, of more immediate concern, what had this possible Ernesto Daniel Aristotle O'Leary Tree Stump Maxwell the Third told Lisa? It couldn't have been anything incriminating, given her good mood right now.

"Oh, yeah. Maxwell. What did he have to say for himself?"

"Nothing much. Said he recognized me because you had shown him a picture. He said you spoke very highly of me."

"There's no other possible way to speak of you."

"He seems pretty nice." She walked in and sat on the sofa. Ragwater took his place next to her.

"I want to apologize for the way I acted in the store today," Lisa said. "Sometimes when something's not quite right, I sort of flash back to the way things were with Roger, and then I start assuming the worst."

"Roger's a real piece of work," Ragwater said. Roger was Lisa's previous boyfriend, an acquaintance of Ragwater's and a semi-regular customer at the store. He had cheated on Lisa quite extensively, and toward the end quite shamelessly. More than once he had gotten himself beaten up after making a pass at the wrong woman. Lisa finally called it quits when she found out he had hit on both her mother and her sister. (Under different circumstances, Ragwater would have understood—both were quite attractive women.)

That Lisa had compared Ragwater to Roger was, at first glance, unflattering. But then again, he had to think that the comparison made him, Ragwater, look pretty good—even with his many flaws.

"Maybe you're up to something I don't know about," Lisa said, "but I shouldn't assume it's something that's a threat to me. Maybe I shouldn't expect to know everything."

Ragwater turned a few replies over in his mind. Not wanting to risk saying the wrong thing, he said nothing.

"Or for you to expect to know everything about me," she added.

Well, that raised a few questions—and at the same time cut off the possibility of asking them.

"I'm sorry, too," Ragwater said, "about the flirting thing. I guess I went too far."

"You're better off not talking about that."

Ragwater was happy to let the matter drop.

He scooched closer, and so did she. He put his arm around her, closed his eyes, and leaned in for a kiss. Funny thing, though. Her lips felt different. They were a little fuller, a little more pliant. For that matter, her shoulders felt a little wider than they should have.

Ragwater broke away and opened his eyes to find himself sitting next to the Redhead. He gasped, blinked, and searched his brain furiously for something to say. She smiled at him expectantly, as if he should have been happy to see her there—as if she was sure he would move in for another, possibly more passionate, kiss.

In the next instant, she was Lisa again. "Is something wrong?" she asked.

"No," Ragwater said. "No, really."

She frowned. "Are you sure?"

"Oh, yeah. Absolutely."

He moved close, tentatively gave her a little peck on the lips, and then jerked back.

"Something's wrong," Lisa said. "Do I have bad breath?"

"No, nothing's wrong," Ragwater said. "I'm just being playful."

"It's an odd kind of playful."

"I won't do it anymore," Ragwater said. That quick, little kiss had turned out all right, so the Redhead... the hallucination?...was probably nothing more than a one-time thing.

He leaned in for another kiss, a bit reserved but giving it some feeling. As he put his arm around her, he felt a thick, luscious cascade of hair that fell to about halfway down her back.

Lisa's hair wasn't that long.

Ragwater didn't open his eyes. Once again, the lips were a bit too full to be Lisa's. Fingers moved slowly down his back, circling around each vertebra with a firm, confident touch as they progressed. Lisa had never done that before—but, he reminded himself, that didn't mean she couldn't have decided to do it now.

Regardless of anything, this was Lisa.

How could she be anyone else?

He kept his eyes closed. He relaxed.

And still, the hair, the lips...he moved his hand up to her earlobe and discovered an earring.

Lisa never wore earrings. Her ears weren't pierced.

Stubbornly, Ragwater kept kissing. The fingers resumed massaging down his backbone. It felt so nice that, well...maybe he didn't care who was doing it.

But it was disturbing to think that he might be that...uh, for lack of a better word, that pathetic.

Ragwater backed away slowly and opened his eyes. He caught a glimpse of the Redhead sitting in front of him—almost immediately to be replaced, again, by Lisa.

He blinked.

Lisa. With shoulder-length hair and no earrings.

"So, how was your day?" he asked.

"What?" She was surprised by the question.

"I was thinking, it might be nice to talk for a few minutes."

"Are you sure nothing's wrong?"

"Well, yeah." Ragwater paused to think. What legitimate reason could he have for interrupting a make-out session? That is to say, what reason could he give her that wouldn't sound bad? After all, men aren't expected to want to talk, especially when things start getting physical. "It's the way I was twisted around," he said. "I got a cramp in my back. I think it'll be all right if I sit up straight, like in a normal sitting position, for a few minutes."

"You want me to rub it for you?"

How could he turn that down? "Sure."

"Lie down flat."

Lisa got up so that Ragwater could stretch out along the length of the sofa. She straddled him and began working on his back. "How's that?"

"Hmmm...good."

"Some old codger came in and insisted we sell him a fishing license," Lisa said.

"Did you?"

"Of course not. Diane kept telling him we only do driver's licenses, but he wouldn't listen. He said we could sell him a driver's license, cross out the word 'driver,' and write in the word 'fishing.'"

"He said that?"

"Yeah. He insisted. We tried to tell him to go down the hall. That was all he had to do, but he wouldn't."

"Old codger, huh?"

"He started talking about John Dillinger. Weird stuff."

"John Dillinger? He wasn't threatening you, was he?"

"Oh, no, not at all. He claimed he went to school with him. I don't know why. I mean, I don't know why he was talking about it right then and there. I don't even think he could have been that old. Wouldn't he have to be, like, a hundred years old to have gone to school with John Dillinger?"

"Maybe he was."

And then, a knuckle pressed gently into his upper back, just below neck level, and began circling around a vertebra. "Shelly's little boy fell asleep during a Little League game," Lisa said. "He was standing in the outfield, and he lay down on the grass and dozed off."

And then, Ragwater could have sworn he heard her say, in a slightly muffled voice, "A man came to my parents' door yesterday and wanted to buy the dandruff mining rights to the land their house is on."

Ragwater tried to roll over.

"Relax."

The massage continued. "I saw some evil spirits for sale at a pet store the other day," Lisa said—if, that is, it was really Lisa. He thought he heard a different sort of quality in her voice.

This wasn't going to work. Ragwater tried once again to roll over. "I think I have to get up," he said.

Lisa stood up. As Ragwater moved around to a sitting position, she sat next to him. "I think this muscle cramp is too much for a back rub," he said. "I think maybe I need to get to bed, by myself, and take it easy."

"That's a shame."

"Yeah, no doubt about it. But I'll make it up to you, I promise. We'll do something really special over the weekend."

Lisa nodded. "I'll take you up on that." She got up and went to the door. Ragwater followed.

"I'm really sorry about this," he said. He gave a little wince for good measure.

Unnoticed by (apparently invisible to) Lisa, the Redhead strolled casually in from the kitchen. She stopped directly behind Lisa, gave Ragwater a sultry look, and began the dance of seven veils.

"It's all right," Lisa said. "You take care of yourself."

"Yeah, all I need is a little dance…uh, rest, that is, and I'll be all right."

"Dance?"

The first veil dropped.

Oh, crap. How could he explain the word "dance" slipping out? "Yeah. I was thinking you might want to go dancing, like for the special thing we'll do this weekend."

"But you hate dancing."

"This one time, I'll make a concession." He couldn't believe he was saying it.

The redhead reached out, tapped his shoulder for attention, and then stretched sensuously, back arched, hands above her head. She closed her eyes and parted her lips in an expression that might have been what she would look like in a moment of passion.

"You don't have to make that much of a concession," Lisa said. "But we'll talk about it later."

Lisa stepped forward. He gave her a hug, and another veil fell over his head. He reached up and pulled it off.

"What are you doing?"

"Oh, I heard a fly buzzing around. Just shooing it away." He was getting tired of making up so many excuses. If he didn't get Lisa the heck out of there, he was going to slip up in a big way.

And then, he could see, behind Lisa, one of the Redhead's breasts was bare. It looked like a C-cup, he guessed, nice and firm.

"I'll call you," he said, eyes on the breast.

The redhead moved around behind him.

"Okay. If you're not feeling better in the morning, stay home."

The redhead's hands were on his shoulders, moving in to caress his neck.

"I can't do that."

"Sure. Call Jason and have him mind the store for you."

"I hate to call him in with no advance notice."

Breasts pressed against his back.

Those fine, firm, C-cup breasts.

"He goes to school," Ragwater said.

"It's summer."

"I think he's taking a class."

"Well, if you go to work, take it easy. Don't do any heavy lifting."

The redhead was nibbling on his earlobe.

"Yeah, I'll take it easy."

Lisa gave him a quick kiss and slipped out the door. A moment later, the Redhead was handing him his phone. And he wondered, was this really his imagination? He liked to think he had a vivid imagination, but this was beyond anything reasonable.

Maybe an apparition? Something that was, objectively, there, but not an actual, physical woman? Like a hologram or something?

He looked at her intently, trying to see whether she was...well, real. She looked *solid* enough; that is to say, he couldn't see any "ghostly transparency" in her appearance. Not that he would know what to look for, anyway. He had no experience with apparitions or hallucinations, or whatever. She certainly *felt* solid.

Oh, did she ever.

Lisa hadn't seen her. That meant something. Was this the same way she had appeared in the store that day? But then, Plow had seen her. He had seen her in the park, too. In those cases, though, it wasn't strange to think that she could have been there. It *was* strange, very strange, for her to show up in his apartment as if she had been there all along.

The redhead gave him a faint smile, barely enough to notice. Was she flirting? Being conspiratorial?

This wasn't what he had had in mind when he and Maxwell talked about being adventurous. Yet he didn't seem to have a choice.

Oh, pish-posh. One always has a choice, even when all the available options are bad.

Ragwater found John Plow's number. "Speak to me, daddy-o," Plow said.

"Hey, John. You want to do something truly weird tonight?"

~ 12 ~

Pulling into the driveway, Ragwater could see Plow sitting on his front porch making occasional gestures of throwing something. He couldn't, however, tell what (if anything) was being thrown.

And as he walked toward Plow, Plow zinged a couple of small, dark objects at him.

"What are you doing?"

"Throwing raisins into the front yard."

"Why?"

"I don't like raisins. I have to get rid of them some way."

Ragwater reached the porch and sat next to Plow. "Why did you buy them?"

"I didn't. My mother did." He looked at Ragwater's car. "Go open your window, and I'll see if I can throw one in."

"Did you happen to think that maybe she wants them?"

"Huh?"

"Your mother. If she bought the raisins, she probably wants them. And here you sit throwing them into the front yard."

"You think so?"

"I'm pretty sure of it."

"Oh. Maybe I should go pick them up."

"I don't think that's necessary."

"Yeah. It's too dark to find them."

***

Armed with spray paint and beer—no, make that beer and spray paint, beer being the necessary lubricant to get the expedition going—Ragwater found the spot for his first strike. He parked on the street, and he and Plow walked a half block to a nearby alley entrance. Suddenly, Ragwater darted around the corner. Plow, taken by surprise, hesitated a couple seconds and then followed.

"What's with all the dramatic skulking about and stuff?" Plow asked. "Do you think you're in a spy movie?"

"If I am, it's a bad one," Ragwater said. "I'm feeling the need to be careful."

"No one's around."

"You can't be sure. Besides, what about surveillance cameras?"

"Are you saying that acting suspicious is the way you want to appear on surveillance video?"

Ragwater had a ready answer to that: "Shut up."

Plow nodded. "I see your point," he said.

"Good. Now, I'm ready to get into some serious vandalism." Ragwater pulled a can of spray paint out from under his shirt and began shaking it.

"You know," Plow said, "if you're all that concerned about getting caught, that little ball in there is rattling around awfully loud."

"Yeah, and your tiny little brain is rattling around inside your skull even louder, so that should cover the noise I'm making."

"Hey, you're the one trying to be sneaky," Plow said.

Ragwater gave the can a couple more shakes, just to be contrary. Then he looked at the wall, an old, dirty brick surface that somehow seemed to lack something because it had no graffiti on it. I'm performing a *service*, Ragwater told himself. He would have preferred a bit more light to do this, but he could get by.

He shook the can again, not thinking about noise, and picked a spot—a spot that screamed out in its need for decoration.

THE MAD VANDAL

Ragwater stepped back and regarded his work. "Not bad, eh?"

"The Mad Vandal?"

"Yeah. Cool, huh?"

"Well, Gilbert, I know you've never claimed to be the guy who wrote the very definition of cool, but still...I have to say that after a late-night phone call and a frantic shopping trip for spray paint..."

"It wasn't frantic."

"Seeing this as the final result is, well...a letdown. You dragged me out here for *this*?"

"You don't like it?"

"It doesn't *suck*, but I'm not feeling it. You know? If you're going to impress me, you need something more... uh, shall we say, spectacular."

"Well, this is what it has to be."

"Why? I say if you're going to paint graffiti, go all-out. I say you should be Vincent van freakin' Gogh."

"Maybe I'll work up to it."

Plow reached for the spray paint. "Gimme that. I want to create some art."

"There's a sentence I never thought I'd hear you say."

Plow pulled himself up into a dignified pose. "I'll have you know, sir, that I'm quite a sensitive individual."

"If by sensitive you mean completely insensitive."

Plow gave the paint a few shakes and stared off into space.

"What are you doing?" Ragwater asked. "We don't want to linger around here longer than we have to."

"Says the guy who took time to crack jokes about my sensitivity. For your information, I'm communing with my muse."

"Nothing good can come of that."

"Ah, I have it. The greatest artistic subject that exists."

"What's that?"

"A naked woman." Plow stepped up to the wall.

"Do you know what one looks like?" Ragwater asked.

"I've seen pictures." Beer in one hand and paint can in the other, Plow proceeded to draw some curves and lines. Then he added a few dots here and there. Finished, he stepped back. "Well? What do you think?" The rendition was crude, showing no trace of talent or training. But the general idea was clear enough.

"What's that?" Ragwater said, pointing to a dot.

"A birthmark."

"Ah, I see. Well, overall, it certainly shows some

enthusiasm for the subject matter."

"I've been practicing a lot in public men's rooms."

"I can tell," Ragwater said. "By the way, I have some news for you. Have you met Sylvia's best friend?"

"No, I sure haven't."

"Well, don't."

"Okay." Plow started walking toward the car.

"John?"

Plow stopped and turned around. "What?"

"Don't you want to know why?"

"Why what?"

"Why you don't want to meet Sylvia's friend."

"Oh, that. I just assumed it's because you think she's ugly."

"No. Quite the opposite, in fact. She's Linda."

"Sure, I know. She talked about her."

"John, she's *Linda*."

"Yeah. I said I know."

"The one you tried to pick up in the park Sunday."

Plow looked down at the spray paint can, as if expecting it to comment, maybe to explain the situation to him in more believable terms. His mouth opened, but no words came out.

"Are you okay?" Ragwater asked.

"No," Plow said.

"What? You don't believe me?"

"No, I *do* believe you. This explains a few things, details about stuff Sylvia said to me. I should have connected the dots myself."

"I don't see why you would expect you should have connected those particular dots. What are the chances you would end up with a picture like this?"

Plow looked straight at Ragwater. "I guess about a

hundred percent, huh?" he said pointedly.

"Hey, it's not my fault."

"I didn't mean it like that."

"Yeah, I know. Listen, we have to get moving. I have to do more Mad Vandal walls."

Plow started walking. "You make it sound like someone assigned you to do all this."

Of course, it was nothing more than an off-the-cuff remark, Ragwater told himself. He couldn't possibly know. "I'm not the one trying to pick up strange women to cheat on my girlfriend with," Ragwater said. Technically, it was true. He was the one getting signatures on a petition and painting graffiti so he could...be *given*, for lack of a better word, a woman to cheat on his girlfriend with. No pickup needed.

"What does picking up strange women have to do with graffiti?" Plow asked.

"Nothing, I guess."

It sounded incredibly *lame* when Ragwater thought of it that way—that is to say, tasks in exchange for making the woman "available." And maybe that was why he had been willing to tell Plow about it only under the pretense that it was an idea for a short story. He, Ragwater, told himself it was because his friend wouldn't believe it was actually real—but then again, it did sorta seem like...well, a lot of people think that dating web sites are for losers who can't get dates the traditional way. Maybe this seemed like the same thing. But on a web site, all you have to do is describe yourself: six feet four inches tall, athletic, nonsmoker, social drinker, MBA from Harvard, financially secure professional with an income above $200,000, love to travel. And so on.

Ragwater didn't have to do that. He didn't have to make a good impression, false or otherwise. All he had to do was sneak around performing strange little tasks that had no apparent purpose. It wasn't something to brag about.

But then, the Redhead would agree to anything he wanted. That wasn't lame, was it? That is to say, from Ragwater's point of view?

Plow would surely understand that. For that matter, Plow would likely agree to such a deal himself.

Yeah, he probably would! And with much less thought and agonizing analysis than Ragwater had put into it.

From around the corner, Ragwater heard footfalls and some kind of scuffling. A skinny guy with long hair and a scraggly beard ran into the alley toward them. "Help!" he shouted when he saw Ragwater and Plow.

The guy ran toward them. He stopped and pointed to the spray paint can. "What's that? Mace?"

"Spray paint," Plow said.

"Just as good," the guy said. "Let me have it." He grabbed at the can. Plow held it away from him.

"Wait a minute!" Plow said.

"Who are you?" Ragwater asked.

"My name's Henry," the guy said, "and my two *ex*-friends want to beat me up." He grabbed at the spray paint again.

"Gilbert!" Plow shouted.

Ragwater stepped over and pulled Henry away from Plow. "Take it easy," Ragwater said.

Henry squirmed out of Ragwater's grasp. At that moment, two figures appeared at the corner, silhouettes under the streetlight, like characters in an old *film noir*. They paused to look into the alley and then, seeing Henry, ran toward him.

As they approached, Ragwater could see that (a) these guys were Aunt Rachel and Sniffy, and (b) they had tire irons. Ragwater thought about his history with them, modest though it was, and tried to figure out whether they would consider him enough of a friend to give him a pass if things got violent.

As soon as they saw that Ragwater and Plow weren't going anywhere, they slowed to a deliberate walk—sort of but not quite a strut.

"Well, well, Henry," Aunt Rachel said. "It looks like the chickens have come home to roost."

"Hey, wait," Sniffy said. "This is the dude from the music store."

Aunt Rachel smiled. "Yeah, the prank guy."

"Cool it," Henry said. "These guys are my friends."

The two guys stopped about ten feet away. Aunt Rachel looked at Henry and Plow as if evaluating them. Sniffy took a long, deep drag off his cigarette.

"Friends, eh?" Aunt Rachel said.

Sniffy flicked his cigarette away and slapped his tire iron into his palm. "We got our friends here too."

"Oh, for crying out loud," Plow said.

"You don't take us seriously?" Aunt Rachel said. "We can fix that."

"He's cool," Ragwater said, nodding his head toward Plow. "He can be a world-class smartass sometimes, but he's cool."

"Back off," Henry said. "We have spray paint." He made another grab for the can. Plow stepped back.

Ragwater was irritated. "What's going on?" he asked.

"I was sitting in a bar around the corner," Henry said, "minding my own business—and that's the key word: *minding my own business*—not bothering anyone—when these two clowns came in and started hassling me."

"Don't call us clowns," Sniffy said.

"Henry, quit acting like you don't know about that Burger Utopia bit," Aunt Rachel said. "Do you think we're stupid?"

"I don't know."

"I almost got arrested in that parking lot. And then that other phone call."

"Phone call?" Henry said. "I don't have a clue what you're talking about."

"Oh, yeah, sure you don't. You're going to reach through the phone line and pull my uvula out, right?"

"Huh?" Henry said. "I though a uvula was a female body part."

"Huh?" Ragwater said.

Many people would have seen that Henry was genuinely puzzled. Most people would have noticed that Ragwater's mouth had fallen open far enough to shove a basketball in.

Aunt Rachel and Sniffy noticed none of that. They had their minds set on attacking Henry, and they weren't about to be distracted.

Aunt Rachel leaned toward Sniffy. "Come on, man. Let's quit fooling around and clean his clock."

And yet, Ragwater couldn't help but feel that if they were going to attack—that is to say, mount a serious, physical attack—they would already have done so. They would have dived right in without any comments about chickens coming home to roost or rehashes of phone calls or threats to "clean his clock"—geez, he didn't think anyone actually said that. No, this cat-and-mouse stuff was strictly from the movies. Real beatings of this sort were quick and vicious, and they never started out with threats.

But then again, maybe they were unsure of what they should or shouldn't do in front of Plow and him. It didn't matter, though. All Ragwater cared about was that no blood was flowing.

"They have black belts," Henry said.

"Don't tell them that," Plow said.

"You're supposed to warn them before you kick their ass, aren't you?"

"Oh, god," Plow muttered. "We're all going to get killed."

"No one's going to get killed," Ragwater said. Then, to Henry's friends: "Listen, we don't know this guy. We just happened to be here."

"That's what I thought," Aunt Rachel said.

"Thanks a lot," Henry said. "No one's willing to help anyone these days."

"I'll help anyone who deserves it," Ragwater said. "What I object to is being dragged into the middle of a fight that's none of my business."

Aunt Rachel and Sniffy moved forward. Henry stepped around behind Plow and maneuvered around. He held Plow by the arms, trying to use him as a shield.

"Watch it!" Plow said, genuinely angry. "You'll spill my beer!"

"You're making it harder on yourself, Henry," Aunt Rachel said. He and Sniffy split up and went around Plow on different sides. Henry made a break for it down the alley, his "friends" in hot pursuit.

Plow was indignant. "Give 'im what-for, guys."

"Are you okay?" Ragwater asked.

"Yeah. The nerve of that guy, trying to get us beat up with him."

"Well, I don't think that was his actual plan..."

"But still..."

"Yes. But still."

"So," Plow said, "you know those guys?"

"They've been in the store a couple times. You know them. They were the guys who went to Olive's and insisted they had an appointment."

"Oh, yeah."

They began walking toward Ragwater's car. "You know who that other guy is, don't you?" Ragwater asked. "The one they were trying to beat up?"

"No. And furthermore, I don't care."

"Oh, I think you do. I think you're extremely interested."

"And I think you're a rutabaga pie."

"He's Henry. Remember when you tried to call Linda, and the guy who answered the phone thought you were..."

"Henry. But that doesn't mean this guy is the same Henry."

"A couple days ago, those same two guys were in the store complaining about Henry, all the flaky stuff he's been doing, getting people in trouble and whatnot. And just now, they were talking about a phone call."

"Yeah? So?"

"That was your phone call to Linda. Or, should I say, your *attempted* phone call to Linda. And you got him all riled up."

"Oh, a phone call. Big, fat, hairy deal."

"A phone call isn't unusual," Ragwater said. "But he quoted the bit about reaching through the phone line and pulling his uvula out."

"Oh, yeah, he did, didn't he?"

"Yeah. And you just saw the results of your handiwork."

"What? So you're trying to make me out to be some kind of jerk? Is that it?"

"No more than I usually do."

They reached the car. As Ragwater was unlocking the door, Plow said, "One of those guys said something about getting arrested at Burger Utopia. I wonder what that was all about. I know I didn't have anything to do with Burger Utopia."

Ragwater blinked. "I don't know," he said. "Maybe another wrong number."

~ 13 ~

Ragwater's door was ajar.

He was sure he had closed and locked it when he left. He was certain of it.

Well, pretty sure, anyway.

He stepped up to the door and leaned forward, his face inches from the opening. A faint light glowed from inside—probably the floor lamp across the room. He couldn't be sure whether he had left it on or not, but going out at night, he probably would have.

Ragwater held his breath and listened. All he could hear was his own heartbeat, the pounding of his pulse through his head, a ringing in his ears.

He was too tense. Too much adrenaline. He stepped back and took a couple of deep breaths. His hands were shaking.

Ragwater walked around the corner and sat down at a bus stop. Now removed from any danger that might be lurking in his apartment, he was able to calm down.

Who could be in there? Those two guys who had been chasing Henry? Not likely. They would have no reason. Maybe Henry himself? Again, why? None of those guys would know where he lived, anyway. Right?

Ragwater dialed 911 on his cell phone and, thumb

poised to push the call button, again approached his apartment. He took a deep breath, held it, and nudged the door open a few more inches. No reaction from inside. Whoever had been there had probably left.

Yeah, that was it. The intruder was gone. All that remained now was to figure out what had been stolen.

Ragwater threw the door open to see Maxwell sitting in the easy chair reading a copy of *Writer's Digest*. "Hi, Gilbert," he said. "I found a bunch of these in your bedroom closet. Interesting stuff. Do they really help you write better?"

An instant of light-headedness passed. "What?" Ragwater said.

"What do you think about these *Writer's Digest* magazines?"

"I saw the door open and thought someone was in here."

"Yeah. I'm here."

"I mean, a burglar. Someone who might be dangerous."

"A burglar? Come on, Gilbert. Get over yourself. You don't have anything worth stealing."

How do you explain things to someone like that? "I don't want you hanging around in here when I'm not home," Ragwater said. "From now on, if you want to wait for me, wait outside." He flipped his phone shut.

"I'd like to think I'm entitled to come in because of our special relationship." Maxwell reached up to the floor lamp; it had a hinged arm, which was positioned so the light was over his right shoulder. He swung it ninety degrees forward and studied it.

"I'd like to think you're not as clueless as you appear to be," Ragwater said. "But it's damn near impossible to think that." He reached back and closed the door.

"Don't you think we're friends?"

Ragwater started to the kitchen. "Friends? I don't know. I'm not sure what word I would use." He opened the refrigerator. He took a beer out and squeezed a handful of stomach. "No, I don't think I would say we're friends."

"Gilbert, I'm hurt," Maxwell said.

"It's business. That's nothing to be hurt over."

"Well, okay. If that's the way you want it."

Ragwater strolled back into the living room. "It's not a matter of want. It's how I see it." He popped the can open. "And I also see a problem. A big one. You've been manipulating me," he said, and took a long drink.

Maxwell waited until Ragwater lowered the can. "Manipulating you?"

"Into doing the Mad Vandal job tonight."

"How so?" Maxwell reached up and grabbed the lampshade. It was sitting on top of a wire framework, not screwed on, so it lifted right off.

"Put that back," Ragwater said.

"Huh?"

"The lampshade. Put it back."

Maxwell looked at the lampshade. It was a faded-looking sort of tan, discolored with age and countless hours of heat from light bulbs. An embroidered pattern ran along the bottom edge. "You mean this?"

Ragwater sighed impatiently.

"There's no need to be like that, Gilbert." Maxwell, still sitting, carefully put the lampshade back in place. "Are you happy now?"

Ragwater flopped onto the sofa. A few drops of beer splashed out of the can and onto his hand. "Thoughts about the Redhead kept coming into my head while I was trying to get cozy with Lisa."

"That's not unusual. You're a healthy young man, full of virility and hormones."

"Yeah, virility and hormones, that's the ticket. Look, the way this happened, it was unusual. It was bizarre. It was so vivid, it was like she was really here."

"Well, Gilbert, you do have quite an imagination, you know. You can't blame that on me."

"This wasn't imagination. I could feel her hands on me. Literally. I felt the physical sensation of her hands on me."

"Gilbert..."

"How does that happen to a guy who hasn't completely lost all touch with reality?"

"To be fair, Gilbert, I don't know what you have or haven't lost touch with, although I'm beginning to wonder." Maxwell looked over to the side and noticed a box of tissues on the end table next to the chair. Stealing a quick glance at Ragwater, presumably to evaluate whether a reprimand might follow, Maxwell reached over and pulled out a tissue. He recoiled as the next tissue popped halfway out. Then he looked at the one in his hand. "Is it designed that way?"

"For another one to pop out like that? Yes, that's what it's supposed to do. Like, if you're about to sneeze, it's easy to grab one quickly."

Maxwell studied the box again, considering. "But neither of us was about to sneeze," he said.

"*If* we were," Ragwater said. "*If*. It's supposed to be like that, just in case."

"Oh, I see. Just in case." Maxwell dabbed the tissue against his nose, as if pretending to wipe snot.

"As I was saying," Ragwater said, an edge of testiness in his voice, "you've already shown me you can read my mind."

"You weren't saying that."

"I was leading up to it. You've shown me you can read my mind. For instance, knowing we were going to watch that movie the first night you showed up here. How did you know that?"

"Lucky guess."

"Glib answers aren't going to get us anywhere."

"Well, really, I don't think that was technically what you would call glib."

"And if you can read my mind, why can't it work in the other direction?" Ragwater sat up and leaned forward. "Maybe you can project thoughts into my head?"

"I think your overactive imagination is at work again." Maxwell began rolling the tissue between his hands, fashioning it into something that resembled a too-long, too-thin, hand-rolled cigarette.

"So first, you want me to think you can read my mind, and now you don't. Get your story straight. Which is it?"

"I'm trying to give you a reality check," Maxwell said. "Think about this: What would your friend John say? The same thing, I'm willing to bet." He regarded his rolled-up tissue and then resumed rolling it some more, apparently trying to tighten it.

"But far more bluntly, I'm sure," Ragwater said. "Here's the thing, though: he wouldn't be seeing it from my point of view."

"Which is?"

"I told you: that you've been manipulating me."

"I can see this notion has you upset, and I want to

keep you with me. So I'm going to offer you a compromise."

"Compromise? I have a serious complaint!"

"Why don't you listen to what I have to say? And then, after I'm finished, is the time to get all huffy about it if you still want to." Maxwell once again looked at his rolled-up tissue. Then he looked at the box. "Hey, that one tissue is still sticking out."

"Yeah," Ragwater said. "It'll stay like that, just in case someone needs it."

"Oh, yeah. Just in case. So, like, if I felt a sneeze coming on now, I could reach over there and grab it real quick."

"You could. Quick as your hand can move."

Maxwell nodded. "Yeah. Okay, then. Compromise. Can I tell you what I have in mind?"

"Please do."

Maxwell put his rolled-up tissue on the end table. He contemplated the box for a moment, and Ragwater *knew* he was considering whether to pull the next tissue out—and then, possibly because he didn't feel a sneeze coming on, decided not to.

Maxwell leaned forward. "First, I want it understood that this offer is in no way an admission of guilt. I'm doing it simply to help things to move along more smoothly. To help boost morale. Okay?"

"Whose morale?"

"Now, now, Gilbert. That attitude simply won't do."

"All right. So, you have an offer. What is it?"

"You're headed for a little crisis tomorrow. If you agree now to complete all seven tasks, with no backing out, I'll get you through the crisis."

"What kind of crisis?"

"Oh, no. If I tell you, you'll be able to prepare for it. You won't need my help."

"I see. You're quite the opportunist, aren't you?"

"Gilbert, a...situation...is about to come up. I could simply sit back and let you wallow around not knowing what to do. But no. I'm offering you a way out. That's worth something, I think." He sat back, reached up, and swiveled the lamp's arm so the light was once again over his shoulder.

"Maybe so, if this problem is big enough."

"You'll consider it big."

Something occurred to Ragwater. "How do you know this is going to happen? This sounds like more of what you would call my overactive imagination."

"See? There you go again, Gilbert. Thinking about things too much. Overanalyzing. Do I trim one sixty-fourth of an inch off my fingernail or two sixty-fourths? Me, I prefer to deal in concretions."

"Concretions?"

"Don't get me wrong." Maxwell paused and then reached over and pulled the next tissue out of the box. Yet again, another tissue popped up through the opening. Maxwell's eyes widened, just enough to be noticeable. "Thinking and analyzing have their place," he said. "If you want to design a new engine that gets five hundred miles to the gallon, you're going to have to do some thinking and analyzing. But you, Gilbert, you're not designing an engine. You're not even designing a box that spits out tissues." He gave the tissue box a quick, sideways glance.

Five hundred half-formed thoughts tumbled around in Ragwater's head.

"By this time tomorrow," Maxwell continued, "I'll

either have rescued you from some sort of crisis you wouldn't have been able to handle on your own, or I won't have."

It all sounded terribly...glib...to Ragwater, but he didn't have a comeback. Maxwell was right: this so-called rescue would either happen or it wouldn't.

"Twenty-four hours from now, if something hasn't happened that fits the general parameters I just described, the deal is off. You can back out completely with no further penalties or obligations. You won't even have to get that petition back." Maxwell looked at the tissue he was holding and then put the corner of it up to his tongue. "Just walk away," he said.

"You know, this kind of thing doesn't go very far toward making me feel I can trust you."

Maxwell wadded up the tissue. "No big deal," he said. "I was curious as to what it tasted like."

"No, not that. I mean, it's a little bit weird, but the thing that gives me doubts about trusting you is this whole deal with the crisis you're proposing. It just doesn't feel completely comfortable."

"See? Now you're going on about feeling stuff. Thinking, feeling. Feeling, thinking."

"What else is there?"

"Live, Gilbert. Just *live*. Walk outside your door, kick a pebble, and enjoy the 'clack' sound it makes when it hits the retaining wall at the edge of the parking lot. That, my fine friend, *that* is the meaning of life."

"That's all very Zen and stuff, but I think you're forgetting that this is supposed to be a business relationship."

"It makes sense to have some concern about the welfare of the people you do business with. I want you in tip-top condition—mentally, physically, and emotionally—did I leave anything out?—and spiritually—so you can do the best possible job for me."

"Yeah, because spiritual well-being is *so* important to painting 'The Mad Vandal' on a wall properly."

"I would almost think you're being sarcastic, Gilbert. There are certain facets to these tasks that you wouldn't understand. But," Maxwell said, "you don't need to. Those facets have nothing more to do with you than a dog peeing on a tree in China." He reached up and took the lampshade down again.

"Why can't you keep your hands off that?"

"I'm not damaging it. What's the problem?"

"Forget it," Ragwater said. "You have another task to assign me, right?"

Maxwell turned the lampshade sideways and looked through it. "Yes, as a matter of fact, I do. You agree to this new formulation of our deal, right?"

Ragwater rolled his eyes and said, in an affected, sarcastic monotone, as if reciting something he had memorized without understanding the meaning, "Yes, I agree to the new formulation of our deal."

"Good. I want pictures of five people, taken by you personally, within a week of each person's birthday."

"Birthday."

"Yes. Well, that is to say, within a week thereof."

"That could be tough."

Maxwell squinted, still looking through the lampshade. "You know, this doesn't make things look any different."

"It's not supposed to."

Maxwell put the lampshade on top of his head. It hung down far enough to cover his eyes. "I know the task sounds difficult, but I'm trying to make it as easy as I can. For my purposes, the pictures would be better if they were taken on their birthdays at the exact time of day the people were born. But I can make do if it's within a week."

"Okay."

"You can take the pictures at any distance, at any angle. If other people are in the picture, the birthday person has to obviously be the main subject. For example, he or she would be out in front of everybody else. Got it?"

"I got it."

"Any questions?"

"Yeah. Can you take that lampshade off your head?"

"Yes." Maxwell sat, unmoving.

"Uh, what I meant was that I would like you to take the lampshade off your head."

"Oh, I'm sorry." Maxwell took the lampshade off and placed it in his lap. "Is that better?"

"Yes, thank you. So about these pictures...I'm wondering how you'll know the people in the pictures are really within a week of their birthdays. But I know that if I ask, you won't give me a straight answer."

"I'm glad we got that cleared up," Maxwell said. He stood up and placed the lampshade over the box of tissues. Ragwater started to say something, but the conversation had already taken too many tangents for his liking. He could fix the lampshade after Maxwell was gone.

"By the way," Maxwell said, "are you making any progress getting the petition back?"

"I've been thinking about it. No ideas yet, but I haven't given up."

"I have faith in you. See, this is where that overactive imagination of yours can come into play." Maxwell looked at the bare bulb in the lamp.

"Yeah, well, should I *think* about it? Is that what you're saying?"

Maxwell touched the bulb and then jerked his finger back. "Ow! That's hot! Gilbert, there's no need for sarcasm."

"Is that how you *feel* about it?"

"I understand you're feeling some frustration. But, you know, in spite of all your complaining, I think we work well together. Like Laurel and Hardy. Like Jagger and Richards. Like Frank and Stan."

"Frank and Stan?"

"Yeah, the guys who built the monster out of dead body parts. It's a very well-known story. I'm surprised you're not familiar with it."

"I'm familiar enough with it to know it's Frankenstein. One name, one guy."

"I must have been thinking of the remake." Maxwell fingered the switch on the lamp.

"And I hope you're not thinking of these tasks as being similar in some way to building a monster."

"Oh, no, not at all. What I think is exactly what I said: we work well together." Maxwell pushed the switch on the lamp, and the room went dark except for the light in the kitchen reflecting weakly off the wall from around the corner.

"I'm awful glad to hear that. But right now, it's three in the morning, and I have to get up at eight."

"I know. You go on to bed. I'll keep the TV down low so you can sleep."

Ragwater sighed, exasperated. "It won't matter to

me how loud you have the TV on—"

Maxwell's face brightened. "That's great! Because I like to immerse myself in the experience—"

"Because you won't be here watching mine," Ragwater said. And then, when Maxwell didn't reply, he added, "Get out of here."

~ 14 ~

It was about noon when Maxwell came into the store, carrying a vase with an elaborate floral arrangement. He strolled over to the sales counter, putting on an act of being oblivious to anything that might be going on around him—although nothing was, indeed, going on—and placed the vase on the sales counter. "Hello, Gilbert. How are you this morning?"

"Yeah," Ragwater said.

"A bit tired, perhaps?"

"Whatever you say."

Maxwell busied himself fixing the flowers, making imperceptibly slight adjustments to the arrangement. "I didn't mention it last night, but you did an excellent job with the graffiti."

"I'm awful damn glad to hear that."

"Absolutely. If this were a traditional employer-employee relationship, I would probably give you a raise for such good work."

"Well, you could make two redheads available to me. I wouldn't mind."

Maxwell smiled. "I would like to, Gilbert, but I'm afraid it's not possible. You don't have any idea of the sheer amount of psychic energy it's costing me to process your tasks."

"Psychic energy?"

Maxwell eyeballed the flowers and removed an orchid from the front and put it in the middle. "Do you think these flowers will do?" he asked.

"Do what?"

"Will Lisa like them? I don't know her very well. I had to pick something on the basis of what caught my eye." He turned a pansy about three degrees clockwise. "That's much better, don't you think?"

"Why did you get flowers for Lisa, and why are you bringing them here?"

"Well, they're not really for Lisa. I just think they make the place a little brighter looking." He gave Ragwater a friendly smile and then moved a few feet away and began looking at a display of pinback buttons. He fingered one with a King Crimson sun-and-moon design.

On cue, the bell over the door jingled. Lisa came in, looking irate.

"Hello," she said icily.

"Hi," Ragwater said. "What's wrong?"

"What were you up to last night?"

"Up to? What do you mean?" Ragwater suddenly felt very apprehensive. Best not to volunteer any information. "I was with you."

"My car broke down after I left your house last night," Lisa said. "I tried to call, but you didn't answer. You had to be home, though. Right? You were supposed to be in bed, asleep. Recovering. I thought you had your phone turned off so it wouldn't wake you up. I walked back to your place, took about ten minutes. I knocked on the door. No answer. I went around back and tapped on your window. No answer. And then when I walked back around front, I realized something. Guess what I realized?"

"What?" Ragwater was afraid to ask, but he had to say something.

"Your car wasn't there. I had been gone for ten minutes, and you were already out somewhere else."

"Well..."

"If you wanted me to leave, you could have said so. You didn't have to lie about muscle cramps."

Maxwell turned around. "You mean he didn't tell you?"

Lisa was surprised to see Maxwell there. "Oh, I'm sorry," she said. "I didn't know you were there."

"Yes, bringing some flowers to Gilbert." Maxwell indicated the vase. "Don't they look nice?"

"Uh, I guess so," Lisa said, unsure about this new turn in the conversation.

"My wife cut her hand with a carving knife," Maxwell said. "Very nasty cut. We don't have a car, so I had to get Gilbert to drive us to the hospital. That's why I'm here this morning. To thank him." Maxwell gestured toward the flowers. "A little something to brighten up the store," he explained. Ragwater noticed he had a Talking Heads button pinned on his shirt.

Lisa looked suspiciously at Ragwater.

"Sure," Ragwater said. "If you had given me a chance, I would have told you."

"I don't know..."

"Go look at the blood stains in his car," Maxwell said. "Backseat."

Lisa looked at him and then at Ragwater. Ragwater shrugged.

"Go ahead," Maxwell said. "You'll feel better."

She hesitated and then went out. As the door swung shut, Maxwell turned to Ragwater. "My, my. She's every bit as suspicious as you are. I don't think it's entirely healthy for both members of a couple to be that way."

"Why did you tell her that?"

"The blood? It's okay. I fixed it before I came in."

"You mean you put blood in my car?"

Maxwell picked up a North Star Music bumper sticker and began slowly peeling the backing off. Ragwater wanted to stop him, but figured that if he did, Maxwell would start playing with a second one. Better to let him ruin the one and leave it at that. "Well, yeah," Maxwell said. "She can't see blood it if it's not there, can she?" Having peeled off about two inches of backing, he peered at the adhesive surface of the sticker. Then he touched his finger to it. "It's sticky," he said with an accusatory tone.

"Yeah, that's the idea. Where did you get blood?"

"I have my sources. And don't worry; it's not much. Just enough to be convincing."

"I hate to think of how much you mean by 'not much.'"

"There you go, thinking again."

"You'll understand if I'm not thrilled with the idea of putting blood stains in my car."

"It was necessary. It's not as if I did it for fun."

"But nonetheless, it *was* fun, wasn't it?"

"Well..."

"Is this the 'crisis' you were talking about?" Ragwater asked.

"Yes, it is." Maxwell put the bumper sticker down and picked up a North Star flyer. He made a few quick folds and held up a little origami piece that looked like an armadillo. "What do you think?" he asked.

"Seems to me that you're the one who caused this whole situation she's upset about. I think you owe it to me to fix it without any nonsense about compromises or deals. For all I know, you sabotaged her car last night. And I'm telling you this without doing much thinking."

"Gilbert, sometimes you amuse me. You need to deal with the situation and not worry so much about meaningless details. You wouldn't have been able to talk your way out of this on your own, right?"

"Probably not on the spur of the moment."

"And this would have been serious if I hadn't volunteered my little cover story, right?"

Ragwater had to agree. By itself, maybe it might not have been that bad. But taken with all the other weird, bad-looking stuff of the previous few days, it could have added up to a huge problem. "Yeah," Ragwater said. "I guess you're right."

"Well, there you go. You needed my help. Why do you have to be so high maintenance?"

Ragwater started to say something, but the door interrupted him. Lisa came back in. "It's there," she said.

Maxwell held up his little armadillo thing.

"Cute," Lisa said.

"It was a very compassionate act on Gilbert's part," Maxwell said. "He was feeling very sick himself."

"But I'm better now," Ragwater added.

"I guess you're in the clear, Gilbert," Lisa said. "From now on I'll try not to leap to hasty conclusions."

Maxwell handed Lisa the armadillo. "To decorate your desk at work," he said. "And now I'll leave you two to kiss and make up, or whatever it is you do in these situations."

After he was gone, Lisa looked at the flowers. "Nice," she said.

"Yeah."

"They make the place a little brighter looking. Listen, Gilbert, I hate to be suspicious so much. I'm sure everything's okay, but you have to understand how some of this stuff you've been doing could look bad."

"Yeah. I think I understand. Did you get your car fixed?"

"It turns out I ran out of gas. Something's wrong with the gas gauge."

***

Later that day, Don Vecht came in. Don was a freelance writer who specialized in company newsletters, employee handbooks, and other business-related work. He was a serious blues collector, and when a check from a client came in, he invariably made a stop at the store as soon as possible. A big payday for Don could mean $100 or more in sales for Ragwater.

Nice.

And Don, being a bit older and more level headed, might have a little wisdom he could impart to a confused friend. Ragwater didn't know how extensive Don's love life was before he got married, but he had the definite impression that Don had learned something from whatever mistakes he might have made. Further, after being married for eight years and still going strong, he probably had an idea of what at least one woman wanted from men. That was one more than Ragwater could claim.

So Ragwater found himself asking Don, "What's the stupidest thing you've ever done because of a woman?"

Knowing, of course, that he couldn't possibly return the favor by telling Don his own story.

"I don't know," Don said. "Are you having woman problems?"

"Well, a guy came in here a few days ago, a psychology student." From there, Ragwater gave Don a rundown of the petition story, including the flirting. He left Maxwell out and told Don the story just the way Lisa would tell it from her point of view. "So what do you make of that?" Ragwater asked.

"I'm not sure I understand," Don said. "What did you do that was so stupid besides screw up the story when you told her about the student?"

"Well..." Ragwater suddenly realized that in leaving out the stuff that made the story unbelievable, he also left out the best of the stuff that made him look stupid. "Flirting with those other women in front of Lisa," he said.

"Oh, I see. I thought you meant stupid like, for example, letting some psycho woman talk you into robbing a liquor store so she could pay for a boob job, or something like that."

"What? Have you done that?"

"It's just an example. It's the kind of thing I think of when you start talking about doing something stupid because of a woman."

"You have, haven't you? You can tell me."

"Well," Don said, "it was a long time ago. Back then I was high on crack all the time. I don't remember much about those days. I've been told I killed some people. I'm lucky to be walking around a free man today in relatively good health."

"So that explains that disconcerting twitch in your eye?"

"Yeah, nerve damage. That's also why I walk with a limp."

"I never noticed."

"Well, I have a limp in each leg. They balance each other out."

"So, other than the liquor store, have you ever done anything stupid for a woman?"

"I think we all have. I've done stuff like spending too much money, telling lies about things that might impress her. I don't think I've ever done anything monumentally, life-changingly stupid. I suppose I'm one of the fortunate few in that regard. Why do you ask?"

"Research for a story I want to write. It's about a woman who has a way of getting men to do stupid things. I mean, yeah, that's lots of women, I know. But this one is going to be world class. She gets men to do the monumental, life-changingly stupid stuff all the time. She doesn't even mean to. They just do it."

"Well, here's what I think. I think you don't need to do research. Make up anything you can think of. Anything you can imagine, no matter how outlandishly stupid, is going to be something that some guy, somewhere, somehow, some way, might have actually done."

"Okay, so let me ask the age-old question: What do women want?"

"Well, in my opinion, I think that asking the question means you're looking at the whole issue from the wrong point of view. I say you shouldn't concern yourself about it. Women are responsible for knowing what they want and finding it themselves. So are men. Therefore, be yourself. If you can win a woman over that way, then she thinks you have what she wants, whatever it might be, and everything's fine. If you can't, you're better off forgetting about her and looking for someone else."

Be yourself. Who could have imagined such a thing? "Is that what you did when you met Alicia?"

"Pretty much."

"But what if, for example, you see an exotic, smokin' hot babe, like in a bookstore or something, and you want to meet her but don't know what to say?"

Don smiled. "Ah, yeah. Well, I guess you'd better become someone who knows what to say."

~ 15 ~

"Contingency coin flip," Ragwater said. He tossed a nickel onto the floor next to the table, and it came up heads. "Okay, rule change. The Canton Bulldog rules are now in effect."

"No, we did the Canton Bulldog rules two changes ago. We should be on the Ragwater rules now."

Ragwater pointed to a spot on the score sheet. "Uh, no. When you rolled those four threes about ten minutes ago, that caused an automatic reversal of the rule-set rotation."

Plow looked. "Wow, that's right. So we've been on the Wake Up Little Susie rules for the last fifteen minutes."

"You didn't know that?"

"Well, I…no."

"You're aware that the rule change means everyone in my advance line gets promoted to second corporal and acquires amazing mindreading powers," Ragwater said.

"But my primary defenders get five-hundred-dollar a month pay raises," Plow said.

"That's good for them, but in the big picture, it won't help you any." Ragwater nudged an antacid tablet a couple of inches to the left, placing it between a church-key can opener and a nine-volt battery. "I think that will effectively block the fomentation attack you're probably planning."

Plow growled. "Okay, you got me this time. But I have other tricks up my sleeve." He picked up the dice and then put one down. "I'm going to roll four," he said.

He tossed the dice onto the table. "Oh, my god! Four fours! A Grand Zrink!" Plow stood up and began slowly walking around the table, studying the layout from all angles and waving his hands over the game.

"Okay, what are you doing?" Ragwater asked.

"This is a rare opportunity. I have to make sure I take full advantage of it."

"By acting as annoying as possible?"

"Well, sure. That's part of it. Get inside your head and psyche you out. I thought you knew that." Plow finished circumnavigating the table and took his seat. He cleared his throat and cracked his knuckles. "Okay, pal, put your driver's license on the table."

"Not the license, man," Ragwater said. "Wouldn't you rather knock my polar bear over?"

Plow regarded the plastic polar bear—decorated with neon orange stripes—in the middle of the table. "As tempting as it is, I don't feel it would serve my long-term interests very well. I have to demand either the license, or you take a bite of celery."

Ragwater considered the celery. It really didn't look appetizing. Well, that is to say, after sitting out on the table for several days, it looked even less appetizing than celery normally looks. He didn't want to bite into it, but the alternative—putting his license on the table—would leave him open to a Phase Two Neopinscer

Maneuver. Plow would need only to roll a six on at least one die on his next turn to move into position for it. Ragwater couldn't take the risk. "How many points for the celery?" he asked.

"Four."

"You've got to be kidding. Look at it."

Plow looked. "Yeah. What about it?"

"That sorry-looking thing? It's more wilted than your mother."

"My mother can kick your miserable ass anytime she wants."

"Yeah, she did last night, for sure."

"But I'm going to kick your ass in this game today."

"Ten points, at least, and another ten if I don't gag trying to get it down. If I take a bite, there'll be only one bite left."

"Tell you what. "I'll give you five for the license."

"I think we both know the tactical implications of the license," Ragwater said pointedly. "I need at least twenty-five points for it."

"I think we both also know that I have you over a barrel here. You have no leverage to bargain with. But since I'm nice, I'll go up to ten for the license."

Ragwater knew that with Plow taking such a hard line, he, Ragwater, couldn't hope for a better deal. "All right, the celery for five."

"I said four."

Ragwater groaned. "Mark it on the score sheet." He picked up the celery.

"And it has to be a respectable bite, too," Plow said. "No dainty, little nibble where you only get three molecules."

"There's no need to count molecules." Ragwater

said. He picked up the celery and quickly (so as not to think about it beforehand) bit in. He gave it a couple of chews and swallowed. "There," he said. "Are you happy?" The dull taste of staleness lingered in his mouth. Or was it the stale taste of dullness?

"Well, my friend, I wish life were simple enough that watching you eat limp celery could be enough to make me happy. But to answer the question you *meant* to ask, yes. I consider the deal to be fulfilled." Plow made some marks on the score sheet. "Guess what?" he said. "Score's tied, fifty-three apiece."

"Last Monday, I had such a big lead."

"I have momentum building up."

"You have *something* building up, but I'm not sure it's momentum." Ragwater got up and went into the kitchen. "Beer?"

"Yeah, sure." Plow picked up his can and finished it off.

Ragwater came back in with two beers. He gave one to Plow and stepped around the table to his own seat. "I have a favor to ask," he said, sitting down.

"If it has anything to do with pulling my first-level drumulans back to neutral territory, I'm going to have to respectfully decline."

"No, it has nothing to do with the game."

"Does it have something to do with push-ups?"

Ragwater had forgotten all about their little fitness talk. "Maybe it should, but no."

"In that case, ask away, dear friend. What are we here for if not to help each other through this strange and wonderful experience we call life?"

"Where'd all that poetic-sounding stuff come from?"

"A wonderful evening with Sylvia."

"Oh? Did you move on to the big event?"

"Not quite, but I think I'm making progress."

Ragwater held his beer can up for a toast. "To progress," he said.

"To progress." They drank. "I found out an interesting bit of news, too. Sylvia was telling me about her friend Linda's boyfriend."

"Yes?"

Plow leaned forward, a gleam in his eye. He was clearly relishing his opportunity to tell the story. "It seems he disappeared last night. They were at his apartment, and he went out to meet a drug connection. He was supposed to be gone a half hour, but he never came back."

"Sounds pretty grim."

"It does. And do you know who he is?"

"Henry."

Plow recoiled. "How did you know?"

"Stands to reason."

Plow studied his beer can and then took a deep drink. "I guess it does," he said. "I bet he was at that bar to meet his connection."

They sat for a moment, silent.

"I'm sure he'll turn up," Ragwater said. "I don't think they would have killed him."

"Yeah, let's go with that. So what's your favor?"

"This restaurant where you work has a birthday thing, right?"

"A birthday thing?"

"Yeah, like, you get something special if it's your birthday."

"Sure. A free dinner. They'll even sing 'Happy Birthday' if you want to call attention to yourself."

"And you have cards people fill out to sign up for the free dinner?"

"I'm not sure I like where this is going, but yeah."

"Okay, so, like...can you get me, say, a couple dozen cards for people who have birthdays coming up in the next couple weeks?"

"What's going on here?" Plow asked. "Graffiti in the middle of the night, stolen birthday cards?"

"It's too weird. If I told you, you wouldn't believe me."

"I already don't believe all this stuff. I think you've lost your everlovin' mind."

"Then there's no point to me telling you about it."

"There is if you want me to get cards for you."

Ragwater sighed. What had happened to trust? Well, he could hope that curiosity would trump trust. "I need to find a few people who have birthdays soon," he said. "No one will connect you to it. I'm going to send out cards that'll look like a typical promotional mailing. As far as the people who get them are concerned, it'll look like they were chosen at random."

"But you're not telling me why."

"I can explain more later, but that's all I can tell you right now."

"You need to find birthday people."

"Yeah. It's easier than finding celery people."

"What?"

"Oh, nothing. Yeah, I need to find birthday people. What do you think? Can you help?"

"Well, if the only way to find out what you're up to is to say yes, then yes."

"You're a champ."

"Yeah, I feel like one. There's only one thing. You

don't actually need the cards, right?"

"What do you mean?"

"All this stuff is saved on the computer in the office. Once a week somebody enters the new data, and then they throw the cards away."

"That doesn't sound very secure. Someone could go dumpster diving and get all the information."

"Sure, if you want to sift through a whole dumpster full of restaurant garbage for a few dozen cards that are going to be soaked full of melted ice cream, coffee, and gravy, to find out people's birthdays. Anyway, what I'm saying is, I could copy the computer file for you. It's on a spreadsheet."

"They give you access to stuff like that?"

"Well, they don't *give* it, but people are in there all the time, like when they're on break or goofing off or whatever, getting on Facebook and Twitter and YouTube. I think I could manage to copy a file without anyone suspecting anything."

"Sounds good."

"The only thing is, it might take me a few days to find a good opportunity. I need to be careful."

"That's fine. But somehow, I doubt that it'll take you that long."

"Yeah, I'm pretty slick."

~ 16 ~

The next night, Ragwater had his laptop out, working on the birthday project. He had to get the copy for his postcard written and polished up, all professional-like, ready to send as soon as Plow came across with the mailing list.

So far, Ragwater had spent more time drinking beer than pounding on the keyboard, but he figured that when the words started flowing, everything would fall into place. And the Public Image Ltd. tunes were flowing, too, which would help. Or so he expected.

Yeah, birthday. Start with the idea of birthdays...

> CDs make wonderful birthday presents, and CDs from North Star Music are the most wonderful of all.

Oh, brother. This was some corny stuff. My CDs are wonderful. They're *wonderful*. Sheer crap.

> CDs make great birthday presents, and North Star Music can hook you up with the good stuff.

Hmmmm...Still corny, and somehow not quite

right, but he was going to go with it. The main thing was the offer. Yeah, offer to give people something for free, and they'll overlook a little stupidity in the way the offer is made.

> We have a wide selection of rock, country, blues, jazz and hip-hop. See for yourself! If you bring this card to the store within a week of your birthday (along with ID to prove it) and let us take your picture for our bulletin board, we'll give you a free CD of your choice. It's our birthday present to you. We're sure that once you've seen what we have to offer, you'll come back for all your music shopping, whether you're looking for the latest popular release or an old, obscure collector's item.

Ragwater stopped and looked at the screen. He read the paragraph to himself out loud. It was a good start, but it needed a little something more.

He picked up his beer and took a long, slow drink. He re-read what he had so far. He drank again. He put the beer down and resumed typing.

> North Star—Where you can get excited about music once again!

Ragwater looked at his work, read it out loud again, and clicked Save.

"Where you can get excited about music once again!" Yeah, nice. He would have to think about using it as an advertising slogan.

***

Plow showed up a couple hours later with a flash drive. "It was no problem at all," he said, laying the drive in Ragwater's hand. "It was almost spooky, the way it worked out. A couple of kitchen people called in sick, and Terry, the manager, had to cook all night. He usually spends most of the night in the office, but he didn't have a chance to get anywhere near it tonight until after closing."

"So you saw the opportunity and jumped in."

"Yeah. It's the whole list, not just people who have birthdays soon. But I assume you can figure out how to get what you want out of it."

"Sure. You're a hero," Ragwater said.

"I thought I was a champ."

"Both."

"Naturally. So what's this all about?"

"Well, you plug it into the computer and use it to store files."

Plow sighed impatiently. "And you want to use the file stored thereupon for the purpose of...?"

"Yes."

Plow groaned. "Come on, give it up."

"Not now. It's best if I wait until the whole thing plays out. Then all will be answered."

"That's your final word?"

"I hope it isn't. I hope my final words are something like, 'Was it good for you too?' when I'm a hundred and fifty years old, talking to a smokin' hot, twenty-three-year-old bimbo."

***

Ragwater went through the spreadsheet and picked two dozen people who had birthdays one to two weeks out and who lived close by (so that it would be, theoretically, convenient for them to come in). He went for an even split, twelve male and twelve female, and chose a variety of ages. He didn't know what difference it would make, but it seemed like the best way to go.

And then he dropped twenty-four postcards in the mail.

***

A couple days later, people started coming in with the cards. The first was a college-age-looking fella who was hanging around outside the store when Ragwater came to open. As soon as Ragwater put his key in the lock, the fella asked, "Do you work here?"

One would hope so, Ragwater thought, if I'm unlocking the damn place. But he resisted the urge to make a smartass remark. "Sure thing."

Ragwater had the fella browse the CDs while he went through his opening routine. Ten minutes later, the fella was waving a copy of The White Stripes' *Icky Thump* at Ragwater, ready to have his picture taken. Ragwater grabbed his point-and-shoot from under the sales counter, reached up, and turned on the work light he had clamped to a shelf on the wall behind him.

He aimed the camera. "Yeah, looks good. Say 'cheese.'" He snapped. Oh, wait a minute. "Let's try this. Why don't you hold the CD up to show what you got?"

The fella held the CD up. Ragwater snapped again.

He reviewed the pictures, and the one with the CD on display looked like a little kid proudly showing off the new toy he had gotten for his birthday. The fella wasn't particularly childish-looking; it was the pose. Regardless, it was far too goofy-looking to post on the bulletin board—even though Ragwater thrived on goofiness.

And then he reminded himself: Who cares? Maxwell hadn't given him any requirements as to how the people should be posed.

"I think they look pretty good," the fella said. "The card says you're going to put them on the bulletin board. Is that all?"

Well, gosh. It really didn't sound like much, did it? A free CD for a picture to put on the bulletin board, nestled among the notices from bands looking for bass players and flyers advertising computer repair services. What was the point?

"It's just to get people into the store," Ragwater said. "It got you here."

The fella considered this. Then, "But it seems you should do something more with them. You have these pictures you could use for advertising, but no one will see them unless they're already in the store."

Yeah, right. "Well, maybe newspaper ads or something. I'm thinking about several ideas." He tried to give his voice a tone that would suggest the conversation had come to a conclusion. As much as he wanted to, he couldn't very well come right out and say, "Shut the hell up." He didn't want word getting around that the owner of North Star Music was an ill-tempered lout who would tell people who were interested in helping promote the store to shut the hell up. Worse, it might give the impression that he had some sort of creepy or nefarious plans for the pictures.

And then it occurred to him for the first time that he had no idea what Maxwell was going to do with them. He had no clue where Maxwell came from, what he did when he wasn't bugging Ragwater, what he did for a living, or who his friends were. It was possible that he knew an arcane, esoteric, secret ritual that would render these people into mindless zombie-like creatures who would exist only to do his evil bidding. Maybe he was working on creating his own version of celery people.

Yeah, sure, it would be cool as hell, in a way, but not if Ragwater had played some unwitting part in getting things started.

Oh, get a grip. They were pictures. Pictures—big, fat, hairy deal. Anyone could pull thousands of pictures of people off the Internet in a matter of minutes, for Pete's sake. As long as they weren't embarrassing, who would care? Or more to the point—since that was the immutable reality, why waste energy caring?

"Well, thanks for the CD," the fella said.

Ragwater looked at his card. It was addressed to Nick Rolinski. "I hope you like the store, Nick. See you again?"

"Yeah, I'll be back."

***

Toward the end of the day, Ragwater had gotten more than enough pictures. He would still have to make good on the offer if anyone else brought cards in, but he was fully prepared to do that.

What he wasn't prepared for was seeing Henry's

"friends" walk in. They stepped inside, looked around, and spotted Ragwater. "Hey," Aunt Rachel said. "How's it going?"

"Pretty well, considering everything in my life is all messed up."

"Cool," Aunt Rachel said. "Check it out, man. I got one of these in the mail." He waved one of Ragwater's birthday cards around in front of his face. "So I came for my CD."

"Yeah, sure. Go find something." Ragwater couldn't help but wonder what he would come back with. Patsy Cline? Duke Ellington? Menudo? Well, he didn't have Menudo in the store, but he wouldn't be surprised if Aunt Rachel were to ask for them.

And the choice was Metallica, *Death Magnetic*.

Just goes to show.

Ragwater checked off the disc on his inventory spreadsheet. Then he posed Aunt Rachel for the picture and snapped.

As they turned to leave, Ragwater had an idea. These guys had done so well with the prank at Olive's..."Hey, hold on a second," he said.

"What?"

"How would you guys like to pick up a little bit of extra cash?"

Sniffy looked at Aunt Rachel. Aunt Rachel shrugged and said, "Okay."

"Good," Ragwater said. "First of all, part of the deal is no questions asked. Nothing illegal is involved in this, but it's kinda like there's a secret involved. I need you to do it and forget about it. Okay?"

"Okay."

"It's easy. Now, you might think this is weird, but

it's no big deal. I need you to make a phone call—you can do it from here, right now—and tell someone you're a psychology student. You left a petition here at the store to get signatures from customers. She has the petition right now, this person you're going to call, and you want it back. Make arrangements to get it from her and bring it to me."

"Petition?" Aunt Rachel said.

"Yeah. You, the psychology student, left it here. It's a weird little petition, asking people to support letting Earth into the United Confederacy of Planets. The story is that it's an assignment for one of your classes, and you're going to contact the people who sign it and ask them to take part in a survey."

"Uh, okay."

"So the problem is that she has it. I need it, but I can't ask her for it. Never mind why; it's a long story, and I don't think you would care. Whatever you want to do about getting it is fine with me."

Aunt Rachel looked at Sniffy. Sniffy shrugged.

"That is to say," Ragwater said, "I don't care what kind of arrangements you make with her. But no breaking and entering, or anything like that."

"Hey, what do you take us for?" Sniffy asked.

"I'm sorry," Ragwater said. "It was supposed to be a little joke." Yet he would have felt uncomfortable if he had left it unsaid.

"How much?" Aunt Rachel asked.

"Ten dollars."

"That sounds about right if we just make a phone call. It's not enough if we have to go get it."

"What sounds like enough?"

"Twenty."

"Okay."

"Each," Sniffy added.

"This is getting expensive," Ragwater said. Maybe he shouldn't have made that breaking-and-entering joke. "I thought we were friends."

"We're doing business," Sniffy said. "There's no such thing as friends when you're doing business."

"I guess you're right about that," Ragwater said. "Twenty each. Payment after you deliver the goods."

"No way, man. Cash in advance."

"What do you mean, no way? You can trust me. You know where to find me."

They couldn't argue with that. "All right." Aunt Rachel whipped out his cell phone.

"Her name is Lisa Novak," Ragwater said. "You know what to tell her, right?"

"Yeah. I'm a psychology student, and she has my petition, and I want to get it back."

"Right. If she asks any questions you can't answer, say you're not supposed to tell her any more than that." As much as Ragwater hated lying, he at least wanted to do it right: keep the story as simple as possible.

Aunt Rachel nodded. Ragwater dictated Lisa's phone number to him. "Hello?" Aunt Rachel said. "Is this Lisa Novak?...My name is Rick Morris, and I'm a psychology student...Oh, yes...I'd like to get it back... Sure, whatever's convenient for you." He listened another moment and then held the phone down and spoke softly to Ragwater. "She wants to leave it with you."

Ragwater nodded agreement.

"All right," Aunt Rachel said. "Thank you." He flipped the phone shut.

"She didn't sound suspicious, did she?" Ragwater

asked.

"Did you expect her to?"

"It's a long story."

"Do we get paid now?" Sniffy asked. "I mean, since we don't have to go get it."

You mean, since all *you* had to do was stand there not doing a damn thing, Ragwater thought. But a deal was a deal, and to be honest, the whole thing was easier this way. How could he complain about that?

"You want it in CDs?" Ragwater asked.

"I need the cash," Aunt Rachel said. "I have to put gas in my car, and stuff."

"Yeah, and stuff," Sniffy said, apparently thinking he was funny.

Ragwater opened the cash register and gave each guy a twenty.

"Thanks, man," Aunt Rachel said.

"Yeah, thanks," Sniffy said. "C'mon, let's go look through my dad's closet before he gets home."

Maxwell sauntered in behind them.

"Yeah, you wouldn't believe it," Aunt Rachel told Ragwater. "His dad has these magazines…I swear, I don't know how they think of some of that stuff." He turned around and, seeing Maxwell, chuckled awkwardly, obviously embarrassed. "Oh, uh, excuse me, mister."

"Enjoy your magazines, young men," Maxwell said with a fatherly attitude, seemingly oblivious to any reason for embarrassment. He stepped around them. "Very ingenious, Gilbert. Get them to come to you."

"What?"

Maxwell picked up a Minutemen CD that had been left out on the counter. He gave it a couple of shakes and looked at it suspiciously. "Your birthday people. You figured out how to get them to walk right in here to get their picture taken."

"Oh, yeah. I guess I did. I believe in making use of whatever resources I have available."

"Admirable."

"Yeah. If you want to wait about five minutes, I can print them out in the back room."

"No need. I'll take the memory card." Maxwell ran his fingernail along the edge of the CD case.

"I paid ten dollars for that card."

"Does this thing open?" Maxwell asked. "It looks like it's supposed to open."

Ragwater grabbed the case and opened it.

"Wow," Maxwell said. "How clever." He took the case from Ragwater and gently fingered the printed surface of the CD. "Yeah, so I'll take the card."

"I told you. I paid ten dollars for that card."

"You paid those two guys forty dollars for a phone call. What's ten more? Besides, I'll bring it back." Maxwell slid the insert out of the case. "Hey, it comes out," he said.

Ragwater popped the camera open. "Forty dollars here, ten there," he said. "Fifteen thousand somewhere else. What the heck? It's only money."

"Yeah, there you go," Maxwell said. "That's the attitude you should have."

Ragwater groaned and handed Maxwell the memory card.

"Are you in pain?" Maxwell asked. "If it's chest pain, you really should get to the hospital and have it checked out. Chest pain could indicate something very dangerous."

"No, it's not chest pain. It's spiritual pain."

"I've never heard of spiritual pain." Maxwell slipped the card into his shirt pocket.

"It's a figure of speech," Ragwater said, hoping Maxwell would let it drop.

"I think you're trying to confuse me."

"What would the point be?"

Maxwell inhaled slowly and deliberately and then pursed his lips. After a moment, "I'd say it's time for your next task."

"All right. Shoot."

Maxwell smiled. "Oh, I get it. Shoot. You've been shooting pictures, and now you say, 'shoot,' asking me to tell you something. Very clever."

"Yeah, clever."

Maxwell fingered the CD again and seemed surprised when it rotated. "Get four stickers with pictures of unicorns and stick them to the walls of men's room stalls."

Ragwater waited for further instructions. Maxwell studied the CD. Ragwater said, "And?"

"And what?"

"Is that all?"

Maxwell looked doubtfully at Ragwater. "I told you to stick four unicorn stickers on men's room walls, right?" He pushed his finger down harder on the CD and rotated it some more.

"Don't do that," Ragwater said.

"Why?"

"You could scratch it."

"My finger is smooth. No chance."

"No, the side of the disc facing down. You could scratch it against the case. We don't want that."

Maxwell studied the CD. He slid a fingernail under the edge and pried it up. It popped out and fell to the floor.

"Now see what you've done," Ragwater said.

"Did it get scratched?"

"It's probably okay," Ragwater said. "Small scratches usually don't cause a problem. But you don't want to get careless with them."

Maxwell picked up the disc and looked at it. "No scratches," he said.

Ragwater leaned over and looked. "Yeah, I think it's all right."

"So do you understand the task?" Maxwell asked. "Unicorn stickers."

"I have unicorn stickers in the store."

"Well, then. See how easy it is?"

"Put them on the walls of men's room stalls? Is that all there is to it? Any other requirements?"

"The stalls have to be in public men's rooms. Not ladies' rooms, not unisex rest rooms, not private bathrooms. Public men's rooms. Each one in a different building. Put 'em where they're easy to see, about eye level if someone is sitting down."

Ragwater stepped over to the display case that held the stickers. He removed a package of four and held it up for Maxwell to see. "Are these all right?"

"Just fine."

Ragwater looked at the package. The stickers were a variety pack, with pictures of different-colored unicorns in various poses. A rainbow arched across the background of each sticker. What interest could Maxwell possibly have in them?

Why should Ragwater care about that? This task

was a slam dunk. He slipped the package into his shirt pocket. Yeah, he was ready.

***

After closing, Ragwater stopped at a twenty-four-hour fast food place for a cheeseburger, a discount store for socks (which he didn't need but eventually would; at any rate, it was a reason for going into the store), and the Stupendous Mart for milk and gas. In each of these fine establishments, he left the men's room decorated with one of the stickers.

Actually, he thought they looked kind of cool there. No, really, he did. They kind of brightened the place up. Let's face it, almost all public men's rooms are fairly drab places. Maybe it doesn't make any difference if people aren't going to stay there for more than five minutes, but still, it doesn't hurt to give it a bit of... flair.

Yeah, flair. Much nicer than someone writing, "Here I sit, broken hearted..." on the wall.

Ragwater dropped the milk off at home, and ten minutes later he found himself at the Slipknot Inn with his last sticker. He sat at the bar with a mug of draft beer—both to create the need to visit the men's room and to celebrate the completion of the task.

~ 17 ~

Ah, but Ragwater's evening wasn't over yet. When he got home, he found Maxwell sitting in his easy chair, feet propped up on the coffee table—outside the front door. He was drinking a beer and reading *Writer's Digest* under the light from Ragwater's floor lamp, which was standing behind his right shoulder. The door was ajar, presumably so Maxwell could run an extension cord outside for the lamp. (And why had Maxwell brought the lamp out, anyway? Why hadn't he positioned the chair so the light mounted on the wall next to the door would shine over his shoulder? Probably because this way, he would see the need to bring one more item outside. Probably the only reason he hadn't brought the television set out was because he couldn't figure out how to disconnect the cable. Yes, and then he could have sat there watching the snow on a set that wasn't receiving a signal, pretending he was getting something out of it. What would Arnie next door think of *that*?)

Somehow, Ragwater envisioned this little scene as a photo for an album cover, most likely some quirky one-hit-wonder band from the mid to late seventies. But no. This was his furniture, out in the parking lot.

In the freakin' *parking lot*, for Pete's sake!

Ragwater parked and approached slowly, trying to give himself time to figure out what to say. He hadn't been able to think of anything by the time he reached Maxwell, so he blurted out, "What the *hell* are you doing?"

"Waiting for you to come home."

"With my furniture outside?"

Maxwell put the magazine down. "Remember last time? I came inside to wait, and you told me from now on to wait outside. So here I am. I don't see the problem, Gilbert."

"My furniture needs to stay inside."

Maxwell considered this for a moment. Then, "Gilbert, your furniture is a collection of inanimate objects. It doesn't *need* anything."

"*I* need it to stay inside."

"Ah, okay. You should have said so."

"Yeah, well, I need for you not to poison my food, but I shouldn't have to tell you."

"I'm not sure what you mean by that. I like you, Gilbert. Why would I poison your food? Are you accusing me of something?" He sounded so impressively reasonable.

"No. The point is, there are certain things I shouldn't have to tell you. Don't poison my food. Don't tear my clothes into ribbons. Don't go into my store and smash all the CDs with a baseball bat. Don't drag my furniture outside."

"Gilbert..."

"Besides, in order to get the furniture, you had to go inside, didn't you? What's up with that?"

"You said not to *wait* inside. When I was in there,

I wasn't waiting. I was getting stuff to bring out here, and then I waited outside. You don't want me to stand around outside your door, do you? That might look suspicious."

"I meant you weren't supposed to come in at all."

"That wasn't what you said."

"I'm saying it now." Ragwater pushed the door open.

"Sorry," Maxwell said.

"It looks as if there was no harm done. But remember, from now on, my furniture stays inside. And you don't go in, for any reason, no matter how short a time, unless I'm already home and invite you in. Got it?"

"What if you need help? What if you're in there having a heart attack, and you can't answer the door?"

"For no reason at all. If I'm having a heart attack and can't answer the door, I'm screwed. If thugs break in and beat me senseless, and they run away and leave the door standing wide open, and a few minutes later you come along and see me there in desperate need of help, laid out on the living room floor with a traumatic head injury, bleeding all over the carpet, but I can't tell you to come in and help me because I'm delirious and disoriented from the injury, well, then, I'm screwed. Got it?"

"If it makes you happy, yes."

"Yes, I think it would make me very happy."

Maxwell gave Ragwater an odd look. "I find it hard to believe that your life is simple enough that leaving your furniture inside is enough to make you happy."

"Okay," Ragwater said. "Now remember, my furniture stays inside at all times. And you stay outside—you don't come in for any reason, not even for an instant, unless I invite you in."

"You don't have to keep repeating it."

"For some reason, I feel I do. Now get this stuff inside."

"All of it?" Maxwell asked.

"What do you mean, all of it? Do you think we should leave something out here? Huh? You think we need a coffee table in the parking lot? Yes, all of it."

Maxwell looked at the furniture and then at Ragwater. "Can you help me with the chair?"

"You got it out here on your own."

"Yeah, but it wasn't easy."

Ragwater wondered what would happen if he were to punch Maxwell in the head. Would he go down and then pop right back up, pretending nothing had happened? Would he morph into some hideous, evil beast and say—in a thunderous, reverberating voice that would seem to come from everywhere all at once—"You shouldn't have done that," and breathe fire on Ragwater?

Best not to risk it. He took a position next to the chair, ready to lift. "Come on," he said.

They carried the chair inside. "Where do you want it?" Maxwell asked.

"How about where it was?"

"Where was that?"

"Probably in that chair-sized empty space over there."

"Oh, yeah," Maxwell said with a hint of doubt in his voice, as if replacing something in the spot it had come from was a strange idea.

They moved the chair into place, and Maxwell started to the kitchen. "That was tough," he said. "I'm ready to relax with a beer."

"We still have a coffee table and a lamp to bring in."

"What? Why now? It's not supposed to rain tonight."

"I want them in here."

"No wonder your store's not doing better business. You're too surly."

"It's a cross I'll have to bear."

They brought the rest of the furniture inside. Maxwell insisted on washing his hands after they were finished. As he came out of the bathroom, Ragwater couldn't resist one more comment. "I can't believe you did that," he said. "I *know* your mama didn't teach you to do stuff like that."

Maxwell looked surprised. "When did you talk to my mother?"

Ragwater sighed. "I didn't. I…oh, never mind." Then he regretted it. Maybe he would gain some leverage if Maxwell thought he had been talking to his mother.

"You seem frustrated," Maxwell said. "Try to remember, I'm going to get you the Redhead."

"All that means is that you get to tell me to do a series of tasks. It doesn't give you carte blanche to do anything you want with my stuff." And then Ragwater realized that he hadn't thought much about the Redhead in the last couple days—in fact, he had thought about her very little since starting the tasks. The little scenarios about life together, of performing comedy routines and traveling all over the country on the spur of the moment—it had fallen by the wayside. He had not so much as formulated a fantasy about a lukewarm phone call between buddies: "Hey, are you busy tonight? Wanna rent *Smokey and the Bandit*?" "No, I don't feel like it." "Okay, well, catch ya later." He had gotten so wrapped up in sneaking around doing weird things and making up weak excuses that now, she seemed like little more than...well, not the goal or the reason for all this stuff, but merely a pretext to do it. (If Maxwell were to point out such a thing, Ragwater would deny it and put on a big show of indignation; nonetheless, he had to admit that it was true, true, true.)

"Carte blanche? Is that some woman? What are you talking about?"

"It's not a person. It's French. It's a..." And here, Ragwater realized he was about to explain another figure of speech to Maxwell—a curiously strange task, to be sure. "It means the freedom to do whatever the hell you want. So what I'm saying is that you don't have the freedom to do whatever the hell you want with my stuff. It's not part of the deal."

"Oh, Gilbert. You're three simple tasks away. Do you realize that? We're in the home stretch, my boy. The light at the end of the tunnel. You're coasting home!" He flopped onto the middle cushion of the sofa. "You know, I should have dragged this thing outside," he said, patting the cushions on either side.

"What do you want?" Ragwater asked.

"Yes, business. All business, all the time. Well, if that's how you want it, that's how it'll be. Your next task is to get four unicorn stickers..."

"I just did that."

"Oh, yeah, you did. And you did a great job, too, by the way. If you ever need a job reference, give 'em my number."

"I'll keep that in mind if I'm ever looking for a job putting stickers on walls." He was doubtful that

Maxwell had a phone.

"Well, then. What I want you to do now is bring me recordings of the last words of three dying people." Maxwell closed his eyes, held his arms out at full length, and touched his index fingers together.

Ragwater didn't say anything. He looked at Maxwell, who appeared to be off in his own little world. Was he really oblivious or just putting on a show of it?

Moments passed.

"Did you hear me?" Maxwell asked.

"Yeah. I was waiting for you to tell me what you *really* want me to do."

"Didn't I say it right? I want you bring me recordings of the last words of three dying people. They can be any three people, recorded at any time, in whatever place you can do it. The only rule is that you have to be the one who makes the recordings you give me."

"You've got to be kidding."

"Why would you think that?"

"I think it should be self-evident."

"I'll admit it's a bit tougher than the others," Maxwell said. "But you're a bright guy. I think you're ingenious enough to pull it off. I mean, it's really very simple if you approach it the right way."

"Oh, yeah. Ingenious. The task is preposterous."

"That attitude won't do, my boy. Think of it as a challenge. Use your creativity."

"How am I going to find dying people? It's not as if they're walking around at the shopping mall. What am I supposed to do? Advertise?"

Maxwell sat up. "Okay, Gilbert. You can either spend all your time thinking up reasons why you can't do it and spouting off clever, sarcastic comments, or you can apply yourself to the task. It's your choice." He picked up a magazine from the coffee table and tried to put it back down like a tent. He seemed disappointed when it fell flat.

Ragwater walked—slowly—into the kitchen for a beer, trying not to think about what Maxwell wanted him to do. He reached for the refrigerator door handle, paused, and then let his hand flop down.

There was no way he could do this.

Ragwater returned to the living room. "What if I tell you to go take a flying leap and forget the whole thing?"

Maxwell closed his eyes and considered the idea. "Is that what you're telling me?"

"I'm asking you: What if?"

"Well, you could do that. But then we get into that pesky little 'forfeit your life' part of the deal. Need I point out, Gilbert, that you haven't put that petition back into my hand yet?"

"It's on its way."

"It's not here yet. You're not clear of the life forfeiture clause at the moment."

"Yeah, and that's another thing. How would it happen?"

"If you had to forfeit your life?"

"Yeah. Would it be quick? Slow? Painful? What?"

"Oh, I can't tell you that, Gilbert. If you really want to know, you'll have to find out the hard way."

Well, that wasn't surprising. Ragwater returned to the kitchen, opened the refrigerator, and looked inside. "You drank my last beer!"

"Sorry about that. If it makes you feel any better, I didn't drink the whole thing."

"Yeah, that restores my faith in humanity, all right."

"It's better this way, Gilbert. You might want to keep your head clear tonight."

Ragwater came back into the living room. "I'm going to walk down to the corner. You need to move it on out."

"What?"

"I'm going to walk down to the Stupendous Mart. For beer. You see, since for some mysterious reason I don't have any in the refrigerator, that's the closest place where I can find some at the moment. You can't stay here while I'm gone."

"Why certainly. I wouldn't want to stand between a man and his beer." Maxwell got up, and they went outside. "I assume you understand the task," Maxwell said as Ragwater tested the doorknob to make sure it was locked.

"I think I understand quite a few things," Ragwater said, trying to imply more meaning than the statement actually had.

"That's good, my boy. That's good." Maxwell stuck out his hand, and Ragwater, purely by reflex, shook it.

Ragwater stood in front of his door watching Maxwell walk away and disappear around the corner. It was then that he noticed the beer can on the pavement, next to the spot where Maxwell had been sitting. That could have been—*should* have been—*his* beer.

He kicked a pebble toward the retaining wall at the edge of the parking lot. It went only about halfway.

~ 18 ~

Ragwater strolled through the alley, taking a shortcut to the Stupendous Mart, rolling the new task around in his head.

The last words of three dying people. Good grief! How on earth could he possibly do something like that? Where would he find them? At a hospital? They wouldn't allow him to walk into a room where someone is dying and turn on a tape recorder. The families would certainly object. Maybe he could slip an orderly fifty dollars? It might be workable if he could find the right person, but he wouldn't know how to find the right person or make the offer. Further, it was possible that something like that could violate some law or ethical rule or something. If that was the case, it would be even more difficult to find the right person to bribe—and the price would be considerably higher.

What else could he do? Kill them himself? No, Maxwell had said, at the beginning of all this, that he wouldn't have to do anything he would consider morally objectionable. Even if he were to decide that he was okay with killing lowlife scum such as, say, child molesters or bank executives, or whatever, he had to allow as how the whole "due process" thing was a pretty good idea. Besides, he would probably miscalculate and kill them instantly, before he had a chance to turn on the recorder. Yeah, it would surely happen that way.

As Ragwater was contemplating all this, he heard footfalls off in the distance. An instant later, someone rounded the corner and ran into the alley. A feeling of déjà vu washed over Ragwater, and he realized this was Henry.

Without thinking, Ragwater ducked behind some garbage cans. He peeked between them and saw Henry trip over something. He went airborne for an instant and came down on his head. Ragwater recoiled; it was painful just to see it.

Henry tried to get up, but he seemed dazed. As he wobbled around, not fully upright, two figures appeared. Even though Ragwater could make out little more than silhouettes in the dim light of the streetlamp at the corner, he knew who these guys were.

"Look, there he is!" one of them said.

They rushed over to Henry, who didn't seem to be aware that they were there. One of them shoved him down. The other punched him a couple times. The one who had shoved him gave him a kick in the ribs.

"Wait," the puncher said. "I think I heard something."

Ragwater, very conscious of the need to be quiet, watched as the two of them stood still, looking alert.

"I don't hear anything," the kicker said.

They listened for a few more seconds, and then the puncher said, "I don't think anybody's coming."

Henry groaned weakly. Ragwater suddenly realized he had been holding his breath, but now he was afraid to exhale.

The puncher looked down at Henry and said, "We've done enough, anyway. We don't want to hurt him."

"Yeah, I think we got our point across." The kicker gave Henry a contemptuous little nudge with his foot, and the two of them walked away with a sort of tough-guy strut, the kind of walk you see a lot in movies but rarely in real life.

As they walked away, one of them said something. Ragwater couldn't make out what it was, but the two of them burst into laughter. The noise gave Ragwater the opportunity to catch his breath.

He stayed still for a few more moments to make sure Henry's "friends" were gone, and then he came out from behind the garbage cans.

Henry, flat on the ground, turned his head toward the footsteps. "Call an ambulance," he said in a weak voice.

As Ragwater approached Henry, he could see a pool of blood spreading out on the ground next to his head. Careful to keep his feet out of the blood, Ragwater looked at Henry's head and saw a horribly nasty gash behind his ear. The beating wouldn't have caused an injury like that; Ragwater was pretty sure no kicks or punches had landed on his head. It must have happened when he tripped.

Ragwater moved around to the other side of Henry, away from the blood, and squatted. "Are you all right?" he asked. Geez, what a stupid question.

"I think I'm dying," Henry said.

Ragwater started feeling nervous. "It doesn't look that bad," he said.

"I think it is," Henry insisted. "It hurts. I feel dizzy. Get me to a hospital."

Ragwater took out his cell phone. His hands were shaking.

"Yeah, that's it," Henry said. "Call nine-one-one."

It came to Ragwater then, that this was a setup. This was a manufactured situation, like so many of the things that had happened to Ragwater since he had met Maxwell. Like the Redhead appearing in the park. Like—he suddenly realized—like Lisa uncharacteristically taking the petition.

If that was the case, then Henry would indeed be about ready to die, right there in front of him, with no one else around. He, Ragwater, could record Henry's last words.

In fact, he had to. If he didn't, Maxwell might very well take it as in indication that he was giving up on the tasks and call for him to forfeit his life.

Yeah, Ragwater wanted to do what he could for Henry (poor Henry), but sacrificing his life would be going too, too far to help a total stranger.

No one could expect that of him. Right?

Ragwater nervously poked at the buttons on his phone. Menu, Tools, Calendar.... oops, Back, Voice Notes.

"Tell them to hurry," Henry said.

"Yeah," Ragwater said. Then, following through on his little charade, Ragwater spoke into the phone. "I need an ambulance. Alley between Lancaster and Noble Street...uh...nine hundred block...yeah, looks like a beating victim. I found him here bleeding...Good. Thanks."

Ragwater paused, and then he put the phone down next to Henry's head. The lie came too easily: "They'll be here soon."

"Oh, god, I don't think I'm going to make it. Look, you saw the guys, didn't you? You saw who did it?"

"Yeah," Ragwater said. "Yeah. I know who they are. I've seen them around."

"The one guy, his name is Rick Morris. And the other, he's Philip Rutherford. You'll remember that?"

"Yeah," Ragwater said. "I'll remember."

"And you'll tell the police, right?"

Ragwater looked away.

"What's wrong?" Henry asked. "You'll tell them, won't you, Promise me you'll tell them who did this?"

Ragwater couldn't make that promise. He knew he could never tell anyone other than Maxwell that he had been there when Henry died. After all, he was letting it happen. (And what kind of irony was that? The person he least trusted was the only one he could trust with this secret.)

If he were to make the promise, Henry would never know whether he kept it, and yet...this was a line Ragwater couldn't cross. "You'll be able to tell them," he said. "I heard the one guy say they didn't want to hurt you."

"Didn't want to..." Henry said. "Didn't want to. I think they miscalculated."

"It's not as bad as you think. You'll be okay."

"How do you know? Are you a doctor?"

"No. I mean, I can tell."

"Promise to tell the police. Please?"

"You'll be able to do it."

"Why won't you promise?" Henry died. Ragwater sat beside him for a moment, and then he pushed the button to stop recording.

~ 19 ~

Ragwater stepped into his apartment and looked around. The place was eerie, unnatural. Corners looked crooked, walls slanted inward. Dim shadows loomed large against the walls in a way that Ragwater couldn't attribute to the lighting. He felt as if he were in an old German expressionist film. At any moment, an ancient, sad vampire might step slowly out from a doorway and size him up.

Ragwater had let a person die. Well, no. Let's call it what it is: he had killed a person. He had put his overactive brain through all sorts of logical contortions to rationalize it. But it gave him no comfort to think that a different decision could have resulted in coming home to find Maxwell waiting for him, ready to accuse him of giving up, ready to require him to forfeit his life. He wanted to think that anyone could understand what he had done, even if they wouldn't condone it.

Would Henry have agreed with his decision?

Ragwater took off his shoes and fell into bed, his heart dark and heavy as a sunken ship.

Promise you'll tell the police who did it. Oh, yeah, Henry himself didn't know.

The phone rang. Ragwater considered letting it go

to voice mail, but then he answered. "Is Bob there?" a raspy voice asked.

"I'm sorry," Ragwater muttered. "You have the wrong number."

Ragwater disconnected and looked at the phone.

Why won't you promise?

He dragged himself up and went to the dining table, where his laptop was. He plugged the USB cable in and connected the phone. A quick drag-and-drop put the audio file on the computer.

All right. Ragwater started Audacity, an audio editing application, and loaded the file for his little recording. Just to look at it on the screen, it could have been a recording of some guy telling a knock-knock joke.

Knock-knock.

Who's there?

Henry, and it's strange that you heard me knock because *I couldn't have knocked* ***because I'm fucking DEAD***.

Ragwater clicked the Play button, and Henry's voice came out. "Tell them to hurry."

And then Ragwater's fake 911 call, followed by Henry asking Ragwater to tell the police who beat him up.

But even if Ragwater could tell the police something, what would he tell them? Certainly, neither Aunt Rachel nor Sniffy had delivered the fatal blow. Henry had tripped and hit his head. It's extremely unlikely that that would kill someone, a one in a million chance, but it *does* happen. Land the wrong way, and it's all over. Freak accident. It wasn't anyone else's fault that Henry was clumsy.

But Henry had been running from them. It would

be impossible to determine whether he was afraid for his life, but to some extent, he was afraid. So they had some culpability. And then...after that, it had to come back around to him, Ragwater. He was the one who had let Henry die.

Yeah, there was plenty of blame to go around.

But then again, maybe Henry wasn't dead. After all, Ragwater wasn't a medical professional. He hadn't taken Henry's vital signs. Maybe he, Henry, had merely passed out. An experience like that would take a lot out of anyone.

Who was he kidding? There was no doubt in Ragwater's mind.

And Maxwell...yeah, he was part of all this—the main part, actually—but there was no way that that could ever figure into an investigation. "Officer, I'm pretty sure this Maxwell guy somehow manipulated Henry into being at whatever place his friends happened to find him. I think he uses some sort of paranormal ESP brainwaves to exert control over people. And whatever it is Henry tripped over in the alley, I wouldn't be surprised if Maxwell put it there precisely for that purpose. He's very tricky, you know, Maxwell is...His full name? I think it's Ernesto Daniel Aristotle O'Leary Tree Stump Maxwell the Third."

Yeah, that would be the way to get them to take him seriously.

And one of the cops might ask, "Do you know where we can find this Maxwell person?" What then? "No, officer, I have no clue. All I can tell you is that he owns a chain of little antique shops that are there one day and gone the next. When he deals with me, he just shows up when it's convenient for him."

Well, that was that. Maxwell wasn't going to show up if he was a murder suspect, was he? It wouldn't matter anyway; the police wouldn't believe a story like that in the first place. He might as well try to blame it all on the Dreaded Mind Reading Yeast.

The recording reached Henry's last words. "Why won't you promise?"

Ragwater highlighted everything up to that point and deleted it, and then he sat back and studied the edited wave form. It looked so innocuous, so innocent. One would never know, would never *guess*, what was actually going on there. Listening to it out of context, it could mean anything. It could be a man pleading with his wife, who's about to go to the hair salon. He loves her long, beautiful hair, and he's afraid she's going to get it cut too short. "Promise you'll at least leave it below shoulder length." "Well, I don't know. I want to do something different with it." And so on. Finally, "Why won't you promise?"

He hit Play one more time. "Why won't you promise?"

Why hadn't he promised? Henry would have felt better when he died.

Try as he might, Ragwater couldn't think of a more despicable thing to do than lie to a dying person. Well, okay, one thing: to let someone die for your own selfish, cowardly reasons.

Ragwater saved the file—with just the one sentence—and got up. As he walked into the bedroom, the phone rang. He slammed the bedroom door shut behind him and fell onto the bed. Sleep didn't come, but it didn't matter. Sleep wouldn't help.

Off in the distance, he heard sirens.

At least the manager at the Stupendous Mart thought he was a decent person.

***

Ragwater awoke to footfalls in the living room. He lay still, listening. The intruder moved around slowly and approached the bedroom. Ragwater looked around, hoping to find something to use as a weapon. The only thing he saw was the clock radio. Maybe he could get close enough to wham his assailant over the head with it. Yeah, right.

"Hello?" It was Lisa.

He sat up. "Yeah. In here." His voice sounded gravelly.

The door swung open, and Lisa stepped in. "Hi."

"Hi. What's up?"

"You...Your front door was open."

Ragwater rubbed his eyes. "Oh, no. Is everything all right? Nothing missing?"

"Not that I could tell. Your computer is still on the table. I assume if anyone had come in to steal something, that would be the obvious thing to go for."

"Yeah, probably so. I'll have to be more careful about that."

She sat on the bed next to him. "You look like seven kinds of hell."

"I'm glad to hear that. The way I feel, I would expect to look like fourteen kinds."

"What's wrong?"

"Uh...sinus infection, I think." Yeah, more lies. Well, at least this one had some credibility; Lisa herself thought he looked bad.

"That can be miserable," she said. "Did you go to the doctor?"

"No. I mean, I will. I'll call for an appointment as soon as they open."

"Do you want me to go with you?"

"You have to work, don't you?"

"I can call in if you need me to."

"Oh, no," Ragwater said. "A cup of coffee, and I can manage okay."

Lisa gave him a doubtful look.

"Okay," Ragwater said. "Maybe I'll need two cups."

"Your friend the psychology student called. I brought the petition back. It's in there, on the coffee table."

"Yeah, okay. Thanks. I'll get it to him. What time is it?"

"A quarter to eight. If I'm going to go to work, I should take off pretty soon." It was a question.

"Yeah, go on to work. I'll be okay."

"Is there anything I can do for you?"

"Ordinarily I would tell you I need help taking a shower, but I don't think I feel like I could properly appreciate it right now."

"You're not going to go to work today, are you?"

"I don't know. I might call Jason and see whether he can fill in."

"That's a good idea." She gave him a quick kiss. "In the meantime, get some rest."

"I don't think I have a choice. I don't feel like doing anything."

She got up. "I'll call later."

Ragwater nodded agreement. He got up and walked to the door with her. He opened it, and Maxwell walked in.

"Well, hello," Maxwell said. "This is great, Gilbert. I didn't even have to knock." And then, to Lisa, "Gilbert and I work well together. Just like Frazier and Ali."

"They didn't work together," Ragwater said. "They fought each other."

Maxwell's eyes went blank for a moment. "Yeah, that's what I meant," he said. "They worked together to produce a great fight."

"How's your wife?" Lisa asked.

"Much better, thanks to Gilbert," Maxwell said. "She'll be back to one hundred percent in a few more days."

"I'm glad to hear that," Lisa said. She gave Ragwater's hand a squeeze and stepped out the door. "I'd like to stay and chat, but I have to get to work."

"Yes, of course," Maxwell said. "I wouldn't want you to get in trouble with your boss."

"I'll be okay. Don't stay long; Gilbert's feeling bad. Sinus infection." Lisa pulled the door shut behind her.

"I hope I wasn't interrupting anything," Maxwell said.

"No, not at all."

"She's a very lovely lady. You're a lucky man."

"Then why have I been doing all this stuff so I could meet some redhead I know nothing about?"

"Only you can answer that, Gilbert. All I did was make you an offer."

"It's a rather blunt way of putting it, but I guess it's true."

Maxwell walked over to the table and sat down. He looked at the computer as if it were a floral centerpiece. "I thought you might want to see me."

"I assume you know what happened."

"Yes, that's a safe assumption."

"When we made the deal, you said I wouldn't have to do anything morally objectionable," Ragwater said.

"That's right. You don't. If, for some reason, you mistakenly feel you must use morally objectionable means to get them done, that's a different matter."

"It amounts to the same thing. I had to let Henry die so I could record his last words. I was afraid if I didn't, you'd think I was quitting, and you'd expect me to...forfeit my life."

"You can't hold me responsible for what you choose to be afraid of."

"I couldn't take the chance. I've seen how everything around you just sort of falls into place the way you want it. This was the first time in my life I've ever been next to someone who was dying, right at the moment of death, and it was mere minutes after you gave me the task. How can I believe that was a coincidence?"

"Well, Gilbert," Maxwell said, "you can point to any two events and make up some kind of story to explain why it's a coincidence that things happened the way they did. Or why it's not. It's a meaningless concept. The real question is, what's your point?" Any other time, the question would have sounded sincere, as if he had really missed the point. Now it sounded like a challenge, almost confrontational.

"You set everything up. You put me in a position where I thought I had to let Henry die."

"I did no such thing. I assigned a task."

"You...you would have thought I was quitting."

"You had no reason to believe that."

"Maybe, maybe not. I don't know what goes on

inside your head. What I *do* know is that I've never entirely trusted you, and you haven't done a single thing to make me feel at ease about it."

"If that's how you felt, you shouldn't have accepted the deal in the first place."

"Yeah, well, I did, and now, here we are. I let this guy die because I couldn't take the chance."

"Gilbert, you don't think I'm that unreasonable, do you? Do you honestly believe that if I were to have any question about what you're doing or why, I wouldn't ask you about it and give you the opportunity to explain?"

"I don't know what you would do, and I couldn't think clearly when it was happening. As I saw it, it was his life or mine. Tell me it's shameful the way I handled it, that I was weak, that it would have been the noble thing to do, to call an ambulance instead of recording what he said. It's all true. But don't try to tell me I should have known anything about what you would do. There was no way for me to account for that."

"I don't think an ambulance would have gotten there in time anyway."

"Doesn't matter. Right now, the thing is that you weren't honest, and I want to quit."

"You haven't finished this task yet. You know what that means."

"I contend that you invalidated our agreement when you set me up to do something I objected to. And I don't know that I won't end up doing something worse if I keep on with these tasks."

"I haven't had a chance to look into it yet, but I suspect you don't have a leg to stand on. Legally, that is. You didn't have to resort to objectionable means to get this done, and it's not my fault that you did."

Ragwater shrugged. How else could he reply?

"Even so," Maxwell continued, "you could cause a lot of trouble and keep the case tied up in court for a long time."

"Court?"

"It's not worth it to me to go through all that. So I'm willing to call off the deal without requiring you to forfeit your life."

"Damn nice of you."

"It is, Gilbert, because I would eventually win. Now, I believe you have a petition for me?"

"I think she left it on the coffee table."

Maxwell stepped into the living room and took the petition. He gave it a good looking-over, moving his finger down the page as if to count signatures. Finally, he was satisfied. "Thank you." He walked to the door and turned to Ragwater. "And Gilbert, watch your mail tomorrow."

~ 20 ~

Ragwater called Jason and asked him to work at the store. He, Ragwater, lounged in bed all day, sleeping, dozing, napping, and in general, lazing about.

Why won't you promise?

Why hadn't he?

Henry lurked in his mind all day. Ragwater tried working on the novel but couldn't concentrate. He tried reading but couldn't follow the story. He tried playing his Gibson SG, unamplified, along with Ramones CDs, but ran out of energy.

The idea was kicking around in the back of his brain that a police detective might knock on the door. It wasn't likely, though. He was pretty sure he had left no evidence of himself behind, that no one had seen him out and about. There was no connection between Henry and him. If things played out normally, Ragwater would never fall under suspicion. He was also pretty sure that even if they could place him at the scene of the crime, they couldn't prove he was there at the time it happened. He took that shortcut all the time.

Yet things might not play out normally. If Maxwell decided to get all hardcore about it, that knock could very well come. An anonymous telephone tip: "I was walking by the entrance to this alley, and I saw a guy clobber another guy with a length of lead pipe. Got a good look at him, too. He's the guy who runs that music store. I think his name's Ragweed or something...Oh, yeah, I could identify him in a lineup, no doubt about it." And the police would probably find a lead pipe with Henry's blood and Ragwater's fingerprints on it.

This wasn't a pleasant line of thought. If he knew some meditation techniques, or somesuch, he could withdraw into himself, make his mind a blank and relax. He had always meant to learn that kind of thing but had never gotten around to it.

Ragwater found Lou Reed's *Metal Machine Music* and put it in the CD player. Four LP sides of guitar feedback, recorded as nothing more than a "contractual obligation" album—certainly not listenable in any conventional sense, yet it was rich with details and nuances if you actually paid attention. Ragwater thought of it as something of an "aural Rorschach test," a way to give his brain a good shaking-up and clean the dust out of the little nooks and crannies of his mind. He could never get through more than a few minutes of the album in a single sitting, but then again, he saw no particular need to.

About five minutes in, it occurred to Ragwater for the first time that he could have gone to the police at no risk to himself. He could easily have told them the whole story as it actually happened with the revision of one detail: Henry was dead by the time Ragwater got to his side. No one would ever know—unless Ragwater, under stress from his conscience, cracked.

He could still do that. But he knew he wouldn't. How could he turn in Henry's "friends" when he himself was more directly responsible for...the outcome? Yeah, Henry had died quickly, probably more quickly than it would have taken an ambulance to arrive. And regardless of when the ambulance might have gotten there—if it could have arrived instantaneously—who's to say Henry would have lived anyway?

Who was he kidding? Even if he had truly known Henry's condition to be hopeless, which he couldn't have, he should have tried. No one—no one at all—would give him a pass just because Henry would have died in spite of his best efforts. Nor should they. If it had been Ragwater lying on the ground with a huge gash in his head, he would want anyone who came along to do everything possible to help.

And maybe Henry could have held on longer if Ragwater had made the promise. It might have given him a little extra boost to keep going until help arrived.

Ragwater had to insist that others shared the blame, but still, he himself had killed Henry as surely as if he had taken a length of lead pipe to his head in a deliberate murder attempt.

Obviously the only right thing to do was to confess, to lay it all out to the police, accept his own culpability, and (firmly and with great conviction) name Maxwell as an accomplice. But no, the police would never find Maxwell. In fact, they might not even look for him—Ragwater would never be able to tell them a story that would make them think Maxwell was anything more than the David Lynch-inspired product of a feverish, possibly drug-addled mind.

Even so, that was what he should do. *That* would be in keeping with the promise that Henry had wanted.

Ragwater wanted to think he would indeed confess

if there were some way he could be sure of taking Maxwell down with him. But there wasn't, and he wasn't about to go down by himself—there would be no justice in that.

Further, there was no justice to be served by Ragwater turning himself in. This had been an extraordinary situation; he posed no further danger to society. He wasn't going to kill anyone else. So what would be the purpose of wasting taxpayer money on a trial and prison time?

Nothing. Nothing at all.

Yeah, that was what he told himself.

***

And then Gustav called. "I need you to come get me, man."

It was the "man" at the end that got Ragwater. It made him want to jam railroad spikes into Gustav's eyes. Every time. Gustav made these calls twice, maybe three times a month. He had been out someplace the night before, and now, hung over and with no money, he needed a ride home. Every time—every single time—he started out the same way. I need you to come get me, man.

Man.

Ragwater knew that no matter what Gustav did or how he did it, he, Gilbert, would find some way to be annoyed by it. But that didn't make it any easier.

"Where are you?"

"At this chick's house I met last night," Gustav said. "On Frankfort Avenue."

Ragwater wondered if she was kicking him out

because they had run out of weed. He pictured her telling him to get more. Having no money, he would want to ask Ragwater for a "loan" they both knew would never be repaid, but he wouldn't have the nerve. "Frankfort Avenue?" Ragwater said.

"Yeah."

"Can't she give you a ride home?"

"She doesn't have a car."

"She can't give you bus fare?"

"Gilbert, you *know* I don't live on a bus line." Yes, he knew very well; they went through this little ritual every time. Ragwater always made these little rescue missions as unpleasant for his brother as he could. In his view, it was only fair. He believed Gustav should suffer some kind of consequences for his irresponsibility, and unfortunately, that was the best he could manage. What was he going to do? Spank Gustav? Ground him? Take his television privileges away? Besides, he wanted Gustav to feel as if calling him was the absolute last resort, an option to be exercised only with extreme reluctance.

***

"The chick" lived on a side street off Frankfort Avenue, on the second floor of a large apartment building that looked to have been built in the thirties or forties. It was a bit dingy, in need of paint, but otherwise seemed to be in fairly decent condition.

She answered the door quickly, apparently having been sitting nearby waiting. She was about five-six with a few extra pounds but not too many, with short black hair, and she was maybe—judging by the way she looked—about thirty-five, although somehow Ragwater got the impression that she probably looked older than she actually was. He figured she was probably divorced because her husband had been a shiftless no-count who wouldn't work and cheated on her when she went out to earn a paycheck. Maybe he had even banged her sister a time or two.

And she tended bar at Oscar's down at the corner, or some similar place, where the regulars had gotten to know her pretty well. As soon as they heard about the divorce, some of them would undoubtedly have been hitting on her. "Hey, since he's been cheating on you, you might as well..."

She brushed them off, finding that kind of opportunism off-putting. Besides, she didn't see that anything good could come of bedding down with them (even though that Clarence guy who came in on Tuesday nights was kinda cute). Keep the work and the social life separate.

So how would she have met Gustav? Ragwater could think of lots of possible ways, but knowing Gustav, most likely he would be one of those regular customers she didn't want to bed down with. That was, by far, the most realistic way to suppose he would meet a woman.

Realistic? Hell, *realistically*, Ragwater didn't know that she was a bartender.

As Ragwater began reshaping his little scenario, Gustav, who had been slouching on the sofa with a drink in his hand, sat up almost straight. "Hi, Gilbert," he said.

"Oh, yeah, I'm Gilbert, his brother," Ragwater said to the woman.

"I'm Sara." She gave him a weak smile.

Ragwater nodded. "I hope Gustav hasn't been too much trouble."

"Oh, no," Sara said. "We had a good time." Ragwater wasn't convinced she meant it, but then again, he didn't detect the kind of tension he would expect if Gustav had indeed been too much trouble.

"Well, that's my mission in life. To make sure Gustav always has a good time," Ragwater said. Gustav shot him a dirty look. Ragwater ignored it. "You about ready to go, big guy?"

On the way home, Ragwater dispensed with the usual ballbusting and asked about Sara. "What does she do?"

"Huh?"

"For a living. How does she get money?"

"You want to know what she does for a living?"

"Yeah. That's why I asked. That's how it works. If you want to know something, you ask. If you don't want to know, you don't ask. I asked."

"There's no need to be like that about it."

"Okay, no, there's not. So what does she do?"

"She's a supervisor at Wayne Printing."

"Supervisor, eh? How do you hook up with someone like that? She's several steps above your social standing."

"Gilbert, you think there's nothing more to me than lowlife scum. It's not like that."

"Where'd you meet her?"

"At Stanley's Tavern."

"If you want me to think there's more to you than lowlife scum, it doesn't help your case to be picking up women at a place like that—even if she's a supervisor somewhere."

"It's not that bad a place."

"It's a dive."

"Whatever." Gustav pouted.

"How does she have a job like that, anyway? It's the middle of the day. She should be at work right now."

"So should you."

"I'm not the topic of discussion. Did she play hooky because of you?"

"She works second shift."

"And what does she see in you?"

"I don't know, Gilbert. I don't care. I offered to buy her a drink, and she let me, and one thing led to another. We're both consenting adults. That was all that mattered. Why do you have to analyze it?"

***

The next day, Ragwater felt no better. The world was a dark, dank tunnel, with a slightly too-cold-for-comfort breeze in his face, and the earth was trembling constantly with the approach of a train, and there wasn't enough room to step aside—yet the train never gets there; it's always bearing down, about to hit at any instant...

He had to go to work. If he was stubbornly going to continue his normal life, he had to make some attempt to be normal. More of this would only render him down to an inanimate blob of goo.

~ 21 ~

It was sunny and seventy-three. Ragwater stepped outside at twenty minutes to ten and had to talk himself into being glad the day was so nice. He wanted it to be overcast and chilly. He wanted a slight drizzle, just enough to make his windshield wipers smear the dirt on the glass.

He wanted weather that would make him feel miserable.

But no, this weather is good, he told himself. This is the kind of weather I should want. He didn't believe it, so he told himself again.

Ragwater walked out to his car. Putting the key in the lock, he suddenly flashed on the idea that he had been so preoccupied with thoughts of how horrible a person he was that he could drive to work and open up the store, *having forgotten to put pants on*, and not realize it until someone came in and said something about it.

He looked down. The pants were there, as expected.

In the car, he caught a portion of Black Oak Arkansas playing "Jim Dandy to the Rescue."

***

At the store, Ragwater went through the motions. A few customers here and there, a couple of phone calls from people asking about releases. He took care of business. He wasn't enthusiastic about it, but he reminded himself that it was worth putting forth a little effort to avoid the hassle that would eventually result from neglecting everything. If he didn't want to deal with ringing up sales now, he wanted even less to deal with going through bankruptcy and living in his car later.

***

A few minutes after noon, Lisa came in with lunch. She began laying out food on the sales counter. "Your neighbor Mr. Maxwell seems like a nice man," she said. "A bit strange, though."

"He's strange, all right."

"Dealing in antiques would be fascinating. And you can make a killing, too, if you know what you're doing."

"Yeah. You can also lose everything if you don't. But I can guarantee you he knows what he's doing."

"You mean you don't think he's completely honest?"

"Well, I don't know. I've never done business with him, having no particular interest in antiques. But my advice would be to approach him with caution."

"I don't think you know him as well as you think you do."

"What?"

"Last night I was at Olive's with my sister, and he showed up. He sat with us for a while."

"Is that right?"

"Yeah. I hadn't talked to him much up until then.

Turns out he's a very interesting man."

"Oh, how so?" Ragwater asked.

"Well, not like *that.* I mean he talked a lot about politics. He had some interesting ideas."

"About politics?"

"Does that surprise you?"

Well, if they were talking about the same Maxwell, this was a man who didn't see anything wrong with dragging a bunch of his furniture outside. What kind of political ideas would a man like that have? "I guess not," Ragwater said, not wanting to talk about it further.

"Anyway, I think he's honest. We sat there and talked, I'd say for about a half hour, and four or maybe five people came up to him and asked him about pieces they were looking for, very friendly, happy to see him. These weren't people he had screwed over. They were regular customers."

But nothing involving Maxwell was the way it seemed. Ragwater, however, didn't want to argue the point. "Maybe you're right," he said.

"His cell phone kept ringing. He must have done about five thousand dollars' worth of business while he was with us. I almost felt as if we were in his office."

Cell phone? It had never rung when Maxwell was around Ragwater. He, Ragwater, would have gone so far as to bet Maxwell didn't know how to use a cell phone.

The bell over the door jingled, and the letter carrier came in. "Looks like you have a feast laid out," he said.

"Fit for a king," Ragwater said.

The carrier handed him a few envelopes. "I hope there's some good news in there," he said.

"I could use it." Ragwater shuffled through the mail. He stopped and stared for a moment at an envelope bearing the single word "MAXWELL" as the return address. He snuck a peek at Lisa to make sure she wasn't paying attention, and then he quickly slipped the envelope to the bottom of the stack and laid the whole thing on a shelf under the sales counter. "The usual junk," he said.

The bell over the door jingled again. Ragwater looked up to see the fella who had come in for the first birthday picture—Nick Somethingorother. He was swishing mightily and holding his hands up high enough to display a world-class limp-wristedness. Ragwater didn't remember him this way. Nick stopped and gave Lisa a very thorough once-over—critically evaluating a rival. "Well, Gilbert," he said in a campy voice, "I can see *now* why you didn't want me to come in here."

"What?"

Nick pranced his way over and inserted himself in front of Lisa. He leaned over, elbows on sales counter, and batted his eyes. Ragwater stepped back, as if Nick had bad breath. And then it hit him: this was a prank. Russ at Olive's had sent him over to do this.

"Look, dear," Nick said. "I came out. *Out*, okay? I asked my wife for a divorce a month ago."

"Yeah, whatever." Ragwater wasn't in the mood for a prank at the moment. His mind was on the Maxwell envelope. Besides, prank or not, shoving himself in front of Lisa was rude.

"Whatever? *Whatever*? Don't give me whatever!"

"Okay," Ragwater said. "You can stop now. Prank's over."

"Prank? You broke up my marriage. You call that a

prank?"

"What's going on?" Lisa demanded.

"It's a prank. Russ sent him over here."

"Russ? I don't know any Russ. Is he some other married man you've been leading on?"

"That's *enough,*" Ragwater said, snapping at Nick like a stern teacher dealing with a sassy child.

"Enough? Oh, honey, I'm just getting *started.* You talked me into breaking up my home! And all *you* had to do was break up with this..." Nick turned his head toward Lisa and sneered, "this *person* you've only been dating for a few weeks. You told me she was nothing but a skanky little tramp." Lisa's eyes widened. Nick went on. "You said you could toss her aside like an old shoe. But here she is, still. What's the problem, lover?" He wiggled his butt.

No, this wasn't a Russ prank. If it had been, Nick would have stopped when Ragwater told him to. These pranks weren't supposed to be anything more than stupid little jokes.

"I think you'd better leave," Ragwater said coldly.

"Leave? You didn't want me to leave when I came over to your place Monday night, did you, big boy?"

"Gilbert..." Lisa started.

But Nick rolled on. "You called me up, nearly midnight. 'Oh, Nick, can I come over and see you? My girlfriend was here, but I was thinking of you the whoooole time.'"

"Gilbert!" Lisa, clearly, realized this was more than a stupid little joke.

"You said, 'I told her I had a muscle cramp and she should go home.' Yeah, Gilbert, you had a muscle cramp all right. And I took care of it *real good.* It was a shame your friend had to interrupt with that phone call when he needed you to take his wife to the emergency room, wasn't it?"

Ragwater's thoughts raced. Lisa could have believed it was a joke if the guy—Nick—had stopped when he was supposed to, but pushing it this far, in this much detail...He couldn't even say, honestly, that he had never seen the guy before. "Who are you?" he asked, trying to put some forceful outrage into it but knowing he sounded uncertain.

"Who am I? *Who am I*? Remember that night I tied you down to your bed and tickled you with feathers for three hours? You sure knew who I was *then*."

Ragwater turned to Lisa. "I didn't..."

"My friend Eric warned me," Nick said. "He told me, a guy like you who puts on a big façade about being straight, all you want to do is get my panties off, and after that I'll never see you again."

"Panties..." Lisa said, her voice empty.

"I don't know this guy," Ragwater pleaded.

"And I said to Eric, 'Eric, this one's *different*! He'll treat me right!' Boy, what a sucker I was—pun intended."

In the back of his mind, Ragwater was thinking that somehow, he should run this guy out of the store, grab him and throw him out on the sidewalk, the way they throw a drunk out of a bar in the movies. Maybe kick his ass or something. But he couldn't quite bring the idea to the front of his mind. The whole situation was too bizarre and too unexpected for him to figure out what to do. A violent reaction probably wouldn't help his case with Lisa, either.

Was Maxwell behind this?

"Oh, come *on*," Nick said. He turned to Lisa. "He knows me as well as he knows you, if you catch my drift. Probably better." He leaned closer to her and lowered his voice. "I didn't realize I was gay until I met Gilbert. He showed me the way. He helped me reach self-actualization."

Self-actualization?

Lisa took a deep breath. Then, "Look, Gilbert. Go ahead and be gay if that's how you are. Who cares? But lying to me, breaking up his marriage..."

"I'm not gay! I don't know what he's talking about!"

"Oh, hon, I'm not the only one," Nick told Lisa. "I found out our little Gilbert here has quite a reputation for being a home wrecker. He won't go for single men *at all*. And what he did at that *party*. Don't get me *started!*"

"You are one seriously depraved individual," Lisa said. She turned and went out the door.

Silence filled the store. Several very heavy moments passed.

"Okay," Ragwater said, "what the hell was that all about?"

Nick gaped at Ragwater. "You mean..."

"What's going on?"

"He said it was a joke. He said you would think it was hilarious."

"Who?"

"This guy at Olive's Coffee Shop," Nick said. "I was in there with a friend, and this guy came up to our table and asked me to help him play a joke on you. He paid me fifty dollars and told me what to say, all the stuff about the muscle cramp and everything. He said I should ham it up. Have fun with it. And no matter what, I wasn't supposed to stop until your girlfriend left. He said it was an in-joke between you guys. He said she would act mad, but really, she would think it was hilarious. It sounded strange, but he seemed to know what he was talking about."

"A little shorter than me, middle-aged, thinning red hair, hyperactive?"

"That's him."

Ragwater sighed. "Me and that guy have kind of a history. I don't think this is going to be fixable, and I don't think he wanted it to be."

Nick's face fell. "Oh, no. I'm sorry, man."

"You had no idea. I'm sure our strange little red-headed friend was quite convincing."

"How about if I talk to her?" Nick said. "I'll tell her the truth."

Ragwater thought for a moment:

What would be involved in telling the truth? Well, for starters, Maxwell had gone to some effort to impress upon Lisa that he was a respectable, level-headed businessman. Ragwater would be asking her to believe that he would stoop to an astoundingly juvenile—and damaging—practical joke for no apparent reason. He was pretty sure she wouldn't go for it. After all the funny business that had been going on, it would be easier for her to believe that the Nick thing had been exactly what it appeared to be. Further, Maxwell had gone so far as to construct Nick's story so that it accounted for the emergency room trip with no conflicts in the timeline, thereby preserving his credibility in Lisa's eyes. It was all fiendishly elegant.

Whom else could he blame it on? Plow? He would probably be willing to admit to it in order to get

Ragwater off the hook, but it wouldn't be plausible. Lisa would surely suspect it was nothing more than a guy trying to help his buddy out. Besides, although Plow played along with some of the assaults on Olive's, for him it was just something to do. He wasn't about to put any energy into cooking up something on his own. His strong suit was being a smartass. Lisa knew that.

So it came back to Russ. He wasn't a particularly good suspect, but he was the "least bad" one. "Can you call her and tell her that Russ put you up to it?" Ragwater asked.

"Russ?"

"Yeah. He owns Olive's Coffee Shop. We have a sort of, uh...what I guess you'd call a rivalry. Practical jokes. Stupid little gags. I think she'll find it easier to believe a story about Russ than a strange man paying you fifty dollars."

"Well, okay. Do you want me to call now?"

Indeed. Should Ragwater give her some time to cool down? If he were making the call himself, that would be the way to go. But with Nick doing the explaining, it somehow seemed better to make the call quickly. "Yeah, let's call now," Ragwater said. He flipped his phone open, found Lisa's number, and handed the phone to Nick.

"Her name's Lisa," Ragwater said. "Tell her you got carried away and went too far, and you're sorry."

Nick nodded. He placed the call, and then, a moment later, "Hello, is this Lisa?...My name is Nick. I was the guy in the store a few minutes ago...Right. I want to apologize. Russ at Olive's sent me here to do it. I got carried away and went too far." Ragwater thought he sounded very sincere and contrite. Good. "I'm not gay, and neither is..." He looked at Ragwater questioningly.

"Gilbert."

"Neither is Gilbert...What?" Nick said. "Who, Russ?...Uh, I'd say he's about medium height...I guess he's in his fifties..." Who, Ragwater wondered, was he talking about? Not Russ. He was short and Ragwater's age. "Uh, sure," Nick said. He held the phone out to Ragwater. "She wants to talk to you."

Ragwater took the phone. "Hello?"

"Why can't your friend describe someone he allegedly talked to no more than a half hour ago?" Lisa asked.

Ragwater didn't know how to begin to figure out how to answer. She had nailed him, dead to rights. "I'm sorry," he said.

"The guy on the phone wasn't even the same guy who was in the store, was he?"

"Lisa, please."

"Gilbert, if this is how it's going to be, I think it's best if we go our separate ways."

"You mean..."

"Yes, Gilbert. If you haven't already gotten the idea, then I'll come right out with it: yes, I'm breaking up with you. I'm dumping you. I'm not going to deal with this kind of crap on an ongoing basis. I don't know what kind of issues you have, but whatever's going on inside your head, I hope for your sake you can somehow resolve it."

"I'm sorry it had to come to this," Ragwater said weakly.

"So am I, but here we are." She paused briefly. "Look, I don't think there's anything else to say, so I'm going."

The line went dead, and Ragwater said, "Okay."

After a moment, Nick said, "She broke up with you?"

Ragwater nodded.

"I'm sorry. I keep messing things up for you. She wanted me to describe this Russ guy. I'd never seen him before. I had to say *something*."

"It's not your fault. I really didn't expect it to work anyway, but it was the best idea I could think of. Besides, it wasn't just this. There was a bunch of other stuff going on."

"If it'll make you feel any better, I'll spend the fifty here."

Ragwater shrugged. "Sure." He wasn't about to turn down the opportunity to sell some CDs.

***

Later, left to himself, Ragwater replayed the scene in his mind. He was sure that in fifty years, he would still be able to replay it perfectly, probably better than the alley scene with Henry. "Well, Gilbert. I can see *now* why you didn't want me to come in here."

And then he remembered the letter from Maxwell. He found the envelope and opened it:

Dearest Gilbert,
Since you've seen fit not to live up to your end of the deal, I felt it necessary to undo the little job I did to rescue you from that crisis with Lisa. Think of it as a little adjustment to fix up everything the way it's supposed to be.
Love, Maxwell.

All right, then...Ragwater found a way out of his deal with Maxwell. So Maxwell decided it would only be fair to break Lisa and him up.

At least he signed the note with love.

On the upside, if everything had been fixed up "the way it's supposed to be" (in Maxwell's opinion), that would imply that Maxwell was finished with him. Maybe he, Ragwater, could move on without the fear that at any moment, probably years later when he least expected it, a whole bunch of weird stuff would start happening because...well, because Maxwell got bored, or something.

No danger of that, then?

Well, he could hope so.

***

After work, Ragwater stopped at the supermarket. He needed to make sure he would have something for breakfast in the morning. Beyond that? Well, he had qualms about a major shopping trip. If he bought enough to last, say, a couple weeks, well...it was possible that he wouldn't leave the apartment for a couple weeks. He reminded himself that that would be bad.

But then again, a major shopping trip would give him something to do.

(Henry didn't need to have anything to do.)

Ragwater made the rounds of the canned goods shelves—canned vegetables, canned fruit, canned soup, canned spaghetti, canned enchiladas, canned beef stew...In principle, he preferred to buy fresh food as much as possible, but in reality, that required more of a commitment to going grocery shopping on a regular basis than he was willing to make.

As Ragwater dropped a can of chili into his cart, he noticed an oh-so-lovely redhead walk across the end of the aisle. She was slender and wore a long, white dress. Her hair was long and wavy, with a gorgeous sheen.

Walk? No, it was more like a graceful, elegant glide, radiating a Zenlike self-assurance.

And then she was gone. Ragwater stood still for a long moment, thinking about the image.

Leaving his shopping cart, he walked to the end of the aisle and looked to his right, the direction she had been walking. No redhead. He looked to the left. Of course, no redhead.

Ragwater started to his right, stifling the urge to rush through the store in a frantic search. He walked slowly, as if he might be casually strolling through the store—maybe a husband looking for his wife after they had somehow gotten separated. No big deal.

He walked past the aisles and took a good look down each one. Frozen foods, household goods, and so on. Finally, he spotted her in the produce section. She was picking out pears, dropping the ones she liked into a plastic bag.

His heart was beating at, maybe, twice its normal rate. Paying more attention to the redhead than to where he was going, he walked over to a bin of fruit about ten feet away from her. He tore a bag off the roll and started pretending to evaluate apples.

Ragwater hazarded a look at the redhead. Her face was turned three-quarters away from him. Intent on her shopping, she seemed not to notice him. Besides the hair, all he could see was the curve of her cheek.

Was this *the Redhead*? The one Maxwell had offered him? The one he had performed those stupid tasks for? The one he had become obsessed with badly enough to screw everything up with Lisa? He couldn't tell. He couldn't get a good enough look at this redhead.

Not wanting to get caught staring, Ragwater looked down and studied the apple in his hand. It had a large bruise. So what? He dropped it in the bag.

He stole a quick glance at the woman and told himself he should give up. He should walk away and forget about it. But his heart was still racing, and he knew that meant he wasn't going to be able to.

She tore off a strip of tape from the dispenser, sealed the bag, and placed it in her shopping cart. Then she moved a few feet farther down to check out the lettuce.

Ragwater sealed his bag, stepped away from the apple bin, and looked around, as if deciding whether he wanted other items. He made his way around the redhead to the celery in the corner. Yeah, celery. It's good for you. Well, at least he thought so. He wasn't sure what vitamins and nutrients it had, but it had to be healthy. Ragwater had heard that you burn more calories eating celery than the celery itself contains. And not having done any push-ups, he still had the beginnings of a pudgy little gut. Even so, he routinely bought the stuff and never used it in recipes. It always ended up as game pieces in Fear and Loathing in Hell.

Ragwater put his apple down and tore off another plastic bag. He scanned the celery. There they were, bright green stalks neatly laid out, chock full of negative calories. He let his gaze drift over to the redhead, who was bagging up a head of lettuce. She placed it in her cart and then glanced over at Ragwater. Their eyes met. Ragwater panicked and looked down. He wasn't there to ogle women; he was there to buy some celery. He picked up a stalk, studied it (having no idea how to judge celery), and put it in the bag.

The redhead pushed her cart over to the zucchini. Still standing at the celery, Ragwater took another look at her. Damn, she looked *sooooo* much like that... temptress, if you want to be melodramatic about it... yet he couldn't be sure. He had gotten the one straight-on look at her face, but he had looked away immediately, before noticing any details.

What if she was? What would he do? What *could* he do?

And then, suddenly, she was coming toward him. She stopped about six feet away, careful to keep her shopping cart between them. She leaned forward. "Okay, you filthy creep," she said in a low voice—almost a sort of hiss, "if you don't turn your sorry ass around and disappear *right this instant*, I'll get store security on you so fast you won't know what happened."

"I'm sorry," Ragwater said. "I thought you looked like someone I knew." For the first time, he was aware that the sound of a thunderstorm was playing, very low, over the PA system.

She glared at him. "The count of three. One..."

Ragwater moved away, feeling an odd blend of frustration and well-deserved humiliation. He found his shopping cart and put his produce, such as it was, in.

It occurred to him that he might never be free of Maxwell. For the rest of his life, possibly, anytime something annoying or embarrassing happened, anytime he encountered someone weird, Ragwater would have to wonder if Maxwell had something to do with it.

And in the stress of the confrontation, if it may be called such, he had not gotten a good impression of what this woman looked like. He still wasn't sure whether she was *the Redhead.*

***

Ragwater sat at his kitchen table and carved the bruise out of the apple. He sat there a moment, regarding the hole, and then bit in.

Later, he did eleven push-ups. Hey, at least he was making some progress in one area.

~ 22 ~

King returned to his hotel room to find the light on. He had left it off.

Having been gone all day on a wild goose chase, King was sure now that that phone call about the defector had been nothing more than a ruse, a ploy to get him out of his room. They had probably been watching and gone in as soon as he left.

Which meant that now, hours later, no one would still be there.

Even so, he couldn't take chances. He drew his gun and took a slow, deep breath. He stepped inside. The quiet in the room was profound. It always is when you're tense.

It didn't look as though anything was out of place. King walked over to the corner and felt under the slit in the carpet. Yes, the flash drive was still there.

But he was going to have to get out of that room, and quick. King figured there were three possibilities as to who could have broken in:

First, it could have been that group posing as Egyptian tourists. King had no idea who they worked for, or where their loyalties lay (if anywhere besides themselves)—and in fact, they might really be Egyptian tourists, although King was highly doubtful—but they had seemed a little too interested in his transaction at the front desk. If they had been in his room, he had no idea what the repercussions might be.

Second, if it was McMillan, there would be an element of uncertainty. McMillan knew what the drive looked like. So it was possible that he had found King's drive and replaced it with an identical but blank one. Or worse, one with false data on it. Not having a computer in the room, King was unable to verify the drive.

Finally, if it was Stepanov, King had a somewhat less than fifty percent chance of getting home alive. Not finding what they wanted, Stepanov's men would be watching for him to make a run for it. They were bulldogs. They wouldn't let up. They would follow him out of the hotel and waylay him at the first opportunity. And if they didn't find an opportunity, they would make one.

Both McMillan and Stepanov were experienced professionals. They wouldn't have left the door open—unless they were trying to provoke a reaction.

Which would mean, then, that King wouldn't want the flash drive on him. But then, where could he hide it? And how? If this was the work of Stepanov's men, they would be watching.

But then, if it was someone else, King would want to keep the drive with him.

What to do?

Ragwater saved, sat back, and gazed at the computer screen with unfocused eyes. King was going to have to find some kind of clue in his room that would indicate what he should do. Yeah, something small and seemingly ordinary, something that would be of no significance to the casual observer.

Ragwater didn't feel like thinking about it any more. He had done enough for the time being, anyway; those few paragraphs represented his most productive day in months. Yes, when it came to uncertainty, Ragwater was prolific.

Someone knocked on the door.

"Who is it?"

From outside, Plow's voice called, "It's me!"

"Come on in."

Plow bounded in, six-pack in hand. "I brought beer," he said.

"That ensures you'll be welcome."

Plow put the six-pack on the table. He opened two and gave Ragwater one. Then he took a long drink of his. "So, what's up?"

"Let me tell you what happened today."

"Yes, yes, tell me what happened today."

Ragwater gave Plow a quick rundown of the Nick incident—leaving out, of course, any suspicions that Maxwell might have been involved. He still didn't want to talk about any of that, and he figured it was very likely that he never would.

He couldn't.

Plow listened to the story, complete with details about Nick's campy behavior, his accusations, and Lisa's reactions. "It was completely out of left field," Ragwater said. "I didn't know what to do."

"Bizarre," Plow said.

Ragwater found the USB cable for the printer he had on an end table in the corner. He ran the cable over to the computer and plugged it in. "How does stuff like that happen?" he said. He worked the computer mouse and clicked. "Why do people want to do stuff like that?"

"It's a mystery," Plow said.

An error message popped up on the computer screen. "I would appear to be out of ink," Ragwater said.

"Why do you need to print, anyway? Isn't the whole idea of computers supposed to be that you don't use paper?"

Ragwater walked to the hall closet and opened it. "Proofreading, my fine, illiterate friend. Proofreading. You will very often find mistakes on paper that you would have overlooked on the computer screen." Ragwater reached up to the overhead shelf and grabbed an ink cartridge.

"What are you talking about? Paper, screen, what's the difference? Words are words."

"Yeah, I thought so too, until I tried it."

Back at the printer, Ragwater opened the top and popped out the old cartridge.

Idly, Plow picked up a few pages from an already-printed stack. "Hey, I like this part," he said.

"What part?"

"Where you have Ohlmann King chasing the tall, skinny guy through the streets of Morocco, and then the tall, skinny guy sees that Eva woman and starts chasing her, and then the guy with the big, dark glasses comes running by because he's already being chased by the woman from the souvenir shop, and they split off and start chasing the tall, skinny guy and the boy who's standing in the doorway selling watches."

"Huh?"

"You don't expect me to repeat all that, do you?"

"Well, I don't know. I mean, I don't think it sounded right. Eva was supposed to be looking for the boy who was selling watches because Hirakuru told her he had killed her partner."

"But I thought the watch boy was with Eva when her partner was killed."

"No. Wait, let me see that." Ragwater grabbed the page, and then he noticed something. "Oh, crap. I have ink all over my hands. That cartridge must have been leaking." He looked at the table where he had laid the old ink cartridge and saw a small, dark puddle around it. "And now I have a mess on my table." He laid the page face-down on the table; two neat sets of black fingerprints decorated the plain whiteness in what struck Ragwater as a somehow elegant Zenlike pattern.

"If you want a printer that's not a cheap piece of junk, you have to spend some money, my friend," Plow said.

"Maybe, but even a cheap piece of junk shouldn't make a major mess." Ragwater went into the bathroom, reached for the faucet, and realized he had a problem. "Come in here and turn on the water for me so I don't get ink on the knobs."

A moment later Plow appeared next to him, and, snickering, said, "Ink on the knobs. That sounds *so* wrong."

"Yeah, wrong. Whatever. Make with the water."

"Hot or cold?"

"Some of both. Mostly hot."

Plow got the water running according to instructions, and Ragwater began washing his hands.

"So," Plow said, "why was Eva chasing the tall, skinny guy?"

"She wasn't. He was chasing her. And I think I might make him a short, hyperactive little guy instead."

"Well, that's an interesting choice. But still, *she* was chasing *him*. If you're going to write novels, you need to know your material better."

"Go look at it again."

Plow disappeared toward the kitchen. Ragwater spent another five minutes at his task, scrubbing more thoroughly than he had in, probably, the last five years. In the kitchen, Plow was reading.

"Am I right?" Ragwater asked.

"She's chasing him, but you got it wrong. He should be chasing her."

"Oh? Why?"

"Because they end up in the kitchen of that café. He wouldn't go there if he's being chased. But she would."

"I'll think about changing it."

"I knew you'd see it my way."

"No, actually, I'm lying. He would go there because, unknown as yet to the reader, he has a friend who works in that kitchen. And the friend slips him a small knife he's going to use to threaten Ohlmann King in the next chapter."

"Hmmm..."

"Yeah, hmmm. I'm trying to stay one step ahead of the reader. Keep 'em guessing."

"But you haven't written that part yet."

"Yes, I have. Thirteen times. And I'll give it a fourteenth try sometime soon. I can't get it the way I want it."

"Just get the words down, man. It doesn't have to be perfect."

"Well, if there's anyone who's an expert on not being

perfect, it's you," Ragwater said.

Plow shook his head slowly. "Someone would almost think you don't want to finish this thing."

"You don't write a good book by rushing through it carelessly."

"You also don't write a good book by never finishing it."

"I want to make sure I do it right," Ragwater said. "I'm not going to put my name on some kind of half-assed job."

Plow rolled his eyes and shook his head slowly. He put down the page he was reading and picked up the page with the fingerprints. "Can I have this?" he asked.

"Why do you want that?"

"I like the way it looks. Sort of like postmodern nihilism or something."

"I'm willing to bet that you don't know what either postmodern or nihilism means."

"No, but I'm willing to bet that in general, most of the people who use those words have no clue."

"Probably not."

"Call it primitive. I know all about *that*, right?"

"No doubt about it."

"Primitive art to put on my refrigerator. Right next to my autographed picture of Dog the Bounty Hunter."

"Put it *above* Dog, and you have a deal."

"All right. And when you become a bestselling author, it'll be worth some money."

~ 23 ~

The Slipknot Inn, Saturday night. Ragwater sat at the bar nursing a beer.

A detective movie was playing on the TV behind the bar. Someone had murdered a man at a gas station, and there was some question as to whether the victim had been involved in criminal activity. A couple of small clues seemed to indicate that he had been living a double life as a respected chief operating officer at a large-ish corporation and as a supplier to drug dealers in surrounding cities. If this was true, his death would cause a major disruption in the flow of illegal drugs through the area—that is, until someone else stepped in to fill the vacancy, which would, sadly, certainly happen fairly quickly.

Ragwater watched as the detective did a tough-guy routine on the victim's son. He was insinuating that he thought the son was a partner in the father's drug business and issuing veiled threats that the son could do some heavy prison time and lose everything he had if he didn't cooperate. The son, as far as Ragwater could tell, knew absolutely nothing about drugs in general or about his father's possible involvement in them in particular. He appeared genuinely mystified by the whole affair.

But Ragwater couldn't help but think about the reality of the movie itself, a "meta-reality" of sorts. Yes, the actor was really nailing it if the character was supposed to be naïve and mystified by all this stuff. But how could Ragwater know whether that was actually the intention? What if the son was supposed to be, say, a worldly kind of guy and wary of this detective? Maybe he was guilty, guilty, guilty. Maybe he was indeed partners with the father, and further, had killed the father himself for some reason—and the actor was simply inept at playing the character.

What if?

Ragwater supposed all this would become clear at the end. If the detective solved the crime, the son would either be led away in handcuffs or he wouldn't.

Maybe the son had once killed a guy under circumstances completely unrelated to this investigation.

Speaking of guilt, Ragwater wondered how Henry's friends would react to his death. Would it bother them? Would they feel it was their fault? Maybe they would turn themselves in and confess. In tears, barely coherent, they would insist they hadn't meant to kill Henry. They had just wanted to make a point. "We went too far! We went too far, and a man is dead, and we can't live with ourselves unless we confess and take whatever punishment society sees fit to give us."

Then he, Ragwater, would be in the clear. Yes, a confession by two guys who couldn't finger him because they never knew he was there!

That was what would happen. Yeah, right.

A hand clapped down on his shoulder. Ragwater turned around to see John Plow flanked by Linda and

Sylvia. Yeah, both of them, and neither was scratching his eyes out. "What's up?" Plow said.

"I should ask you that."

Plow put an arm around each woman. "I know you've met Sylvia. This is Linda. Linda, meet Gilbert."

Ragwater stood. "We've met," he said.

"I was in the store a few days ago," Linda said.

"How 'bout that?" Plow said. "I'll tell you what. Why don't you two get that booth over there. I want to have a word with Gilbert, and I'll be with you in a couple minutes."

"Sure," Sylvia said. "Don't be long." Plow and Ragwater watched the two women walk across the room.

"You know," Plow said, "I'm fully prepared to admit that I'm a pig, but I never get tired of watching shapely women walk away from me."

"I'm sure you've seen a lot more of it than most of us," Ragwater said.

"Ha, ha, ha." Plow took the stool next to Ragwater. "So you want to know what's going on."

"Well, if you want to tell me how you got those two together without getting yourself brutally dismembered, I'm curious to hear about it."

Plow's face took on a self-conscious, half-grin-half-frown kind of expression that looked painful to Ragwater. "Well," Plow said, "see, this is where it gets kind of awkward."

Ragwater had an awful feeling that he already knew the story, but he didn't want to think about it. He certainly didn't want to hear about it.

"I took over a job you left unfinished," Plow said.

Ragwater nodded. "Yeah, that's what I thought."

Plow squirmed around like a first-grader who's too

timid to ask the teacher for permission to go to the bathroom. "He...uh, that guy...Maxwell...offered me the deal to finish your tasks. I mean, I felt bad about it, but..." He paused and made furtive gestures toward the women. "I mean, c'mon, man. What would *you* do?"

"Don't worry about it."

"He didn't say you had been involved. He said someone quit, and he was looking for someone else to take over. But the deal...It was exactly like that alleged short story you were talking about in the park that day. I'm no mathematician, but I can put two and two together."

"But when we were talking about the alleged short story, you didn't like the fact that our hero didn't know anything about this strange guy."

"True. But you had made it through some of the tasks without any big disasters. Besides, he's persuasive."

"It didn't occur to you to wonder why I had quit?"

"I figured your conscience got the better of you, sneaking around behind Lisa's back and all that."

"Yeah," Ragwater said. "It looks like you made out pretty well. Did he make you do the last words thing?"

"That's what I started with."

"How did you do it?"

"I found a web site that collects black box recordings from airplane crashes. A big list of them in mp3 format."

"You can find that on the net?"

"Don't act surprised. It would be surprising if you couldn't. So anyway, I picked one that had a three-man flight crew, and that was that. Three guys, all at once."

"He told me I had to make the recordings myself."

"See, there's the loophole. He said, 'You have to make the recordings *that you give me.*' So I made a copy."

"You figured that one out nicely."

"Yeah, well, I bet you would have if you had given it some more thought."

"How much thought did you give it?"

"Well, I came up with the idea pretty much immediately."

"Stands to reason. What else did you have to do?"

"Superglue the receivers of two payphones to the hooks."

"Which was challenging because there aren't very many pay phones around anymore."

Plow smiled weakly. "I managed to find a couple."

"I bet he put the pressure on really hard for you to do that one immediately when he told you about it."

"You got that right. He handed me the glue."

"And then, the last task was..."

"I'm not sure you want to know," Plow said.

But Ragwater already knew. "Get a set of someone's fingerprints."

Plow nodded.

"And for that," Ragwater said, "you get Linda."

"Not just Linda. Sylvia, too. Both."

Ragwater gave a low, appreciative whistle.

"It pays to haggle," Plow said. "I also asked for a great job as a roadie with a metal band, but he wouldn't agree to that."

"Two women at once aren't enough for you?"

"Well, I figured, why not ask?"

"Yeah, why not? But I'm willing to bet he didn't understand what a roadie for a metal band might be."

"Now that you mention it, he might not have. Maybe I should have asked for winning lottery numbers. That would be a simple enough concept for him, don't you think?"

"I don't think there's any way to know. But how did he arrange for..." Ragwater nodded toward Linda and Sylvia across the room.

"Simple. He said all I had to do was ask them whether they would be interested in something with all three of us together. I would never have the nerve to ask something like that on my own, but Maxwell told me it would be all right. They've never done anything like this before, but it turns out the idea intrigued them."

"But Linda didn't like you. She gave you that fake phone number."

"Yeah. I made a bad impression when I tried to pick her up in the park. But when she found out Sylvia liked me, she was willing to give me a second chance."

Ragwater paused and drank from his beer. "You know," he said, "the ironic thing is, I never really believed Maxwell would come through on his end of the deal. I didn't trust him. I blew it big-time with Lisa, and I knew I was blowing it even when I agreed to the deal, and I did it anyway." Yes, if he hadn't been honest with anyone else, he was at least going to be honest with himself now. He could accuse Maxwell of lying to him. He could accuse Maxwell of putting on the ol' hard sell and trying to push him into the deal against his better judgment. He could, maybe, accuse Maxwell of exerting some degree of psychological manipulation.

But he, Ragwater, was the one who had said yes. He, and he alone, had made his big mistake when he said, "I agree to the deal. Please, dear sir, tell me what the first task is." He couldn't blame that on Maxwell.

Plow sat quiet for a moment and then said, "I don't think that's ironic. I mean, not by definition. I think it's just plain stupid."

"Yeah."

"I'm pretty sure you knew from the start that your tendency to agonize over every little thing, your obsession with analyzing stuff to an impossible level of detail—all your little neuroses and anxieties pretty much guaranteed you would cause this to blow up in your face. You could almost say it was self-destructive."

"I'd have to agree. Fear of commitment." But it wasn't the usual, garden-variety fear of commitment, often seen in sitcoms, in which a guy looks with dread at the prospect of giving up his life of partying at will and sleeping around (or, at least, the perceived possibility of being able to sleep around) and, in general, behaving like a heathen—the prospect of taking on a partner who could make him go to the ballet and squash his plans to buy a $700 barbeque grill.

No, it wasn't anything like that. Ragwater's fear was that he would lose his ability to withdraw into his own little world, to wallow around with Ohlmann King for hours on end writing pages and pages of story he would soon throw away, to lose himself in marathon sessions of Fear and Loathing in Hell. That occasionally, he would have to open up and talk about something serious.

But then again, had that really been a concern with Lisa? She had gotten into the spirit of writing the novel—she had been right there with him. She had given Fear and Loathing in Hell a try, and even though she bailed would probably have tried it again eventually.

Opening up? Well, it was great that she had understood him as well as she did. How much better could it have been if he had put some real effort into it?

Lisa was a keeper, as they say, but it was only now—too late—that he was realizing it.

"Whereas you, on the other hand..." Ragwater began.

"Yeah, me, the guy who spent three minutes half-assedly thinking about pros and cons and then made a decision. No agony, no deep analysis. No made-up short stories. And I was fully prepared for Sylvia or Linda—or both—to tell me at any time, 'get lost, jerk.' I would have apologized, they would have thought I was a jerk, we would have moved on with our lives, and I would hope for better results next time. End of story."

Ragwater nodded. "But now, at this point, would you be prepared to do something that might make them think you're a jerk?"

"No, but things are different now." Plow glanced over to the booth where Sylvia and Linda were, and Linda signaled to him. "Listen, I'd better get over there," he said. "You want to join us?"

"No, I'd be a third wheel. Or a fourth. Or something. Go ahead; I'll be all right."

Plow went to the booth and sat down. Ragwater picked up his mug and took a deep drink. On television, the detective was talking to the murder victim's widow. She seemed to be in some distress. "I have money," she said. "How much do you want?"

"What?" the detective said. "You think this is about money?"

She placed a hand on his chest. "Is there something else you want?"

He looked her up and down, appraising her with something of an arrogant expression on his face. "What can you show me that I haven't already seen?" He spoke the line like a jaded, cynical man who had "seen and done it all"—and further, who had "seen and done it all" in every possible variation and permutation one could imagine. So now, he found a perverse amusement in the attempts of various women to pique his interest. Ah, Perverse Amusement. A good addition to Ragwater's list of band names. Some sort of neo-punk group, maybe. They wouldn't have a bass player.

And who, he wondered, was Maxwell? Some sort of demon? A ghost? A figment of his imagination that had somehow become real? A mischievous being from the fifty-ninth dimension?

And why had he chosen Ragwater? That was a better question; the answer might tell Ragwater something about himself that he should know. But he wasn't likely to find out now.

Maybe everyone has his or her own Maxwell.

What about Plow? Ragwater was certain that Plow had not been so "high maintenance," as Maxwell put it, when he did his tasks. He was sure of himself; he trusted his instincts. And these tasks had worked out well for him. If he had his own Maxwell who would lead him astray, it would be someone—or something—different. It wouldn't be so easy to lead John Plow astray. He had a pretty good sense of who he was, what he wanted out of life, and all that crap. He didn't feel he needed things he couldn't (or shouldn't) have.

Well, then, maybe Maxwell's purpose for Plow wasn't to lead him astray.

It was quite possible that "leading him astray" had

not been Maxwell's intention for Ragwater, either. Let's face it: In no way had Ragwater been *led* astray. He had *wandered* astray.

Maybe, even now, Ragwater was thinking too much. How much thought does it take to understand that you should be honest with people? To realize that if you're sneaking around and working your brain overtime to rationalize why the things you're doing are all right, and then lying to cover your tracks...well, then, you shouldn't be doing what you're doing, and you're not, in fact, being honest? Shouldn't it be self-evident? Well, yes. It *should* be...

"Hey, man. How's it going?"

Ragwater turned to see Don Vecht taking the stool next to him. "Woman troubles," Ragwater said.

"The petition thing you told me about?"

"Yeah, but there's more to it than that."

"Did you do something monumentally, life-changingly stupid?"

"It's too complicated to talk about here and now. Suffice to say I should learn to appreciate it if I have something good."

"Congratulations," Don said. "A lot of guys never learn that."

Ragwater nodded.

"I'll buy you a beer," Don said.

"I'll let you."

Across the room, someone dropped coins in the jukebox, and Al Stewart's "Year of the Cat" started playing.

~ THE END ~

PS: Sara, Gustav's erstwhile partner in crime, sat at a table in the back corner at Olive's. She had just gotten off work at Wayne Printing and was talking to an odd, hyperactive little man. He was trying to insert his fist into an otherwise empty beer mug.

"Have you made up your mind?" he asked.

"It's tempting, but I can't get over the feeling that it sounds too good to be true."

"What are you risking?"

"Well..." She drew a blank.

"See? You're making it more difficult than it has to be."

Sara paused a moment and then took a deep breath to gather her courage. "Okay," she said. "Let's do it."

"You agree to the deal?"

"Yes," she said.

"A mere formality, but I need to hear you say it—as a full, complete sentence."

"All right. I agree to the deal."

The man smiled and shoved a sheet of paper across the table. "Your first task is to get seven signatures on this petition."

If you liked *Open Stage*, try these other books by Ray Holland:

The Hermit: A dedicated career hermit becomes mixed up with a promiscuous young lady from a nearby village in this kinda-sorta parable-fairy-tale-type story. Who, if anyone, lives happily ever after?

Goliath: It's a tale of good and evil, of trust and suspicion, of the power of love and loyalty. Little Goliath and his friends face adversity from within themselves, from one another, and from the forces of evil as they work to foil the Neuralgia Sisters' nefarious plot to achieve world domination.

The Hookie-Pookie Man: His mother was from Earth, and his father was from another planet. He doesn't fit in anywhere, but he knows a woman of similar origin is out there somewhere—and he's determined to find her.

Soft White Underbelly: Join Thor and his friends as they overthrow the government from the comfort of Thor's home, go to a yard sale and find a weapon so powerful that it can't be used, encounter a soul-stealing snack machine at the airport, take inventory of everything on the planet, circulate a petition for a Better America, embark on a plot to assassinate Satan...and more. Much, much more!

www.ingramcontent.com/pod-product-compliance
Lightning Source LLC
LaVergne TN
LVHW091034080826
845145LV00002B/485

9780615327877